Lonely Hearts

on Lilac Lane

BOOKS BY KAREN COULTERS

YORK HARBOR SERIES NOVELS
Hope from Daffodils
When Cookies Crumble
Patchwork to Healing

YORK RIVER SERIES NOVELS
Lonely Hearts on Lilac Lane

Lonely Hearts
on Lilac Lane

A York River Series Novel by

KAREN COULTERS

Howland
Press

Howland
Press

18 Loudon Rd. # 494
Concord, NH 03302

This is a work of fiction.
All of the characters, organizations, and events portrayed in this novel
are either products of the author's imagination or are used fictitiously,
and any resemblance to actual persons, living or dead, business
establishments, events, or locales is entirely coincidental, unless
otherwise stated.

LONELY HEARTS ON LILAC LANE. Copyright © 2024 by Karen
Coulters. All right reserved. No part of this publication may be
reproduced, distributed, or transmitted in any form or by any means,
or stored in a database or retrieval system, without the prior written
permission of the publisher. For information, address Howland Press,
18 Loudon Rd., #494, Concord, NH 03302.

WWW.KARENCOULTERSAUTHOR.COM

Library of Congress Cataloging-in-Publication Data
Names: Karen Coulters, Author
Title: Lonely Hearts on Lilac Lane
Book 1 in the York River Series
Description: First edition. | New Hampshire: Howland Press, 2024.

Identifiers: LCCN | 2024911271

ISBN 978-1-7336460-8-6 (softcover) | ISBN 978-1-7336460-9-3 (eBook)

Our books may be purchased in bulk for promotion, educational, or
business use. Please contact your local bookseller or Howland Press
via email @ HowlandPress@KarenCoultersAuthor.com

First Edition: 2024

Cover and Book Design by FormattingExperts.com

PRAISE FOR LONELY HEARTS ON LILAC LANE

Five Stars! A captivating story that takes you down a path of self-discovery of a mother and daughter navigating the rough waters of grief. Karen Coulters does a wonderful job in writing powerful scenes that thoroughly and beautifully express the many different phases of grief; the anger, the guilt, the sadness and eventually the healing. The relationship between mother and daughter is fraught with so much tension, anger and blame you can't imagine the two will ever get to a place of forgiveness and love. But they do, and the journey you are taken on as they both rediscover each other, letting go of the man that hurt them both, and finally learning to love not only themselves but others, is nothing short of perfection.

Michelle Windsor,
Award-Winning Contemporary Romance Author

Lonely Hearts on Lilac Lane is a truly satisfying novel set in the charming town of York, Maine, along the York River. From the moment Janice meets Vincent, I was hooked. Janice's transformation from a belligerent, cantankerous woman to a patient, forgiving woman is captivating. Vincent, a compassionate and honorable man, never gives up on helping Janice find peace, despite his own grief. Madison, Janice's daughter, returns home to care for her mother after an accident, battling her own grief over losing her father. There were moments where I felt anger, laughter, and tears; and then there were times I wanted to shake Janice and tell her to smarten up and see what she has in front of her! Any author who can evoke such emotions is truly amazing, and Karen Coulters does just that! This book was a joy to read from start to finish.

Lori DiAnni,
Author of the Misty River Series Novels

This story discusses suicide.
If you or someone you know is having thoughts of suicide,
please contact the Suicide & Crisis Lifeline
Call or Text 988

ACKNOWLEDGMENTS

Many days and hours are spent putting words to the page. Oftentimes, the words flow, but there are days when each word is a struggle to find, as every single word is important. They aren't written simply to meet a desired word count. The words carry a huge responsibility; they are meant to bring you, the reader, to a place of joy, sorrow, laughter, tears, anger, hope, and reflection. The words on the page may move you to understanding the past and present, to process empathy, humility, forgiveness, thankfulness, and more. These words may be moving to your soul. They might bring up memories, be they bad or good. But in the end, a writer's hope is that you will be touched in some way, and the words will linger, leaving you to ponder and reflect.

Writing *Lonely Hearts on Lilac Lane* challenged me. I always write about emotionally charged subjects resulting in happy-endings, but there are times when imagining the scenes tugs at my heart in ways I'd never have expected. It's in these times I struggle because I know my readers may have experienced one or more the subject matter: suicide, loss, brokenness, estrangement, forgiveness, PTSD, anxiety, and loneliness. These themes flow like a ribbon throughout the storyline. My goal is to bring light to these sensitive subjects in a respectful and tender way that ushers in a new day filled with hope.

I'd like to thank my constant companion, my husband, Michael, for his steadfast support and welcomed critique of my writing. I would be remiss if I didn't thank my daughter, Sara, for using her expertise with the English language and teaching me a thing or two, or three… Thank you as well to my brother Dan for his invaluable input, and to my sister-in-law, Cathy, for her continued support and allowing me to crash at their home in York and for the many walks and car rides through town, so my writing locations can ring true and I may flourish in my endeavor. I can't imagine my life without the love and support of my entire family; I feel truly blessed.

I owe a special thanks to my accountability partner, author Sylvie Kurtz. You have guided me, encouraged me when I hit a wall, and help expand my thinking, for which I will be forever grateful. Lisa Baron and Louise Thompson, there aren't enough words to express my gratitude for your support. You stand by my side at multitudes of events and book signings; you cheer me on in this crazy journey I find myself in, and I'm indebted to you. Thank you to my family of authors in the Weare Area Writers Guild, and fellow authors I've met along my writing adventure; you inspire me and help guide my path.

Thank you, Formatting Experts team, for taking my vision for the cover to its beautiful fruition. Thank you as well to my editor, Elaini Caruso, without whom this work wouldn't be the very best it can be.

My dearest readers, where would I be without you? Your words of praise for my works, be they in person, email, social media, or on review sites, encourage me more than you could ever know. You keep me pressing forward, and I can't thank you enough. I've often thought my writing would be void if it didn't move my readers in some small way, for writing isn't just for me to fulfill a passion; it is for you.

With deepest gratitude and a humble heart,
Karen

Let today be the day you learn the grace of letting go
and the power of moving on

– Steve Maraboli

one

$\mathcal{J}$anice Gable often wondered what her last days on earth would be like. Would she have advanced warning, or would this world snatch her in the blink of an eye? Would she suffer, or would it be painless? One thing's for certain, she wouldn't die like her husband had. In an instant, he'd ripped their family's world apart.

. . .

Janice pulled into Hannaford's supermarket and put the car into park, eyeing the market doors with disdain. She loathed grocery shopping. Everything about it brought out her anxiety. She feared her car door would dent its neighbor's vehicle, or theirs would ding hers. She would usually end up grabbing a cart with a loose wheel, and that squeak would bring attention to her. Janice knew she should count her blessings at the vast selection of foods, but too wide a selection only caused her jitters to go into overdrive.

She adjusted her cap to cover much of her shoulder-length hair, which desperately needed a shampoo, then stuffed her shopping list in her worn cardigan pocket and trudged through the parking lot. The hustle and bustle the moment she stepped inside the store caused her breath to hitch. She closed her eyes for a moment to gather her nerve and maneuvered toward the dairy section, just praying she wouldn't run into anyone she knew.

As Janice slowed to turn into the baking aisle, a cart behind her rammed into the back of her leg. She turned with a jerk. "Watch where you're going!"

It didn't matter that it was a young mom with a child sitting among the groceries they'd collected. It didn't even matter that the mother appeared apologetic. Janice needed her personal space, or her heightened anxiety would surely set her over the edge.

She used to enjoy shopping and running into people she knew. Everyone liked her back then—before the unthinkable happened. Now her former friends stood clear. She still imagined the whispering behind her back, giving her sad eyes of sympathy, or even worse, the shaking of their heads in pity. And even though it had been nine years since her husband's death, the pain of his passing and the rawness felt like an open wound. She'd heard the murmurs, and their voices haunt her today. *I bet she drove him to it. How can she go on knowing what he'd done? Such a shame. Poor thing. They seemed so happy.*

Janice had buried herself with the incrimination. Had it really been her fault that her husband had killed himself? Did she drive him to it? In the end, it didn't really matter who did what because it didn't change anyone's perspective or opinion. She would have preferred to wear a big letter A on her chest, instead of the label she now wore—a widow by suicide. This label filled her with shame and an unbearable regret for not being able to see the signs and preventing it from happening.

Janice swallowed hard and exhaled, willing herself not to cry right there in front of the ice cream section, but Charlie's favorite mocha chip ice cream seemed to mock her. Her legs shook, and she braced herself against the cart's handle. An overwhelming need to escape bore down on her. With only half of her shopping list checked off, she ran toward the checkout counter and dumped what little purchases she had on the conveyor belt.

Her desperation to get out of there grew in earnest. She needed to be home in her safe space, hidden away from the world. She dashed through the parking lot and felt as if she were a child that had to run and jump on her bed before the monsters could grab her. And by the time Janice unloaded the groceries into her trunk, she could no longer fight back her tears. She shoved the cart to the side, then hopped into her car. In her haste, she backed out before looking.

Smash!

The sound of metal, glass, and broken plastic cut through the noise in her head. Janice's hands gripped the steering wheel, and she froze. *No, no, no. This can't be happening.*

"Not here, not now. Just breathe." She inhaled deeply through her nose and blew it out just as a burly man tapped on her window, but she didn't move.

"Ma'am," shouted the man, "are you okay?"

Janice nodded even as tears streamed down her cheeks. She was fine physically, but her insides were screaming at her to get away now.

"Then I need to ask you to get out of your car."

She couldn't bring herself to look in his direction, and shook her head. "I—I can't."

Janice's hands froze to the wheel, and she couldn't unclamp them. Her chest tightened as if a heavy weight lay across it, and it took her breath away. She feared she might be having a heart attack. *Have to go. Home. Now!*

"You damaged my pickup, and I want you to see it for yourself." He leaned into the glass. "We need to exchange insurance."

She wanted to shove the car into drive, but her hands wouldn't obey. She didn't budge. "I'll have to call the police if you don't get out."

No. She shook her head. *No police.* She couldn't bear the sight of flashing cruiser lights, and having them question her, as if she were some kind of criminal. *I'm not a criminal! I'm not.* Janice didn't know where it came from, but in that instant, she gathered her inner strength and threw open the car door. In doing so, she knocked the man off balance, and her anxiety morphed into fury.

"Go ahead! Call the police!" she screeched. "I don't care. Just do whatever you want." Her temper grew. This accident was her fault—everything is and was her fault, and she couldn't hold back. She grabbed her purse, dug in, and yanked everything out. She tossed the items to the floor, into the passenger's seat, and on the dash. Then ripped open her wallet and threw her driver's license and insurance card at his feet. "There! Now you have it! Satisfied?"

"Ma'am. I don't mean to upset you, but—"

"Then don't!"

"It's just that—"

"I get it," she said gruffly as she turned in her seat and set her feet on the ground. "I'm not an idiot, you know."

"I didn't say you were," he said tenderly, almost in a hush, as he lowered himself to her level and plucked the two cards off the pavement.

His hazel eyes questioned as they gazed into hers, as if he were genuinely worried about her. He held her attention, appearing sincere and caring. She couldn't recall the last time anyone had expressed genuine concern for her well-being. He had a calming manner in his voice. It was soothing, almost meditative.

"Are you sure you're not hurt?" he asked. His gaze held hers.

Janice's blood pressure had nearly come back to normal, and she once again nodded that she was okay. "I'm sorry. I completely lost my temper—it's been a bad day. I'm frustrated, and I…"

The stranger's kind eyes still held their gaze. "I've had days like that, too." He waved her license and insurance card in his hand as if he were holding a deck of cards. "What do you say I go write this stuff down, and take a few pictures of the damage, then you can be on your way?" He glanced at her name. "Does that sound okay to you… Ms. Gable?"

"Please." She gestured with a flip of the hand. "Sounds good. Go do what you need to do."

She caught sight of him in her rearview mirror. His light brown hair was graying at the temples and matched his well-manicured whiskers. He had a sturdiness to his frame. He was about her age and slightly taller than her.

Janice continued to watch him snap photos of her back bumper with his phone. He was handsome, she concluded, and she felt her cheeks warm. She shifted her gaze to her own reflection in the mirror. As if she were seeing herself for the first time, the image she saw stunned her. Janice didn't recognize herself. She squinted to take in her sunken eyes and thinning lips. *What has happened to me?* With a sigh of resignation, she sat back and waited for him to get done so she could finally head home to her safe place and escape the madness.

After a few minutes, he once again stood at her car door and handed her license and insurance card through the rolled-down window, then gave a quick open-handed thump on the window frame.

"I hope the day improves for you," he said with a gentle grin.

"Thanks. I hope yours does, too."

He gave another thump of his hand and retreated to his pickup. Janice watched him walk away.

With frayed nerves, Janice cautiously put the car into reverse. She had the jitters all the way home, and they didn't settle down until she was pulling into her driveway.

She sat there, staring at her dilapidated home, and slumped. Even her house seemed depressing. She was exhausted and had made a fool of herself and now faced the expense of a deductible on her insurance; an expense that she couldn't afford.

two

incent Clark watched the old Toyota Camry pull out of the parking lot. He glanced down at the notes he'd taken. *Janice Gable, what's your story?* He couldn't help but feel bad for the poor lady. He realized she was in some kind of pain; a pain that seemed familiar to him. *She's suffered a loss.* His instincts tended to be spot on, and he had the urge to reach out, but to do so would appear rather odd, and so he pushed the thought away.

Vincent shoved the note into his front pocket, climbed into his now damaged truck, and reluctantly made a call to his insurance company.

The sunshine he'd been enjoying turned to a gray overcast, the warmth dissipating into a damp feeling that crept its way into his sore bones. Once again, Ms. Gable and her sad state rolled through his thoughts, as if she had brought the gloom of the day into focus. For some reason, she'd pulled at his heartstrings. He didn't feel sorry for her. No, it was more empathy than pity. Perhaps the hollowness of her eyes had struck him. They had been dull and almost lifeless, and yet, at the same time, intense, as if they were pleading for help.

He knew that look full well, as it had been in his own eyes back when his beloved Cheryl was nearing the end of her life. Cancer had eaten away at her body, but her essence that made her love, feel, hope, dream, and adore him remained, until at last, even that was taken from her—from him, until she was no more. He closed his eyes, and allowed his mind to savor the memory of her.

Cheryl had been his writing muse, and after her passing, a decade ago, his passion for writing waned, and he no longer had the creative will for it. The only thing that seemed to bring him any kind of solace was to dig in the dirt and bring dead things back to life.

Vincent unloaded his groceries, along with the seedlings and soil he'd bought at the local Agway. He looked forward to spending time in his makeshift greenhouse, which was formerly his writing sanctuary in his private backyard overlooking Short Sands Beach.

York, Maine, had been his and Cheryl's home since he'd carried her over the threshold nearly forty years prior. Back then, the small cottage boasted two small bedrooms, one bath, a rough kitchen, and a tiny living room with windows to a screened-in porch, but it was their home. Over the years, they'd updated and expanded it into the beautiful estate it now was.

They'd envisioned each of the four bedrooms filled with children, but it wasn't meant to be. And so, the rooms sat silent, those on the second floor furnished and adorned with the very best linens, drapes, and décor, as if waiting for someone to bring them to life. Until then, those rooms remained shut off from the rest of the house.

Vincent sighed, then trudged down the hallway to his makeshift office and pulled the scribbled notes he'd taken at the scene of the accident out of his pocket. *Ms. Janice Gable, what's your story?*

three

$\mathcal{M}$adison ran her feet over the coarse metal boot scrusher to scrape the horse manure and hay from the bottom of her muck boots. Dew lay across the fields, and a welcomed warmth filled the air. Her chores were done, for now, and her hunger grew as she clomped through the squeaky kitchen door.

Nathan stood tall and leaned in front of the stove. The morning sun shone brightly across the wide pine floor and reached for his golden hair, which shimmered in the light. He could still take her breath away after all these years. She stood back and watched him maneuver onions, bacon bits, and potatoes around the cast-iron skillet with a large wooden spoon before she broke the spell and stood at his side.

"That smells amazing." Madison removed her leather work gloves and rested her hand on the small of Nathan's back. "I'm famished."

"Good, because I got a little carried away with the portions." He shoved a spatula under the mound of fried potatoes and nodded toward the refrigerator. "Mind grabbing the eggs?"

"Ah, but of course," she said with a grin. "Juice?"

"Absolutely."

Butter now sizzled in the pan, and Nathan cracked open

four eggs as Madison poured juice into their glasses before refilling her coffee cup.

"Lily's getting close," she said as she added cream to her cup. "We should see her foal before too long." Madison leaned around Nathan and dropped the spoon into the porcelain sink. "I'm thinking we could start taking turns watching over her at night."

Nathan picked up the plates and plunked them on the kitchen table. "She'll be fine. You worry too much."

She had never told Nathan about her childhood horse. The mare had been a chestnut brown quarter horse, also named Lily. She wasn't sure why she'd felt the need to keep it a secret. She supposed it was because it brought up too much grief. Although she found it puzzling that she would then choose to name this Lily after her first Lily.

Madison wouldn't forget the look on her mother's face the day she'd come home from high school to learn her beloved horse was gone. Her mom had a firm expression with pursed lips. She'd had her hands on her hips and held a wide stance before stating coldly, "I had to sell her, Madison. I couldn't afford her anymore."

Madison sighed as thoughts of her former Lily ran through her mind. *I will not lose another horse.*

"I'm trying to do the responsible thing here, Nathan. What if something goes horribly wrong, and Lily, or her foal, ends up dying? I'd never forgive myself."

Madison leaned back in her chair and pushed her plate away. "Now, I've gone and lost my appetite."

Nathan shook his head and rubbed the bridge of his nose. "Okay. Alright, we'll take turns sleeping in the barn if that will rest your mind."

"It will. Thank you." She gave a nod and picked up a piece of potato with her fingers and popped it into her mouth.

Nathan gave her a sideways glance. "I gotta tell you, if this is how you are about the birth of a foal, I can't imagine what you'll be like when we have a kid someday."

Madison shifted in her seat and gulped her juice in an effort to evade the topic. They weren't even married, and the thought of being a mother was the furthest thing from her mind.

Madison despised her mother. Janice Gable was a bitter, angry woman who drove everyone away, including Madison's beloved father, and eventually, even her younger sister, Hannah, who had been their mother's favorite. Madison couldn't blame her mother for favoring her. Hannah was prim and proper, and had followed her mother around like a doting puppy. Madison, on the contrary, was a barn rat and tried to avoid her mother at all costs. They were the proverbial oil and water.

Madison recalled the day she'd finally turned eighteen. She'd packed her belongings and moved in with her best friend, Francine Murphy. Madison and Franky had only a few weeks left of their senior year at York High, and without hesitation, Franky's mother had welcomed her in until she graduated, but to her great relief, allowed her to extend her stay through the summer, so long as she'd gotten a job. The last time Madison saw her mother's face was on graduation day, and that was eight years ago.

Madison looked on as Nathan devoured his breakfast, oblivious to the fact that she wasn't eating. She could have done a backflip and he wouldn't have noticed. Her mind went back to thinking of her mother. What had made her mom's heart harden? Her mother used to laugh and smile. She even recalled a time when her mother sang as she'd folded laundry or set the table. Madison smiled at the memory of seeing her father gathering her mom in his arms as they danced in the living room. He'd twirled her around, and she'd giggled. They were all happy—until they weren't.

Nathan picked up his plate and placed it in the dishwasher. He gulped the rest of his orange juice, gave Madison a peck on the forehead, and without so much as a word, trotted off to get ready for work.

Madison played with the rest of her potatoes and eggs. *Has it really been eight years since I've been home?* A small part of her longed to be back on the New England coast. She missed the smell of the ocean, lilacs, rosehip, and the sound of squawking seagulls, but she'd ventured off to Ohio in search of a new life away from her past—her family's past.

Madison scraped her uneaten breakfast into the trash and headed out the door toward the barn. She needed to feel Lily's soft muzzle and take in her strength.

She slid the door open, and the fresh scent of hay wafting through the barn filled her senses. Lily leaned over the stall's door, and Madison caressed the horse's neck. Lily's big brown eyes stared back at her, as if to say, *I'm here for you.*

"I know, my sweet girl, and I'll be here for you, too. You're going to be a momma soon." Madison picked up a brush that hung on a hook, opened the stall door, and scooted inside. The brush clung to her palm, and her hand slid over Lily's broad belly as her thoughts shifted to Nathan.

Meeting Nathan had been a stroke of luck. He was staying

the summer in York, Maine, with his family—his mother was originally from York Harbor. That year, Nathan got a job at the Stage Neck Inn because he wanted more spending money than his family was willing to give. He had to earn it. Madison had watched him clock in for the first time, just as she had. Her heart fluttered, and her palms grew sweaty at the sight of him. His green eyes crinkled in the corners because of his broad smile. He had a bronzed summer tan, and his blond, sun-bleached hair appeared to shine like golden wheat swaying in a field. He didn't wear his good looks with airs. He seemed kind-spirited—a happy-go-lucky type, and she'd needed some happy in her life, never mind luck. Madison was smitten from the start, and training him as a server was her responsibility. Just knowing he'd have to follow her around, watching her every move, made the task near impossible.

"You like him, don't you, girl?" Lily's tail swished in agreement as Madison set the brush down and nuzzled Lily as she continued to reminisce about their past.

Over that summer, they'd fallen in love, and following Nathan and his family back to their home in Woodsfield, Ohio was a no-brainer. The timing was perfect because she sensed she'd overstayed her welcome at Franky's house.

Madison's family wasn't the type to travel. Her mother would always pooh-pooh Madison's preposterous requests and say everything that was worth seeing was right there; they lived in Vacation Land. So why leave when it appeared everyone else on the planet seemed to think Maine was the place to be? Even so, Madison had heard exciting stories from her friends of seeing the Grand Canyon, having fun at Disney, crossing the ocean on a Caribbean cruise, and many other far-off places. Thinking back now, Madison supposed they'd stayed home because her mother was a penny pincher, even though her father had a well-paying job. So, it was with great anticipation that she'd traveled to the Midwest with the Hawking family.

"You're going to be a good momma, aren't you my Lily girl?"

Madison stroked Lily's mane and her hand caught the silver necklace that she'd worn every day since she'd moved to Ohio. She rubbed her fingers across the twisted knot at the hollow of her neck. It was more of a sideways, elongated figure eight, with two tiny birthstones inside each oval: an amethyst for her birthday, and a sapphire for her sister, Hannah. She'd eyed the matching necklaces at Whispering Sands Gift Shop, in the heart of Short Sands Beach, and hoped by the time she could afford them, they'd still be there. To her delight, they were.

Madison could clearly remember the day she'd given one of them to Hannah.

She'd packed what little belongings she'd had into the mustard-yellow suitcase Franky's mom had given her as a going away gift. She had little reason to go to the family home before she left, except to give her little sister the gift, a hug, and kiss her goodbye.

Madison's throat tightened, and she tried to push down the memory of Hannah clinging to her with jagged sobs of *please don't go.*

"I miss her, Lily. I miss her so much."

Madison rested a carrot on her open palm. "Hopefully, you'll get to meet her someday." Lily snatched the treat. The feel of Lily's velvety muzzle, in her palm, momentarily calmed her sense of loss.

four

anice sat on her overstuffed sofa, peering out the window. She held an ivory-colored knit pillow across her chest as if it would protect her from her fears and anxiety. The skies were gray and waves smashed angrily onto the rocky coastline. A storm was brewing, and Janice shivered with an uneasy feeling. She closed her eyes, willing whatever storm was about to come her way to pass her by.

Her seaside home in York Harbor, Maine, had been in the family for four generations. The large colonial with a wrap-around porch was once a stunning example of a stately New England home. Now, the home's weathered cedar shake shingles needed repair, along with the roof. The broad porch with its broken balusters and wide sagging staircase led to a rolling lawn that overlooked the seascape. A dilapidated arbor stood in the foreground. Unruly grapevines engulfed the frame as though the shriveled leaves and vines were devouring the once pristine arch. Her previously manicured rose gardens were now overgrown with weeds. A footpath to the water had crumbled with each passing storm, and an overgrown pathway behind the house led to a small barn.

Janice had let the former beauty of her surroundings overwhelm her since Charlie's death and her daughters' leaving home. She'd hoped each season to have the energy to putter in the yard, but to her dismay, she simply hadn't had the will to do so. But every day she put off maintaining the house and the grounds, the harder the tasks became, which created a cycle of depression, self-loathing, embarrassment, and resentment. So she gave up.

Loneliness and sorrow crept in, consuming her. Janice no longer had the strength to bury her pain. Her profound hurt and anger bubbled over when she'd least expected it, fraying her every nerve. Life was easier hidden away because outside, there were too many reminders of everything she'd lost.

Janice beat herself up because she'd been a stickler for order and had always maintained her gardens with pride. By now, she would have had rows of canned jams, vegetables, and fruit lining the shelves in the root cellar. All the pruning to prepare for winter would have been done, along with fall blooms and harvest décor meticulously staged at the entrance for her two daughters, Madison and Hannah, to enjoy. Instead, it had been years since holly wreaths had adorned the front door. No Christmas trees, no festive music had coursed through the veins of the big house that bore ghosts of once happy lives. Now spring was upon her. The drifting snows were merely trickling streams, sinking into the earth. Crocuses burst through, awaiting the sun, but Janice grew weary, thinking summer would never appear. And even when it did finally come, she was certain her sorrow and loneliness would still be with her. *It always is.*

Janice winced, knowing there wasn't much need for the house's upkeep; she had no one to impress. She was the only resident, and after what her husband had done, she rarely, if ever, had any company.

Janice bit down hard on her lower lip. She thought missing her family would get easier over time, but it had only metastasized and made her feel deserving of their betrayal. The ugly voices of judgment and guilt played in her head like a scratched record.

Her body ached with longing for the past. A time of better days, of unruly daughters eating chocolate pudding off the mixing beaters and arguing over who'd get what was left in the bowl. Janice could see Charlie grabbing the gallon milk jug from the fridge and drinking directly out of the container. She'd slap him with a hand towel. It was a disgusting habit her husband had, and one she couldn't break him of. He'd laugh as he invariably jumped out of her reach.

A seagull caught her attention outside the window. It stood stoically on a tree stump as if it were waiting for its long-lost mate. Perhaps, she thought, the gull would give up and fly away, feeling just as rejected as she did.

Janice turned from the seagull, inhaled air into her lungs, and held it before releasing it. She resigned herself to the knowledge that she'd pushed her family away. She'd failed as a wife, and she'd taken her anger and frustrations out on her girls, so much so, they both left her when they'd turned eighteen. Madison, her eldest, hadn't spoken to her since the day she walked out the door. At least Hannah would call from time to time, but the calls were brief, as if they were made out of obligation. And Janice hadn't laid eyes on her since she joined the military three years ago.

Janice's anger with Charlie caused her life to spiral out of control. She couldn't even hold down a job because her anxiety would shoot through the roof every time she left the house. Her one saving grace was her inheritance, but that was dwindling. No matter her effort to seek professional help, no matter how much she tried to move forward, she couldn't escape the losses, and her heart ached with the knowledge of being a failure. She'd made the bed she was now lying in. A bed of emptiness, and with each passing day, her bitterness set in deeper and deeper.

five

adison sank into the tufted cushion of the cottage's front porch swing. The warm evening set off a chorus of crickets chirping around her. It felt more like mid-summer than early spring, and so she shed her sweatshirt and held it to her lap as she gently swayed back and forth. The swing creaked with each push of her heels. Stars lit the full-moon sky, and the haunting sound of a barn owl hooted in the distance.

She tipped her head back and closed her eyes. In the barn, horses shuffled and neighed. There wasn't any distress to the sounds. No, she thought, simply nature preparing for the night.

Madison loved this land. A twelve-acre tract of rolling fields and pasture with a brook that rambled along the side of its boundary, which had swelled after the recent rain. They'd had their first cut of grass and the scent lingered in the air.

She was content, and yet, thoughts of New England continued to press on her mind. Maine would be cooler than Ohio as the weather ran about a month behind. Soon, her childhood home would smell of lilac, and gangly yellow forsythia would flow along the banks. Crocuses, daffodils, and tulips would hint at the surface of the frosted earth, bringing hope of warmth and new beginnings. The blur of the crickets transformed into the clattering of peepers…the first sound of spring in New England.

Nathan's parents had once lived in the cottage while they'd built the main house; a rambling ranch-style home that sat perfectly nestled to take in its surroundings of perennial gardens, Rose of Sharon, and the decorative motif of an antique wooden push plow and wagon wheel on the front porch.

Early on, she often took the lengthy walk to the Monroe County Fairgrounds just to be close to the horses who boarded there. When she'd felt the far away memories of her beloved Lily seeping in, seeing those horses had cheered her.

Once she'd made a habit of showing up at the fairgrounds whenever she'd had spare time, volunteering to brush the horses and nuzzle their noses, Marge, one of the horse owners, would often let her take her quarter horse for rides around the track. This continued for quite some time and Val Hawking, Nathan's mom, took notice.

Madison swayed to the creaking swing's rhythm, as she recalled a pivotal conversation she'd had with Val so many years ago.

"Madison, dear. What is your fascination with those horses?"

The question had taken Madison aback. How could anyone not be fascinated by the majestic animals? She'd told her they made her feel grounded, safe, and provided her with a sense of peace as she brushed their manes. And when she rode them, well, nothing would compare. She would become one with their movement, rhythm, and power. They didn't judge, and they had an incredible capacity to sense our needs—our pain. They brought her joy.

"Perhaps," Val started hesitantly. "Perhaps you might consider bringing Nathan with you sometime."

Madison remembered a heat rise within her. Did Val feel she'd been neglecting her son because she was spending so much time with the horses? But, if that were so, wouldn't she just ask her to not go so much?

"It's just that—well—that he's been so moody." She said the word *moody* as if it was a term that should never be spoken aloud.

Nathan hadn't been himself in a long while. Maybe it was because of the long hours he spent working for his father, and being a district manager for his family's heavy equipment sales and distribution facilities wasn't the same as being a firefighter. Madison hoped with Nathan burying himself in work it would ease the grief of a life he felt responsible for losing. But in the back of her mind, part of her thought Nathan's moodiness was born from something else altogether—maybe she was the catalyst that brought on his mood swings. She didn't want to get married, or have children, like Nathan did, and that possible truth weighed heavy on her heart. She'd seen her own father—up one minute and down the next.

Val had thought that maybe being around horses might be good for Nathan.

Madison had heard about how horses could help with PTSD, disabilities, and depression; they'd certainly helped her. Maybe they could also lift Nathan's spirits.

She'd responded with a resounding yes, and told Val she thought caring for a horse and riding was a great idea. To Madison's delight, the idea had worked, and the following summer, the Hawkings built a four-stall horse barn on their property. It sat back just between the cottage where she and Nathan lived and the main house where his parents resided. Unlike the rustic one-stall barn she had growing up, they'd fully equipped this stately designed barn with the latest advancements. The tack room was ample and carried all the essentials. The day she'd met her sweet, new Lily, she had no doubt the horse had been an answer to her prayers. And so, Madison made sure the stalls were pristine and cared for, and didn't mind mucking, hauling, haying, or feeding. She treasured it.

Nathan seemed to relax when he was in the barn. Madison had missed his carefree whistling. Whistling was a habit he'd done without realizing, but that was before his workload weighed him down, and before the tragic fire. After they'd acquired Lily, his melodies filled the air once again. Madison's heart sang when she saw him brushing Lily because he'd occasionally slipped back to the Nathan that she'd once fallen in love with.

Headlights approached, snapping Madison back to the present. Her heart rate ramped up. *He's home.* This trepidation, in his presence, would usually dissipate or escalate, depending on how his day went, or what may have triggered him. She caught herself picking at her nails, then stuffed her hands in her pockets to try to stop the habit.

Nathan's black pickup truck wore the white-lettered logo of Hawking Equipment on the doors. She was proud that he'd opened himself up to working for his father. Hawking Equipment wasn't necessarily Nathan's dream, but it was work, and it thrilled his father to have him be part of the family business.

Nathan took a few stairs in one leap. "Hey beautiful," he said before planting a kiss on her lips.

He's had a good day. Her insides calmed.

"I'm surprised to see you here," he said. "I figured you'd be in the barn taking care of our new momma. How's the little guy doing?"

"For a two-day-old, he's doing great." She brought her hands to her heart. "He's so stinkin' cute. I love his wobbly little legs."

He leaned over her and squeezed her knee. "I love your wobbly little legs," he said before taking a seat and joining in on the sway of the swing.

Oh, how she loves *this* man on his good days.

Madison snuggled in and rested her head on his shoulder. "I want to live in this moment forever, Nathan."

He squeezed her hand with his and caressed her hair with the other. "That would be nice, wouldn't it?"

Nathan jumped with a start. "Hey, how'd it go with your potential riding student?"

"She's not my new student yet because Lily isn't ready for a rider. She needs time to heal. But I think it went pretty well."

"That's my girl." He gave a wink and a grin. "They'll hire you."

Madison leaned back into the swing and gazed out into the night sky as she replayed the day. The girl's mother had a particular teaching style she thought would work best for her daughter, but Madison wasn't worried about that. She was both confident and competent in her ability to teach dressage, Western, and English-style riding, so there should be no problem there. Her biggest issue was having the time to instruct, as doing accounting and payroll for Hawking Equipment sucked up most of her weekdays. She worked mainly from home, which was nice, but Mr. Hawking had a knack for popping in and asking more of her than she cared to take on. Being a riding instructor was Madison's side gig, and she loved every minute of it. She just hoped her potential new student would wait the six to eight weeks for Lily to be ready. But by the end of the interview, both mother and daughter were full of smiles and shook her hand enthusiastically. She thought that had to account for something.

"I will not get my hopes up. If it happens, great. If it doesn't, then I guess it wasn't meant to be."

Nathan nodded and wrapped his arm around her shoulders. They sat silently as the swing swayed back and forth, and while the squeak of the chains harmonized with the chorus of the night, Madison's mind continued to drift back in time.

Nathan's father, Winston Hawking, had been the one to recognize her ability with numbers and business when she'd taken a job with his company. He told her she had a gift, and she'd chuckled, but the fact that he'd seen something special in her had thrilled her.

Winston had challenged her to go to school and further her education. He was so confident in her ability that he'd offered to pay for it and said he'd promote her when she graduated. After quite some time, she could no longer resist the urge to pursue his offer of higher education. However, Madison insisted she'd one day pay him back in full, with interest, as she didn't want to feel indebted to Hawking Equipment, in case she decided to pursue other options. And for the first time, she had hope that she'd make something of her life.

Now, that life, the life she'd been making with Nathan, was mostly pretty good. They were comfortable together despite the occasional awkwardness between them when he used to press her to get married. She only had to remind him they were fine just the way they were. Sure, he could be moody and aloof, and at times, he'd lose his footing, but they'd found their groove and made it work. She just wished his bad moods were less frequent, as her angst was also getting more frequent.

six

Janice's grumpy disposition waned a bit as she thought of the gentleman whose car she'd hit. He had every right to be angry with her, she thought, as she opened a can of tomato soup and poured it into the pot.

Janice retrieved some whole wheat bread from the cabinet and buttered two slices, then flicked on the burner. She placed the buttered sides down into a small skillet and stirred the soup. The scent made her stomach growl, and for once, she had an appetite. Janice reached in the fridge for a cheese single when she remembered she'd chosen to forgo that item at the store.

"So much for grilled cheese." She turned off the burner and tossed the partially grilled pieces of bread out the back door for the birds to eat.

Janice ladled some soup into a chipped bowl and added a handful of oyster crackers. She smiled as she remembered when she and Charlie bought the set. The sixteen-piece place setting, which now only comprised three bowls and two plates, had been their first purchased household item.

She scooped up a spoonful of soup and slurped. Janice instinctively threw her spoon into the bowl with a splash as she spit the mouthful of the scalding soup back into her bowl. Pain seared through the roof of her mouth and her lips.

Janice shoved her chair back. "That's it! I'm done."

She left the piping-hot soup on the table, then stomped out of the kitchen and into the bathroom to scrub the speckles of splashed soup off her shirt. She caught a glimpse of her reflection. "What have I done to myself?" Not only did she feel miserable, she looked miserable. *I need to pull myself out of this black hole like a weed in my garden.* "Step one: take a damn shower."

Janice wiped away the steam that had built up on the bathroom mirror with her towel and stared at her reflection. *Ghastly.* She leaned closer to the mirror to examine her wrinkles and noticed unruly gray hairs on her eyebrows and sagging eyelids. She ran her finger over her closed mouth. Her lips appeared thinner with smoker's lines, even though she'd never smoked a day in her life. *Who is this woman staring back at me? How did I let this happen?*

Her thoughts shifted to her daughters. She wondered what they'd look like now. She quickly did the math in her head. *Madison would be twenty-six. Yes, that's right. Hannah, well, let's see—she'd be twenty-one now.*

Janice's throat tightened, and a tear escaped and ran down her cheek. She wiped the dampness away and tried to shake off her despair, while Johnny Cash's song, *Hurt*, repeatedly rolled through her mind—*everyone goes away in the end.*

She pulled on her navy-blue T-shirt and adjusted it at the hips, then tugged on her once tight-fitting jeans that now bagged at the waist and rear end. *What happened to my butt?* She rolled her eyes in search of a belt; she hated belts. *Nope, not doing it.* Off came the jeans. She yanked her sweatpants out of the overflowing laundry basket that sat in the middle of her bedroom floor, grateful the pants had a drawstring.

Janice combed out her tangled, damp hair and stared into the mirror again. "Something's gotta give, Janice Gable." She just hoped somewhere within her she'd find the courage to move forward.

She selected a book from her nightstand—a book she'd tried reading for the umpteenth time—and trekked down the stairs to her favorite tufted chair. Janice had no sooner turned a page when her mind would take her out of the storyline because the words on the page invariably seemed to trigger the past.

What were his last words to me? Janice had tortured herself with this same question since the day her husband's lifeless body hung from the rafters. No matter how many times she'd played that day over in her mind, she hadn't any clearer answers. Maybe she'd never know. Maybe the last words he'd spoken were unheard as she often ignored his sputtered mutterings toward the end.

If only I'd listened.

She tucked a worn leather bookmark between the pages, shut the book, and dropped it on the couch. It was too early for her to sleep, but there wasn't any point in staying awake. No, it was easier to close her eyes and hope tomorrow would be a better day.

Janice slogged into the bathroom and removed a Tylenol PM bottle from the medicine cabinet. She filled a paper cup that sat on the counter, popped two pills into her mouth, and washed them down with a gulp. Before long, she hoped to be tired enough to head to bed, drift away, and forget the ordeal at the grocery store and the accident had ever happened.

The sound of tires crunching along her gravel driveway

came to a stop. *What on earth? Who could that possibly be?* It was too late for the meter reader or fuel delivery, and she certainly wasn't expecting anyone. Janice considered they might have made a wrong turn until the car door shut.

She pulled the slats of the bathroom window apart and peeked out, but all she could see were headlights, so she crept down the stairs hoping it wasn't anyone planning something nefarious. Everyone in town knew she lived alone.

Bang! sounded the door. Janice's heart nearly jumped out of her chest. *Bang! Bang!*

"Go away!" If someone wished her harm, she wouldn't want them to think she would make an easy target, but all the same, her adrenaline kicked into overdrive.

"Ms. Gable. I don't mean to trouble you."

Janice's mind raced, trying to figure out who this could be. His voice sounded familiar, but she couldn't quite place it. "I'm not buying whatever it is you're selling."

"No, Ms. Gable. It's me, Vincent—Vincent Clark—from the supermarket."

Mr. Clark? Janice collected her composure, but his presence here still perplexed her. *Why would he come here?*

She flicked on the front porch light and slowly opened the door. A smile greeted her.

"Hello, Mr. Clark," she said, as she clutched the drawstring of her hood.

"Pardon me. I considered the time, and hope I didn't misjudge." He cleared his throat. "I realized after you drove away today that I'd forgotten to give you my contact information, and I didn't have your number to call, so I thought it best for me to stop by—in case you needed it."

"Oh." She shook her head in dismay. The last thing she wanted was to invite him in, but under the circumstances, she didn't know how she could object. Janice eyed the baseball bat resting in the corner; her only means of self-defense. She inspected his stance; he didn't seem threatening. His eyes held a kindness, and his jaw relaxed. Against her better judgment at this odd encounter, she opened the door a bit wider between them. "Would you like to come in?"

Mr. Clark nodded and cautiously entered. He appeared shy, unlike when they'd had their first encounter. He held his elbows close to his side and clinched his hands together with a note securely in his grasp. "Please pardon the interruption at this late hour, Ms. Gable."

Janice glanced at the clock that hung above the fireplace mantle. It read nearly seven p.m. "No, it's fine. I won't be settling in until later anyway," she said as her eyes grew heavy. She was kicking herself for taking a sleep aid. "Can I get you a coffee?"

He hesitated and made a slight rise in the corners of his mouth. "Perhaps another time."

Janice was taken aback by her disappointment at his response. She hardly knew this man. What was it about him that set her befuddled, she wondered? "Yes. Another time might be best."

Mr. Clark handed her the note with his contact information. "I'm so glad to see that you're alright. I was worried you might have gotten whiplash."

Janice brought her hand to the back of her neck and gave it a rub. "Nah. Truth be told, I suffered nothing more than a little bit of embarrassment."

His kind eyes and grin said he understood.

"Well, I guess I better be going then." He gave a nod and backed away.

"Of course," she said, then rushed around him to open the door.

He stepped across the creaking porch and tripped at the top of the stairs from a loose plank. His grasp of the railing did little to stop his momentum, and he went down with a thud. A gasp escaped his mouth. Janice raced to help him up.

"I'm so sorry!" Panic rose in her body. *Twice in one day. I'm a lawsuit waiting to happen.* "Are you okay?"

"Just a bruised ego," he said with a huff as he came to a stand.

"Are you sure? I feel horrible." Horrible was putting it mildly. First, she crashed into the poor man's car, and now he just about killed himself on her porch.

"Never you mind." He brushed himself off. "Truly, I'm fine." He took to the stairs. "You have a good rest of your night, Ms. Gable," he said, and with that, he waved goodbye.

"Good night," she whispered, hoping it wouldn't be the last she saw of him.

Janice stared at the ceiling and noticed a watermark that hadn't been there earlier. The house was decaying before her eyes. She needed repairs done before anyone got seriously hurt. She got lucky this time. But the problem was, Janice had let the house go for so long, she hadn't the money for big repairs. As it was, she barely had enough left of her inheritance to live on, let alone an insurance deductible for her car.

The sleep aid kicked in, as did her restless dreams.

seven

Vincent pulled out of Janice Gable's driveway. "You buffoon!" he shouted into the night, as he took the turn onto Lilac Lane. "The woman invites you in for coffee, and you chicken out. Right there on the spot, you chicken out."

By the time he reached the turn near the York Harbor Inn, he'd berated himself enough that he'd gotten his heart rate up. At least he was feeling something, even if it wasn't the best of feelings.

The moon shone brightly over the water, and the streets were quiet. He pulled his car over and stepped out to take in the view of Long Sands Beach and its briny scent, which never got old. The Nubble Lighthouse shone brightly in the distance and it appeared he was the only person to witness it, so he soaked in the chilly night air and slowed the rhythm of his heart with each deep breath.

What was it about that woman who pinged at his heartstrings? His wife would have said it's because he had the need to fix things—to help.

Vincent was an introvert. He knew that much about himself, which was why being a writer suited him. He could cocoon in his own little world, tucked away in his writing studio, where he could create heroes, solve mysteries, or help a damsel in distress. *Damsel in distress. Hmm, is that what this is about?*

He wished Cheryl were standing at his side so he could talk it out. She'd been his sounding board, his muse, his heart, and soul. She'd been the very air he'd breathed, and now she was gone, floating within the waves of the waters he gazed upon. "I miss you, my beloved."

A breeze billowed, and his cap took flight as if his wife had lifted it off his head in her former teasing way.

"*You fool.*" He could hear her whisper with the wind. "*She's what you need, so find your way back to her.*"

Vincent picked up his cap and brushed off the sand. A knot grew in his throat, and he tried to swallow it down as he walked his way back to his car. He sat, hoping to hear her voice again, but she was gone. He could no longer feel her presence, and he wiped his tears away with his calloused fingers.

With the turn of his key, he knew what he had to do.

eight

Madison swept the front porch of its debris, then plucked the stray tom cat out of the empty window box. The black-and-white cat darted across the lawn and into the rolling green fields before her. She looked forward to the hayfields that followed, the sweeping hay in the wind was mesmerizing. It stirred a peace in her that was far too rare. Until then, she was grateful that the harsh winter was over, and the warmth of summer was just around the corner.

She eyed a nest of newly hatched robins, and as she approached the barn, a few swallows swooped near to say hello.

"Good morning, Lily. How's my new momma doing this morning?" She patted Lily's side and gave her a good rub and a kiss on her soft nose. Lily, in return, lapped up Madison's cheek with her tongue. "I'm glad to know you're happy to see me, too."

She poured grain in her food trough and turned on the water spigot.

"How's my favorite little colt doing?" Madison squatted down to see the foal face to face. "What shall we name you, sweet boy? Hercules?" she said with a giggle. "How about—Journey?"

The foal neighed his approval and nudged her on the chin.

"Journey it is, then, because I have a feeling about you." This feeling had crept over her in the night. She wouldn't say it was divine, or would she? She hadn't quite decided.

Madison turned off the water and was laying fresh hay down in the stall when her phone rang in her pocket. *It's Franky.* She hadn't spoken to her in quite some time, and usually on a holiday. She tapped the phone to answer.

"Hey, Franky. What a surprise. What's up?"

"Not much. Same old, same old. You?"

"About the same as you," she said as a handful of hay fell to the floor. "Oh! I do have some news, though."

"Do tell."

"Lily foaled."

"Oh, no! How terrible. What happened?"

Madison laughed but was touched by Franky's ignorance. "No, it's good news. She had her baby!" She traipsed outside the barn and came to lean on a fence post of the corral. "He's the most precious little guy. I'll send you a pic."

"Oh, that is good news. Sorry, horses aren't my thing, but you already know that." She laughed, then brought the laughter to a more serious tone.

"Franky, is everything okay?"

"Yeah—probably—maybe. I'm not sure."

Madison's impatience grew, and she was on high alert. "Whatever it is that has you perplexed, just spit it out."

"It's your mom."

Madison closed her eyes, inhaled deeply, then slowly let it out.

"Madison, are you still there?"

"Yeah, I'm here. Who has she pissed off now?"

"I'm not sure how to answer that, Madison. That's a pretty loaded question."

"What then, if not that?" Madison asked with her irritation rising.

"I saw her at Hannaford's yesterday—she didn't look so good."

Madison mulled over Franky's statement, "As in sickly?"

"That's what I'm not sure about. Your mom was really pale, and she's lost a ton of weight since I last saw her. Plus, she looked like she hadn't showered in weeks."

"So, you saw her, but didn't actually talk to her. Right?" Madison asked with concern. She remembered her mom was usually dialed in. She would never see her mom in public without looking her absolute best.

"That's right. I'm sorry, I suppose I should have said hello, but she seemed—I don't know—troubled. She was mumbling to herself. Honestly, it's been such a long time that we'd seen each other that I doubted she'd even recognize me."

"I understand. Thanks for letting me know." Madison swatted at a fly buzzing around her head, not sure what she was supposed to do with the information. Her mother probably wouldn't welcome a call from her. Madison could imagine the cold reception and the rebuke to mind her own business. "Why are you home?"

"It's my mom's birthday. We're having a girl's weekend and, while I'm here, I'm going to look at houses."

Madison sighed. "That sounds really nice. I bet she's thrilled to get to spend some time with you. Wait a minute. You're moving back to York?"

"Sure am. Call me crazy, but I miss living here," she hesitated. "You know—Madison?"

Madison could sense where this was going. Somehow, asking her to take a trip home always managed to come up during their conversations. Which was precisely why she'd rarely kept in touch.

"Don't you think it's time?" Franky fell silent.

"I'll think about it. But, hey, enjoy your weekend, and please tell your mom happy birthday for me."

"Madison, I'm sorry. I didn't mean to…"

"No, it's all good. Thanks for letting me know about my mom—truly." She cleared her throat and lied. "But I should get going. I have a deadline at work I need to meet."

"Sure thing—it was good to hear your voice, Madison. I miss you."

"Miss you, too, Franky, but gotta go. Love ya," she said, then ended the call.

Madison stuffed her phone back into her pocket and paced. Over the years, she'd gotten accustomed to being away from her mom. After all, it's what she'd wanted. It's what she'd promised she'd do as soon as she was able. She never considered herself as having run away from her troubles. No, she simply removed herself from a volatile relationship.

Her mother had become more bitter and angry, especially leading up to her father's sudden death nine years ago. But, after his passing, her mother was impossible to be around. In a way, she could understand her anger, but not the way she thrust that anger on everyone around her. At least Madison was grateful that Hannah was spared the bulk of their mother's wrath. Unconditional love a parent has for a child, well, that wasn't quite the case in the Gable home. Hannah was their mother's favorite, and Madison was their father's. Madison, unfortunately, got the brunt of their mother's anger anytime their father had pushed her buttons. But sadly, after Madison left, their mother's anger shifted to Hannah.

Madison recalled a time when she was about twelve. Her

father had come home from work in a bad mood. By dinner, he would have had a drink or two under his belt and snapped out of the bad mood and into a jovial man. He'd started singing to the top of his lungs, and grabbed her by the hand, as they danced to his silly tune. Her mother stormed out of the room and took her anger out on the pots and pans until Madison felt guilty enough to go in and help.

Madison used to see him as funny and free spirited when he'd had a few, but as time went on, her mother said he'd become nothing more than an embarrassment. Looking back now, she supposed those times had become more frequent, but as a twelve-year-old, she had thought little of it. He'd called it his happy juice, and who was she to question that? To her, he seemed happier, and she thought that was a good thing. Her mother not so much.

Franky's call was unsettling. She couldn't picture her mother the way Franky had described. A sinking feeling washed over her. Maybe the time had come to go home. Madison shut the stall door. "What do you think, Lily?"

nine

*J*anice met the morning as she often had, with pessimism. Try as she may to be positive, something would inevitably cause her to stumble. It could be something small, like running out of water in her Keurig, and she'd have to refill it before she could satisfy her thirst. Or she'd watch the news, which rarely seemed good. Or it could be that her phone no longer rang. Whatever the case, she'd end up stewing with bitterness for the rest of the day. "I need a hobby. Something I can do to help me relax." Janice thought for a minute about what she used to do. She concluded that cross-stitch could do the trick. Janice was certain she had a handful of kits in one of the spare bedrooms. *Maybe something happy, like flowers.*

She pulled the curtains aside to bring in the light and made her bed for a change. She threw on some clothes, then clomped to the kitchen to fry an egg and fill her mug. *Maybe I'll just have toast with strawberry jam.* At least she'd remembered to buy the bread, which was a good sign to start the day. As she reached for the jam, the familiar sound of tires crunched up the gravel drive. Janice clunked the jar back on the refrigerator shelf and scurried through the house in time to see Mr. Clark lifting a long wooden plank, and toolbox, out of the bed of his truck.

So much for relaxing. "This is too much. I'm not some kind of charity case, you know!"

Janice pulled the door open wider and took up the door-way. "Excuse me, Mr. Clark, but what do you think you're doing?"

"Good morning, Ms. Gable," he said with a broad smile. "I'm making myself useful, if you don't mind?"

"My name is Janice. Please stop addressing me as Ms. Gable." She hadn't felt like Ms. Gable since her girls were in school, and even less so after Charlie had died.

He set his tool bag down and sized up the plank. "Very well, Janice."

Janice shook her head. She couldn't fathom why this man would attempt to fix her porch. She couldn't help but wonder what his ulterior motive was.

"What is it you're attempting to do here, Mr. Clark?"

"Vincent." Again, he smiled and rocked onto his toes. "You can call me Vincent."

"Mr. Clark, I don't know what you think you're up to, but I can assure you, I don't need your help. In fact, I find this quite insulting."

He stepped back. A dejected expression rose on his face. "I'm sorry. That wasn't my intent."

"Then what is your intent?" She knew her tone was cutting, but she couldn't fathom any other reason for him being here than wanting something in return.

"I was just trying to be nice. You seem…"

"I seem like what? Pathetic? Do you feel sorry for me? Because if you're feeling sorry for me, then you can take all of that"—she waved her arm in a sweeping arc—"and leave. I am not a charity case where you can feel you did your good deed for the day, and…"

"I don't think that at all. What I'm trying to say is that you seem, well, like me, not too long ago, and frankly, how I still am. So, I was thinking I could do something useful to get my mind off my troubles, and figured you could use the company."

Janice didn't know how to respond. What troubles could he possibly have? And why would he choose her to help and befriend? But something was telling her she could trust him, so long as he stayed outside. "I can't pay you."

"I don't want your money."

"Fine. Fix the lifted floor board if you must." With that, she turned and shut the door behind her, leaving him to his task, and leaving her to wonder what his story was.

Seeing him working on her porch made it impossible for her to sit still, so Janice tried to make herself busy by cleaning up the stacks of mail that sat on her kitchen table. She'd no sooner picked up an envelope when she found herself peering out the window to spy on Vincent. Again.

He appeared to know what he was doing as he nailed down the plank. Vincent stood back, then studied his work. He nodded, as if to acknowledge that it fit perfectly, then went about the business of hammering the extensive number of nails that stuck out of the rest of the decking.

Janice held her breath. *He's not Charlie.* If he were Charlie, he'd be barking out the tool he needed from his toolbox, or be blaming her if he measured a board wrong because she'd distracted him. He'd swear a blue streak, then have her get him a beer. Charlie had no patience for carpentry.

She strolled back to her stack of mail, hoping Vincent wouldn't lose his temper and throw the hammer into the yard only to break a flower pot. *He's not Charlie.* Still, a prickle ran down her spine, thinking at any moment, Vincent's temper could flair just as Charlie's had. Janice paused. *Just as mine does.* The weight of that fell upon her shoulders. She tried to shake off her regrets as she forced her finger through the seal of an electric bill, opened it, then chucked it back into the pile of other unpaid bills before realizing that the hammering had come to a stop.

Janice hesitated, then tiptoed back to the window to see what Vincent was up to now. He stood with a clump of the previous year's weeds in his hands as he surveyed the untamed and overgrown flower beds, then turned toward the house. Janice ducked behind the curtain, hoping she didn't get caught, and waited for her adrenaline to subside before attempting to spy again.

Vincent was kneeling on the ground by the stairs, yanking fistfuls of dried-up perennials that had long ago gone to seed. She considered, for a moment, joining him with the task, but to what end? She certainly would not tackle one flower bed and leave the rest of her yard in utter disarray. The task would be too great for her, and he wouldn't possibly continue beyond the one he'd started. Still, it seemed rude to not help. Besides, she thought, what good would become of only having one flower bed looking nice when the rest of the beds remained an eyesore? As the fleeting thought of how her yard had looked in the past flooded her mind, Janice opened the front door. "Can I get you something to drink?"

Vincent looked up. He had smears of dirt on his brow and cheek, and as he came to a stand, she could see dirt caking the knees of his jeans.

"That would be really nice, Janice."

"I have Lipton iced tea or water. What do you want?"

"Water sounds great. Thank you."

Again, with the smile. She jutted her chin at the pile of weeds. "I suppose a rake and wheelbarrow would help."

Vincent brushed his gloved hands together. "I suppose it would."

"They're in the barn." She gestured toward the backside of the house. "Help yourself while I get you your water."

Janice pulled a plastic cup down from the cupboard, then filled a pitcher with water. She glanced at the clock that hung on the yellowed, wallpapered wall. It was past noon and she figured Vincent must be hungry.

She opened a can of tuna, squeezed out the water into the sink, and used a fork to pull it from the can into a small bowl. She diced some onion and a stalk of celery, then stirred in a couple of plops of mayo and built the sandwiches. Janice was happy to see there were enough Lays potato chips in the bag's bottom to add to Vincent's plate, then forked out a couple pickles for good measure.

Janice looked at the two plates that sat on the counter. She couldn't remember the last time she'd made two plates of any-thing, and she fought back the knot building in her throat at the realization. She set the lunch on a tray and made her way through the living room and out the front door.

Vincent wasn't there, nor was the wheelbarrow or rake. She glanced over the yard from the porch toward the barn. *What is keeping him?* She set the tray on a shaky-legged table near the porch's balustrade, then ventured toward the barn. As she approached, she could see the silhouetted image of Vincent standing inside the barn with his hands on his hips and looking toward the roof rafters. Panic entered. Visions of Charlie hanging there flipped to Vincent, then back to Charlie. Her heart pounded with each step, and before she was aware, she was sprinting toward the barn.

"Get out!" she shouted, "Get out!"

Vincent turned to face her and stepped out of the open door frame. His silhouette disappeared as he reached toward her. His eyes were as wide as saucers.

"What's wrong?" he asked as he peered into the barn. "I see nothing but a…"

Janice wasn't concerned about the barn. Not Charlie. Vincent. He wasn't dead. But she couldn't seem to make her pulse slow or the nausea subside. So she fell back on anger—her savior of sanity. "Why are you here, Mr. Clark?"

"I was getting a rake and the…"

"I'm not talking about the stupid rake," she snapped. "I'm talking about why you are here—at my house—in the barn."

His brow furrowed, and his eyes narrowed. "I don't understand."

"Just get out!" She thrust her arm in the driveway's direction. "I'm done with playing games. I don't know what yours is, but if you think you can get your kicks out of my family's pain, then you can get your sick thrills somewhere else."

"I don't—I'm not…"

"For the last time! Get. Out."

Janice stepped aside as he walked past her. He tugged off his work gloves, slapping them at his thigh, and didn't turn back.

She watched until his pickup was no longer visible. Dust fell in its wake.

Janice sank to the barn's floor. Her body shook and she gasped for air. She screamed into the barn. "I hate you Charlie

Gable, and I hate this damn barn!" She felt as though she was losing her mind. Her outburst toward Vincent was over the top, and her extreme behavior was irrational. Vincent wasn't about to kill himself, she knew that, but when she'd seen Vincent's long silhouette in the pivotal spot of the barn, all sense of reality went out the window. Even so, Vincent *was* looking toward the beam where Charlie had taken his life, and he certainly wasn't looking for a wheelbarrow up there.

ten

Vincent's head was spinning with utter confusion. He wasn't sure whether to be angry or sad about the drastic turn of events. "See what happens when I try to be nice, my love?" he shouted into the wind. "That woman is impossible!"

Once again, his attempt at helping someone in need left him feeling ill-equipped and mercilessly unprepared to handle any kind of emotional trauma. His efforts were futile. All he wanted was for his life to go back to the way it used to be before cancer took his Cheryl away from him. *What's the use?* His emotions battled a raging war within him, when he sensed Cheryl's presence. "I tried! What else do you expect of me?" He never felt he did enough for Cheryl. He couldn't take away her pain or her tears. All he could do was be at her side as she slowly withered away, and Cheryl was his wife. So why was he feeling as though he were being pushed to help a complete stranger? The hairs on his arms stood up. "I'll try harder, but I don't know what to do. For crying aloud, I don't even know what I did wrong."

Vincent enjoyed digging in the dirt and fixing things. He could handle that. It brought him fulfillment. He could yank a weed and get instant gratification. Pluck the dead and pitch it away. As if he could sense the earth breathe a sigh of relief with the strangling weeds removed by their roots. With every yank, he, too, found himself able to breathe a bit easier.

He thought about what Janice had said. Was he helping her out of pity? Was he being selfish? He couldn't understand his own motives, so how could he possibly explain them to her? He was only trying to figure out where to find a stupid rake in a dilapidated barn—a barn he wasn't sure he should enter out of fear it would collapse on his head. He had a fleeting thought of adding that as another project, but with the outburst from Janice, he couldn't imagine that happening—ever.

Vincent's stomach grumbled as he entered the house. He peeled a few slices of bacon out of its package and laid them on a cast-iron skillet to fry, then sliced a tomato and pulled off a couple of lettuce leaves, slathered two slices of bread with mayonnaise, then flipped the bacon.

He longed for the days when he'd cooked for Cheryl. Again, he thought about making something out of nothing. Yes, it was in his blood. That need to create and nurture made him thrive. Without it, he, too, would wither away, just as his beloved Cheryl had done. Yet, through her pain, she could still bring herself to smile. Her smile was his last memory of her before she drifted off to an eternity of slumber.

Cancer had a way of devouring everything in its path. It consumed Cheryl's essence, the one he held so near and dear to his heart. Her ever-present zest for life held strong until the end. He knew she'd stayed on this earth as long as she had for his sake. *Yes*, he thought, *I am the selfish one. I wouldn't let her go.*

Vincent's wandering memories came to an abrupt halt as smoke billowed over the stove. He snatched up a dish towel and grabbed the pan's handle with both hands before second-guessing his actions. Vincent let go of the handle and turned off the burner as the bacon grease continued to flare. He swiveled his feet along the floor tile, trying to recall where Cheryl had kept the baking soda—she was the baker, not him. He hastily opened a couple of cabinets, spilling their contents onto the counter until he found the yellow box and dumped it into the flaming pan, then covered it with an ill-fitting lid.

Vincent opened the kitchen door and windows to allow the smoke to clear. He dumped the bread, wilting lettuce, and tomato in the trash, and pulled a three-day-old slice of pepperoni pizza out of the fridge. He then sat on a kitchen chair with, yet again, contradictory feelings. This time, the feelings were that of failure and success. He'd failed today, but somehow, he'd figure out a way to succeed with Janice Gable. He had to.

eleven

anice tossed and turned throughout the night. She was too hot, then too cold. Even her hair around the nape of her neck bothered her. She could feel her heartbeat. *Thump thump, thump thump.* Like a ticking clock, the metronome thumped until she thought she'd go out of her mind.

Janice sat up in bed and caught the full moon through the blinds. Its light cast over the fullness of the barn and corral. She detested that barn. It was a beacon whose sole purpose was to taunt and torment her. When Janice tried closing her eyes, she could almost hear the creak of the barn's rafter and the slide of a rope going back and forth, back and forth. Janice despised Charlie for what he'd done. For, as long as she lived, she would never get the image of him out of her mind, and she couldn't take it anymore.

She scooted off the edge of the bed and stepped into a pair of jeans, then pulled on a sweatshirt that she'd earlier flung to the floor. She grabbed the hair tie off her nightstand and put her hair into a sloppy bun as she traipsed down the flight of stairs leading to the living room. Janice slid her feet into her pull-on muck boots and stomped toward the barn—her nemesis.

"Enough is enough!"

Janice eyed the interior of the barn. She took in the scent of mildew from the old hay that remained in the loft. She ran her hand along the edge of the horse stall's half-door, recalling Madison's pride and joy. The stall was just as it was nine years ago. Lily's bridle draped over a peg just outside the stall. Its worn leather had become stiff to the touch.

Too many bad memories lived here. Memories she needed to destroy. "It's you or me."

Janice stepped through the tool closet's entrance in the barn and picked through the small, cluttered room. She retrieved the wheelbarrow, then loaded it up with a rake, a spade, hose, and both the garden and snow shovel. The grooved floor boards sagged as she pushed the wobbly wheelbarrow through the barn and out into the night.

She was winded by the time she reached the back door of the house, but went back to the tool closet. Janice considered removing the lawn mower but figured it no longer worked, then picked up the gas can. The slosh of gasoline moved in the can. *Good, it's nearly full.* Outside of that, she determined, there wasn't anything else worth keeping.

Janice held the gas can and tried to will herself to pour its contents throughout the barn and strike a match. She wanted to set the barn ablaze, watch it burn, watch it disappear. Janice pictured flames consuming the barn boards. She envisioned the red-hot flames lapping up the structure beams and rafters. Janice wished she could smell the smoke and hear the crackling of timbers. She wanted the barn to become nothing but ash.

But the last thing she needed was for the fire and police to show up, as she would undoubtedly be arrested for arson. Thus, causing her family name to once again be tarnished.

She recalled them showing up all those years ago. They'd lowered her husband's lifeless body to the dirty planks and determined it was suicide. Still, her desire to see the barn turn to ash and rubble overtook her senses. She tore through the barn toward the tool closet and retrieved the sledgehammer she'd seen earlier and hoisted it over her head and swung.

"Take that, you piece of shit!" With each blow of the hammer, she let out a guttural scream. "And that!"

Sweat pouring down her brow, Janice was near exhaustion but had made little progress in her attempt to bring the barn down. *I can't let it win.*

Then she thought about Charlie's old tractor. She'd used it this past winter to clear snow. It sat near the double doors at the back. She checked to see if there was still gas in its tank. To her relief, gasoline shimmered. Janice straddled the seat and turned the key. Nothing. She pulled the lever for the throttle and tried again. The engine sputtered and spit, before the machine shook and engaged. Janice put the tractor in reverse and pressed the pedal to the floor. She slammed into the shed's door frame, then tore through the barn, and rammed into a support beam before coming to a stop. She jammed the gear into reverse, then forward and struck another beam.

With each and every hit of a wall or beam, she felt more alive. She grew giddy as the wood splintered and lifted from their supports. Her adrenaline peaked as the barn listed and swayed with each attempt. "I'm not going to let you win."

Janice was in the moment, and didn't think of what would come next. Euphoria had taken over, and she hadn't noticed the tremendous shift of the structure until it was too late. Down came a side wall with a crash. Janice and the stalled tractor became trapped in the timbers.

Pain seared through the right side of her body. Her arm

and leg wedged between the tractor and a wooden beam. Janice clenched her teeth and attempted to pull herself from under it, screaming as white heat shot through her leg and she felt the blood drain from her face. She shivered uncontrollably, and her pain intensified with each shiver.

That's when the realization of her predicament set in. She could die there, and no one would come to her rescue. The barn was going to win after all.

Janice took in her surroundings. She thought if she could start the tractor again, she might be able to drive out from under the pile. She turned the key, and it sputtered, then backfired. The bang sounded like a gun going off, and she jumped in the seat.

"Help!" she screamed until her throat was hoarse.

What's the point of yelling? There was no one to hear her. She even considered her closest neighbors might be within earshot, but remembered they rarely came back from snow birding until mid-May. Despair swept through her. *I can't die in this barn.*

Once again, she screamed into the night's air. Her arm throbbed and her leg felt as though it were on fire. *So, this is it.* "Is this my punishment? Is this how I'm to die?" she said with a whimper. "Are you satisfied, Charlie Gable?"

She pictured her husband laughing at the irony that the beam that trapped her was the same beam he'd swung from.

Janice pounded the beam with her free hand. The pain didn't matter; she screamed through it. And it didn't matter that with each strike, she did more damage to her wounds. "I'm sorry I didn't help you when you needed me, Charlie!" Janice continued to strike the beam until she hadn't an ounce of strength left. "I'm so sorry."

That's when she convulsed with tears. Her body was purging all her pain, anguish, regret, and guilt. She mourned for Charlie and for driving her girls away. Her guttural cries spilled with remorse for the life she wished she'd had. Then she closed her eyes and attempted to control her breathing. *In and out. In and out.*

"I can't die here. Not here. Not now. Not like this."

Janice was still angry with God for taking Charlie, but He was all she had right now. "Please help me, God."

Time ticked by, and she could hear a barn owl hoot in the distance. Still the metronome beat on. In the quiet. In the dark.

"I'll try to do better. I'll be better."

Tick, tick, tick.

I want to see my girls again.

The moon cast its light across her body as a dreamlike state moved through her. She couldn't feel pain anymore. *I want to live. I want…*

twelve

The shrill of a phone awakened Madison. She breathed a heavy sigh at realizing she'd forgotten to put it into sleep mode. As she reached for it on the night table, she inadvertently dropped it to the floor. "For Pete's sake."

Nathan stirred. "Is everything okay?" he said with a groggy voice.

"I'm not sure." She leaned over the edge of the bed and felt around in search of the phone. "I can't find the stupid thing. I can almost touch it—ooh, got it!"

Madison sat up and peered into the blue light. She dimmed the screen. "I missed a call from Franky."

"Why would she be calling?"

"I don't know, Nathan. I missed the call." She didn't mean to snap, but Franky wouldn't call this late unless she had a reason. Then she wondered if it wasn't Franky at all, and someone was using her phone because something had happened to her. Fear thundered through her body like a shock wave as she recalled when she learned that her father was dead.

"Well, did she leave a message?" Nathan asked.

Madison looked to see if the voicemail icon had changed status. "No."

By now, she was wide awake. Her heart pounded, hoping that if there was something wrong, she'd call again.

Nathan adjusted his pillow and flopped his head down. "Must not have been important, then. You should try to go back to sleep."

"You don't know that, Nathan. People hardly ever leave messages anymore," she said as she willed the phone to ring again, then sighed in frustration. "I can't sleep." She hopped off her side of the bed. "I'm getting a glass of water. Want anything?"

His response was a loud snore.

Madison didn't bother to tiptoe her way out of the bedroom, as she debated whether she should return the call or let things be. For all she knew, the call might have been made by mistake.

She took a large gulp of water while she peered out the kitchen window. The sky was bright, and if she hadn't known better, she would have guessed it to be near dawn.

Nathan's right. If it was important, she'd call back.

Madison refilled her glass, then grabbed her jacket that was draped off the back of the kitchen chair and slid on a pair of Sketchers. It was too beautiful a night to go back to bed.

She curled up on the cushioned chaise lounge that sat on the back porch. The quiet of the night invited her in. She took in the skyline and the silhouette of the barn, whose shadow cast across the sprawling field. She inhaled deeply, allowing the cool air to enter her lungs. Still, her heart wouldn't settle. Something was off. She could feel it.

Madison's thought went to Franky's call about seeing her mother looking sickly, and yet, all she focused on was that Franky had been home for her mom's birthday party.

Madison struggled to recall a time when they'd celebrated

her own mother's birthday. There was one time when she, Hannah, and her parents went out to dinner, and she vaguely remembered a piece of cake with a candle on it. The memory left her thinking it was a sad occasion instead of a happy one. Her parents had argued. Madison closed her eyes and played that night out in her head and the memory came back in a rush. *Yes, it was for Mom's birthday.*

They'd gone somewhere fancy in downtown Portsmouth, New Hampshire. *The Martingale Wharf Restaurant.* They sat at a table inside with a white linen tablecloth near the windows where boats floated by on the Piscataqua River, coming and going between the two bridges. They'd ordered their food. Then her father said he saw someone and stepped away from the table.

Their family had a rule that everyone had to be seated at the table with their food before anyone could eat. She remembered this because he hadn't returned when the food arrived, so they sat there waiting, and Hannah whined because she was hungry. Their mother had finally given in when they'd both complained and carried on, and the three of them had finished their dinner before her dad returned. By the time he came back, his food was cold. The server had placed a small chocolate cake with one lit candle in front of her mother, but instead of blowing it out, her mother had plucked the candle out of the cake and stuffed it, flame down, into her father's uneaten entrée, then demanded they leave.

Hannah was crying, and Dad yelled that he'd been doing business. Her mother shoved her chair back, stood up, and walked away with Hannah following behind. Once her sister and mother were out of view, her father had picked up his fork, winked at her, then ate her mother's cake. Embarrassed and uncomfortable, watching her dad eat her mother's cake, she hadn't known what to do. Madison tried to justify her father's behavior: he'd been working. But the explanation felt wrong. Her mother would be livid when they would finally reach the car. She wasn't sure if there'd be a screaming match, or if it would be utter silence on the ride home. All she knew for sure was that her mother would take her anger out on her, and she wanted to crawl into a hole and disappear.

Yep, she realized, that was the last birthday celebration she could remember in their family's household. Looking back now, she almost felt sorry for her mother. It had been her mother's birthday, and her father turned it into a joke.

Madison yawned and rubbed her puffy eyes. She was exhausted, but it was too late to go back to bed since it was nearly time to feed the horses. She picked herself up from the chaise. Her legs tingled, and she gave them a rub to help her circulation return when her phone rang, startling her. It was Franky.

Madison swallowed hard. "Hey, Franky. What's up?"

"Oh, good." She puffed on the other end. "You're awake."

Franky's voice seemed stressed and worried. "Are you alright? You don't sound good." She held her breath, waiting for Franky's response.

"No, I'm good, Mads." Franky hesitated. "I'm sorry to have to tell you this, but it's your mom."

Madison's mind reeled, and she sat back down on the chaise. She knew something hadn't felt right, and she kicked herself for not calling Franky back earlier. "Is she..."

"She's going to be okay."

Madison breathed a sigh of relief, but part of her still felt as though she were teetering on the edge of a ledge, afraid to see what lay below. "What happened?"

"She had an accident—in the barn."

An accident? A sickness crept in and nausea filled her abdomen. A world of scenarios flooded her mind. Was it really an accident? Did she try to kill herself, too? How? When? Why? Madison couldn't breathe. She dropped her head between her knees and tried not to pass out.

"Madison, did you hear me?"

Just breathe.

"Mads?"

"I'm here, Franky. What happened?"

"She was in the barn when it collapsed. A beam fell on top of her and it pinned her beneath it. And Madison—honey— she was found two days later."

Two days? Alone? In the barn? As much as she detested her mother, she wouldn't have wished what had happened to her on anyone. Madison's built-up tears ran down her cheeks. "You said she was okay, though, right?"

"Yes. My brother was on call and ended up being one of the EMTs that helped your mom. He said she's in the York hospital with a broken collarbone, and her leg is pretty messed up."

"Messed up?"

"I guess they had to remove some kind of giant nail or spiky thing from her thigh. It was attached to the beam that fell on her."

Madison knew that spike. Nausea crawled up her throat. It was where she'd looped her horse's bridle, and lead rope, the same rope her father had used to tie around his neck.

"Franky," she said with labored breath. "Was she trying to kill herself, too?"

"I don't think so, Mads."

Madison gasped for air between jagged breaths. None of this was making sense. "Who—who found her?"

"I think Ryan said it was some guy named Vinny or Vincent something. The man was still there when they arrived at the scene."

Madison pulled herself together enough to blurt out her response. "Vincent?"

"I'm pretty sure it's the name Ryan mentioned. Why? Do you know someone with that name? It meant nothing to me."

"No, but then again, I haven't been home in—well—forever."

"True enough," Franky said with an undercurrent of sarcasm that wasn't lost on Madison.

"So, are you coming home?"

Madison tightened the coat around her suddenly cold shoulders. "I'm not sure just yet—but I'll tell you when I know. Oh, and Franky?"

"Yeah?"

"Would you let me know if you hear of any changes with my mom?"

"Sure thing."

Madison had disappointed Franky, but even if she decided to visit her mother, she doubted anything would change between them. They were like opposite ends of a magnetic force; never the two shall meet eye to eye on anything. And yet…

"Okay then," Madison said, unwilling to commit to anything right now. "I'll talk with you later."

With that, Madison ended the call.

She leaned back in the chaise and pulled her knees up. Her arms wrapped around them for warmth. Who was Vincent? His name didn't ring a bell. Had her mother finally moved on? Were they an item? He obviously wasn't living there with her, or he'd have found her sooner. Unless, of course, he was someone else her mother sank her teeth into then destroyed. But then again, why would he have been there to find her? Regardless of how she felt about her mother and this unknown man, Madison was grateful he'd discovered her in time.

The porch door squeaked open and Nathan stepped onto the porch, balancing two cups of coffee in his hands, then shut the door with his hip.

"Saw you were on the phone," he said as he handed her a cup, then took a seat next to her. "Franky?"

Madison shot Nathan a weak smile as she held the hot cup. She leaned into his shoulder and took a deep inhale of the steaming brew.

"Yep. It was Franky," she said, then filled Nathan in on all the details of the call.

Nathan listened intently. He'd nod here and there, grunted an *mmm*, and an *oh*, now and again. She couldn't have asked anything more of him in that moment until he shattered his understanding with the words: *you should*.

Madison cringed when anyone told her she should. Those two words meant she didn't have good judgment, that she was lacking, that they were smarter than she was. She'd heard it too many times from her mother. She could still hear her mom's cutting tone. "Madison! You should be smarter than that. You should know better. You should cut your hair. You should stand up straight. You should do as I say. Madison, you should study harder. You should be more like your sister."

The list of shoulds went on and on. What's worse was the fact that the list of shoulds came from the woman who should have been a better wife and mother. For that matter, she thought she should have simply been a better person.

Madison came to a stand. "Ya know what, Nathan? I wasn't asking for your advice, and I think I know what I should and shouldn't do regarding my mother."

Nathan rolled his eyes and took a sip of his coffee.

"Seriously! That's your response? Rolling your eyes like a child?"

Nathan ran his hand through his hair, then turned toward her. "What do you want me to say, Madison? Because nothing I say or do lately is good enough for you."

His words cut deep. He was right. Her tolerance was horrible lately, but she couldn't seem to help herself. She'd been on edge because she couldn't get her head out of the past, and found herself resenting everything and everyone. In that moment Madison came face to face with her greatest fear.

She was becoming just like her mother.

thirteen

*J*anice lay in the hospital bed. Her mind was foggy as she came in and out of a deep sleep. *Was it a dream?* No, she thought. It was real. As real as the throbbing in her leg and the sling that wrapped over her arm and shoulder. She remembered ramming the tractor in the barn, and the thunderous sound of timbers crashing down around her. She remembered unmerciful pain and being trapped.

Janice listened to the beeps and buzzes that now surrounded her. In the hallway, shoes squeaked and voices murmured in the distance. A grease board with the date, a nurse's name, and the words *needs assistance* prominently highlighted with red marker. *Why would I need assistance?*

She tried to adjust her legs in the bed, but the minimal effort caused her pain level to spike, nearly taking her breath away. She gasped and beads of sweat formed on her forehead. *That damnable beam trapped me beneath it.*

She peered at the grease board and noted the date, and calculated that nearly four days had passed since she'd gone to the barn, but she couldn't for the life of her figure out how she ended up in the hospital.

A smiling woman wearing scrubs traipsed through the room. "Well, now, would you look at who's awake? Good afternoon, Janice. How are we feeling?"

How are we feeling? How cliché. "Just peachy."

"I've come to give you your pain meds and a little something to keep your leg from swelling, and a little something to keep the infection from getting worse," she said as her icy hand rested on her own. The name on her lanyard read, Jodie Fox, RN, the same name that was scribbled on the grease board that hung on the wall.

"Are you hungry?" she asked as she adjusted the IV cords.

Her mouth was dry, she knew that much, but hungry, she had to think about that.

"You'll have to keep your diet somewhat simple to start. How about some soup? The chicken noodle is pretty good."

Janice's stomach churned. "Sure, chicken soup sounds great."

"It sure is nice seeing you more alert today," Jodie said with a smile. "Mr. Clark will be happy to hear it."

Alarm bells rang in Janice's head. *Mr. Clark.* "Are you talking about Vincent Clark?"

"Why, yes, I am. He keeps calling in to ask about you."

"Oh, really?" Janice asked. She couldn't fathom how he'd know she was even here, or why he'd care one iota about her well-being. Especially after the way she'd treated him.

"Is that a problem?" A crease formed between Jodie's eyes. "We just assumed that it was okay," she said as she pulled the blanket up over Janice's feet. "He told us he was your special friend, and, since he was the one that found you and called for help, we thought we could talk to him."

Jodie placed a fresh, cold compress on Janice's bandaged leg, then tucked the blanket in. "Would you prefer we remove him from your contact list?"

Vincent found me? But how?

"What would you like us to do?"

Janice considered her question. *My special friend.* She was grateful that Vincent had found her, but calling himself her *special* friend had crossed the line. Even so, she supposed it wasn't any harm to fill him in on her condition, whatever that was.

"That's fine," she said when it occurred to her that Nurse Jodie had said *list.* "Who else is on my list?"

"I'll have to check, but as I recall, Ryan Murphy is on it. He's the emergency tech that brought you here. Oh, and your daughters, Madison, and Hannah. I think that's it, but I can take a peek, to be sure."

Janice wasn't sure with whom she was more surprised. Vincent, Madison's childhood friend's brother, Ryan, or Madison.

The pain meds kicked in, and Janice succumbed to her overwhelming grogginess. She realized she hadn't even asked about her injuries. Maybe she had, but she couldn't remember. She had questions—so many questions—but her eyelids grew heavy, and she drifted off to sleep.

Images of Madison swam through her dreams. Charlie was swinging Madison around. Her tiny hands clutched tightly to his with her arms extended as they both laughed. Other images of Charlie and Madison included reading stories together in her worn-out recliner; Charlie holding a tether rope so Madison could ride for the first time; Madison, running into Charlie's arms after a win in basketball. Fishing gear. Charlie and Madison—the dynamic duo. Then Charlie's body was limp, hanging from the rafter, Madison's red face and tearful eyes burning with hatred toward her. "You did this to him." Madison's face weaved back and forth, each time getting angrier, closer, as Charlie's head bobbed from side to side. "I needed you." He bobbed. "You let me down." Janice couldn't escape the dream. She couldn't run away.

"Mom."

Janice stirred, but she couldn't open her eyes. She willed herself to open them, hoping if she could, the dreams would stop.

"Mom, it's me, Madison."

Janice felt the weight of a hand on her calf, and the sinking of her bed as if someone were sitting on its edge. In her sleepy state, she licked her lips. They were chapped. She must be dreaming—these feelings—these words weren't real. Madison couldn't possibly be here.

"Mom, wake up. You need to eat."

The aroma of chicken soup and the fresh scent of shampoo wafted through the air. She opened her eyes, and a blurry vision of her daughter stared her in the face. Madison *was* here? "Madison?"

A second chance, she thought. *I have a second chance to make things right.*

fourteen

Madison gazed upon her mother lying in the narrow hospital bed. Her once bright green eyes appeared faded with time. Her complexion was ashen, and her graying matted hair clung to her neck. Had she looked like this before the accident as well? Was this what Franky had seen at the supermarket? If so, she could certainly understand Franky's concern.

Madison braced herself. "Hello, Mother."

Her mother's eyelids blinked, as if she were trying to focus. "Is it really you?" she asked, with a quietness to her tone. Her mother's free hand reached toward Madison's cheek and tenderly touched it as if she were blind and needed to sense each curve to fully take her in.

A lump formed in Madison's throat, and she tried to swallow it down. Her mother's tender touch moved her, a touch she'd been missing from her mother for most of her life. Madison wasn't sure if she should be happy or sad. It was as if the woman that lay before her was a different person. Maybe she'd mellowed with age and time. Something inside told her differently. It was just the meds.

Madison pulled away and cleared her throat. "The nurse said you need to eat. It will help you get your strength back."

Madison stood and maneuvered the wheeled tray table away from the side of the bed and located the remote. She held the button down and the head of the bed inclined to which her mother grimaced.

"Stop," she said with a groan and adjusted herself. "Okay, try again."

"How's that?"

"If you really want to know, it's terrible," she huffed.

"Do you want me to…"

"No!" she said with a dismissive wave of the hand. "You've done enough."

Madison's shoulders tensed, reminding her of the stress that would be sure to follow. *There's my mother.*

"You know what, Mom?" She needed to get out of here and regroup before she said something she regretted. She grabbed the soup bowl. "I'm going to see about getting your soup warmed up."

"Don't bother. Whether it's hot or cold, it won't do anything to change the nasty flavor."

"So, you've already had some soup then?" Madison wheeled the cart closer to the bed and swung the table over her mother's lap.

"No, I haven't, but it's hospital food. How good could it be?"

Madison watched as her mom fought to open a small bag of oyster crackers. Against her better judgment, she opens herself up to more rejection. "Want some help with that?"

To her surprise, her mother shrugged and handed over the packet of crackers.

"Don't suppose you'll be sticking around for too long."

The turn of conversation took Madison aback. In her haste to get there, she never considered the question. Nathan hadn't even asked about her plans when she'd packed to leave Ohio. The only thing on her mind was to get there. She had no expectations and no timetable. She figured she'd see what happened, guessing her mother would either push her away, or Madison would simply lose all patience and bail, just like she'd done eight years ago.

"I'm not sure." Madison fidgeted with the ring she wore on her thumb. The hammered, white gold band had been the first gift Nathan had given her, and the habit of spinning it helped to calm her nerves. "Figured I'd play it by ear."

"Suppose you're wanting to stay at the house."

"Hadn't really thought about it, Mother," she said, but she *had* thought about going to the house. She wasn't looking forward to going there. The past already haunted her, but to be back at the house was sure to bring back more memories she'd just as soon forget. Still, staying there was her best option. "Seems to make sense."

"Do as you will," she said, then slurped her soup.

Madison wanted to face the elephant in the room. The problem was that it was no longer one elephant; it was a whole herd, and she didn't know where to begin. She glanced up at the clock. It was getting late. She was exhausted, and she wasn't mentally prepared to deal with her mother. Her questions would have to wait.

Janice wiped her face with the napkin, then stuffed it into the now empty soup bowl and pushed away the table. "I'm tired, Madison. It might be best if you head out."

Madison watched the table roll with her mother's dismissive shove, much like she was feeling—dismissed and unimportant. "Of course, you must be tired," she said, unsure of herself, and came to a stand. "I don't imagine you have your house keys here with you?"

Janice scowled. "Why would I have my keys? The door wasn't locked."

"I see. It's just that Ryan Murphy told me the house had to be checked for safety purposes. You know, in case you had something on the stove or something." Madison cleared her throat. "And they locked the house up when they left—for security."

Janice sighed. "The hidden key is in the same place as it's always been, but you'll have to dig around for it. Things are a bit overgrown."

Overgrown? What did Mom mean by that? Madison pulled her handbag strap over her shoulder and clutched it to her side, then turned to say goodbye. Her mother was already fast asleep, so she whispered goodbye and retreated from the room. This time, as she walked away, her mother didn't shout in fury. No, she thought. This time, she felt as though she was leaving someone she'd known from a distant past, much like a stranger, and her heart ached with that newfound insight.

The thought of walking into that house again weighed on her. It had been such a long time since she'd lived there, and she couldn't imagine how she'd feel stepping back in time. *Has it changed?*

Madison took the corner of route 1A onto Lilac Lane. The house was only a few quick turns away, and sweet memories flooded in like the tide. The Wiggly Bridge and Steedman Woods brought her to a place of longing for the innocence and happier days of her youth. A time when she and Franky rode their bikes and played make-believe in the woods. Their fortress of fallen twigs and branches was their safe place, where their imaginations could take them anywhere, and they could be anything they wanted to be.

She rolled down her window and inhaled, taking in the seacoast's scent. Oh, how she'd missed this, she thought with a sense of longing.

Within a few moments, she'd drive by Franky's family home. She wouldn't stop just yet. She wanted to settle in first. As she approached Franky's house, it occurred to her she wouldn't recognize Franky's car if she saw it. She certainly wouldn't still drive the old Ford Pinto they'd bombed around in, back in the day. Madison chuckled at the thought. They'd sung Gavin DeGraw's "Chariot" at the top of their lungs.

Madison slowed as she passed Franky's place. Their house looked the same as she remembered and she noticed there weren't any cars in the driveway as she picked up speed. *Just another half mile to go.* Her hands sweat on the steering wheel. *One more turn of the road.* She held her breath.

Madison sank into her seat, stunned, as she stared at her childhood home in such disrepair. Her parents had taken such pride in its appearance, and she'd been proud, too. Its once pristine landscaping, sprawling porch, and structure of the past were no more. Now, the beautiful home sat looking as if it wore the family's veil of shame. She felt sick to her stomach. Madison hadn't realized how deeply her father's death had affected her mother. Her mother and their home were broken; their wounds hadn't healed. They'd only gotten worse. At that moment, Madison realized how lucky she'd been to escape when she had.

She put the rental car into park and climbed out of her seat. The trunk popped open with the click of the fob. She lifted her suitcase out and lugged it toward the front steps, noticing a few new planks here and there. *Somebody's been doing some work.* She heaved the bag up the stairs and wheeled it next to the door before attempting to search for the key.

Madison was knee-deep in weeds, shoving overgrown vines out of the way. She reached for the stone that hid the house key, pricking her finger on a thorny branch.

"Ouch!" She shook her hand, then stuck the injured finger into her mouth and gave it a suck before kicking the stone over. To her relief, a rusted key ring held the prize. She just hoped it still worked.

Madison shoved the key into the lock, but it wouldn't turn. She jiggled it, pulled it out, then tried again, to no avail. In her frustration, she banged on the door and gave it a kick for good measure before she thought about trying the back door.

She stomped around the side of the house, and the red barn caught her attention. Madison hadn't forgotten about the barn; she'd pushed it out of her mind. She stepped toward the barn and slumped to her knees. Seeing it in front of her, she held her stomach with the shock of the destruction. Remorse flooded her senses. *Mom could have died.*

Madison felt as though the ground were swallowing her up. The image of her father's lifeless body came back as if she'd witnessed it yesterday—stark and in full color. She remembered Lily's frantic shuffling and shifting of hooves. Lily moved from side to side as if she knew something was terribly wrong.

Madison could almost hear her mother's long-ago guttural screams as she ran full speed in her direction.

Her lungs expanded with a deep intake of air, and she pressed her palm against her chest. She wished she could lock the moment away in her memory and throw away the key. She pulled herself together and tried to see what was real and present.

The small barn's outer wall had caved inward. The entire building was listing to the left. That it was still standing surprised her. So much of her wished it had fallen completely. Perhaps then she and her family could move on.

She strode to the back door with the rusty key in hand. Madison's spine prickled. Was she imagining things? She could swear she saw a shadow move. Her muscles tightened. Footsteps came up behind her. She swung around and came face to face with a man.

His eyebrows raised with interest. "Hey there."

Madison took a couple of steps back. Her mind reeling with questions. "Hello."

"The name's Vincent. Who might you be?"

Having recognized the name as the man who'd saved her mother, she let her guard down. "Vincent—you found my mother."

"The one and the same." He stuck his hand out for a shake, and she grasped his full grip. "How's your mother doing?"

"I'm sorry." She shook her head. "You say your name's Vincent, but that means nothing to me." She pulled her hand away and stuck it in her jacket pocket. "Who are you, and how do you know my mother?"

"I'm not exactly sure myself." He chuckled. "The thing is, we pretty much just met last week. She hit my car in the Hannaford's parking lot."

"She did what?" Her head spun, trying to make sense of what this man was saying.

Vincent explained how they'd met, and why he'd come by, then ended up helping around the house. "Your mom, well, she got upset with me. Not sure why, but she asked me to leave."

Madison's defenses triggered. She pulled her hands out of her pockets and took a broad stance. She could only imagine why her mother could have been upset, but then again, her mother was a hothead. Even so, what if she'd been justified by *his* behavior?

"All I did was go to the barn to get a rake, and the next thing I know, she was kicking me out. It was the darndest thing."

Well, that could explain her anger. With her mother's reaction, she guessed there hasn't been another man in that barn since her father. So seeing Vincent in there probably set her off, and with good reason.

Madison dropped her heightened alert. "How did you come to find my mother in the barn?"

"Well, a couple of days after I left here, I realized I didn't have my hammer in my tool bag, so I came back to see if I might have set it down on the porch, but I couldn't find it. Your mom's car was here. I knocked quite a few times. When she didn't answer, I walked out back to see if she was outside. That's when I saw the barn. It wasn't like that when I was here last. Then I saw her on that tractor with a beam laying across her," he said as he scratched his head, eyes widened. "It scared me to death."

Madison swallowed hard. She had to tell Hannah.

Madison rested her hand on his shoulder. "Thank you, Vincent. You saved her life."

"So, she's doing okay then?"

"She's just as grumpy as always. Did you ever find your hammer?"

"Nope." A grin formed across his face. "That's why I'm here."

Madison gestured toward the barn. "Please feel free to look around, but be careful."

He grimaced. "Will do." He walked away before coming to an abrupt halt. "You said you're Janice's daughter, but I didn't get your name."

"Madison." She could tell he was rolling her name around in his head.

"Thank you, Madison. Please give your mom my regards." With that, he headed toward the barn.

Seeing a man, other than her father, trudging through her yard felt strange. He seemed nice enough, but part of her questioned why her mother made him leave. Was her mother just being her typical crotchety self, or was there something more to the story?

She stood there until he was out of view, then went to see about the back door.

Her earlier trepidation at entering the house had waned. Now she just wanted to be inside and get settled. Her stomach was growling, and her bladder was nearing its capacity.

Madison wiggled the key in and turned it to unlock, and once again, it didn't work.

"You stupid, crappy, good for nothing…"

"Having some trouble getting in?" Vincent shouted.

Madison slumped, kicked the door, and tried it again. "No, I'm good, thanks." But she wasn't good. The key was now stuck in the lock.

Vincent's footsteps landed at her side. "Found my hammer." He gave it a wave. "I can break the lock and fix it for you after, if that will help."

She considered his suggestion, as her urgency to use the bathroom was now near panic. "Sure," she said as she backed away from the door. "Go ahead."

Vincent's aim was right on, and with the rot near the locking system, the door easily pulled open. "Looks like I'll have more to fix than just the lock."

"Yep." Madison scurried by him in a hurry. She didn't take the time to look around as she skidded around the corner toward the bathroom, then slammed the door shut.

"Will this crappy day never end?" She sputtered a stream of profanity while she searched for a roll of toilet paper.

"Is everything alright in there?"

Seriously? "I'm fine—thanks."

Madison opened every cabinet, but no paper would be found. "Drip dry it is."

"Pardon?"

"Nothing!" she shouted through the closed door. "I'm just talking to myself!" She hurriedly washed her hands and stepped into the hallway, then peeked around the corner. Vincent's hands rested on his hips as he eyed the door.

"Think you can fix it?" She rubbed her damp hands on the front of her jeans.

"It seems to have quite a bit of dry rot around the frame and the threshold." Vincent scratched his stubbled chin. "The sill could use some help, too."

Madison stood back to measure the stranger before her. "Did my mom hire you as a handyman?" She shifted her weight to her other foot. "Is that how you know each other?"

"No, ma'am. Just as I said before, we ran into each other at the supermarket."

Madison shook her head, trying her best to not lose her temper with his vagueness. "I'm not following."

"Honestly, we've only met briefly two, no, make that three

times." He ran his hand over the wooden door frame. "But when I tripped on one of her floorboards. I came back to fix it."

"So, what you're telling me is, you were helping her, and she kicked you off her property." She had a hard time wrapping her head around what he was telling her. Was there something more than her mom seeing him in the barn, that caused her to send him away?

"That about sums it up." He brushed his hands together and nodded his head. "I'll have to grab some tools from home and make a stop at the Lowes, but I'll have this better than new in no time."

Madison chewed on her lip, then gave a sigh. "I'm just going to come right out with it."

"Okay." He cocked his head and raised eyebrows. "What's on your mind?"

She stared directly into his eyes. "Can I trust you?"

Vincent leaned back and gave a belly laugh. "Believe me, I only have the best of intentions. Woo-wee, if my wife were here right now, she'd be rolling on the floor."

"So, this is funny to you, mister—mister—Clark?" Prickles went up her spine. If he said one more word making light of this, she'd karate chop him right in the throat.

"My goodness, no. I didn't mean to suggest that your question was funny. It's just that I don't think anyone has ever thought of me as intimidating, or, for that matter, untrustworthy." His lips turned up into a smile. "Ms. Madison, you have nothing to fear with the likes of me. I'm just here to help, in any way that I can."

"Why?"

"Because it's how I was raised, and because my wife told me I should."

Madison weighed his answer. He seemed genuine, and he did appear to have the knowledge to fix the broken door, but skepticism remained.

Vincent picked up his hammer and shoved his free hand in his pocket. "Well, I suppose I should get the materials to fix your lock before it gets dark."

"Sure. Um, thanks for helping me get into the house." She thrust her hands in her pockets and teetered back and forth. "Be sure to get me receipts."

Madison looked on as he trudged through the unkept lawn. *I'll be keeping my eye on you, Mr. Vincent Clark.*

Madison closed the door as best she could, then her gaze took in the fullness of the kitchen. The wallpaper had yellowed. Most of the overhead lighting bulbs were out. A moldy bowl of soup sat on the table. A musty washcloth draped over the handle of the stove and baked-on food filled the electric burners. Dead plants sat in dried pots on the dusty windowsill, and it appeared as though the coffee pot hadn't been washed since she'd left home.

As much as she held animosity toward her mother, her heart broke to know she'd taken her father's death so hard. She must have loved him to become so shattered.

Madison ran her hand over the height measurements of her and Hannah on the kitchen pantry's door frame. Their measurements were taken every year on their first day of school. Next to the M, in her mother's handwriting, was the same year her dad died. There were no lines of measurements after.

Madison slumped down on the yellow floral cracked-vinyl kitchen chair, and sobbed.

fifteen

Janice awoke from a nightmare she tried to shake off. Her sheets were damp, and her hospital gown twisted around her waist. It seemed so real, she thought as the dream flooded her mind.

Madison wore a pair of jean-skirted bib overalls, and she was twirling in the backyard, between the barn and the kitchen door. As she danced and twirled, vines grew wildly and entangled her feet, inch by inch, until she could no longer move. Madison was trapped as the vine thickened and wound around her throat. Charlie ran from the barn and tugged on the rope to remove it, but the rope tightened with each yank.

Janice breathlessly tried to reach them, but she, too, got entangled in the weeds and vines. All she could do was fight to save her eldest daughter, but the fight was a losing battle, and she was too late. Charlie turned to dust and the wind carried him away, while Madison's body lay motionless on the ground, except for one hand that reached out to her with a last effort to be saved.

Janice's pulse raced and her heart rate spiked as she relived the nightmare. She gripped her gown and tugged on the hem to free herself from its suffocating hold on her, but when she moved, pain shot down her leg, and she let out a scream. Frustrations grew to a crescendo as the night nurse burst through the door.

"Get this off of me!" Janice's hand yanked at the gown's laces, and as she pulled, the intravenous tubing came out.

"Ms. Clark! Janice! Please try to calm down."

"Calm down?" she barked. "Can't you see? I'm trapped—we're all trapped." She wiggled and strained to free herself. "We are all being strangled to death!"

The last thing Janice remembered was a loud noise, much like a horn, and a couple of white-jacketed people gathering around her, holding her down. A pinch in her arm carried her off to dream once again.

sixteen

As tired as Madison was from her travels and the events of the day, the last thing she wanted to do was house-keeping, and yet, she yanked the sheets off her childhood bed with a huff and gathered them into her arms. She stormed down the hall from her upstairs bedroom to the bathroom, pulled the towel off its hook, then made her way to the laundry room.

Next, she'd see what there was to eat, but feared there'd be nothing until she remembered her mom had just recently gone to Hannaford's. Unfortunately, all she could do was muster up some Cheerios. She took a whiff of the container of milk in the fridge. To her surprise, it seemed okay. *Cereal it is.*

She plunked down at the kitchen table, and a rush of nostalgia crashed in like a wave of the sea. Her sister, Hannah, would sit to her left at the round Formica-topped table for four, as their mother served up shepherd's pie. She could see Hannah's grimace as the brown gravy and potatoes commingled with the ground beef and corn. Madison, on the other hand, loved her mother's shepherd's pie. Madison snapped out of her reflection as she spooned a mouthful of Cheerios into her mouth.

Her mind wandered once again, seeing the house as it had been so long ago. Has the house always appeared this sad? Had she never noticed because her teenage self had been wrapped up in her own wants and needs? *No,* she shook off the thought. Her mom was meticulous back then, even after the "event" happened, or at least until she left home, so why had her mother let everything fall apart? She wanted to ask Hannah about that, but suspected she wouldn't have the answer. The last she knew, Hannah hadn't been home since she'd joined the military. She still couldn't believe her baby sister had done that.

Madison reached for her necklace at the hollow of her throat. The necklace was gone. "No!"

She jumped up from the table, retracing her steps, searching as she took each tentative step, until she realized she could have lost it anywhere. At the airport, in the rental car, or at the hospital. For that matter, she thought, it could be in the grass, or in Ohio.

Her neck felt empty, and she ached for her sister to be with her. The necklace, in its own way, seemed to be the only real, tangible link to her sister because their paths hadn't crossed in years. She wished she could pick up the phone and call her at will, but phone calls had become few and far between. When Madison tried to reach her, to tell her about their mother, she got the runaround. All she could gather was Hannah was on some foreign soil, under heavy restrictions. Simply put, their worlds had separated by more than a physical distance, and now, she could only hope Hannah got the message.

seventeen

Vincent's loaded truck bumped along the lengthy driveway of Janice Gable's home. The sun was quickly setting over the horizon. Bursts of orange and yellow glowed across the water. This sight was something he never grew tired of seeing. He and Cheryl would often sit along the seawall to watch the sunset's breathtaking splendor. It had filled his soul with inspiration as Cheryl talked about all the sunsets they'd cherished together and all that were yet to come. Now, he was alone, and the beauty seemed a bit dimmer, a bit less dramatic. The sun setting reminded him of all the sunsets he'd never see with his beloved Cheryl.

He turned the corner, and the Gables' home shone in the distance. Each window glowed as if it were an open invitation to a grand party. It appeared alive, but he sensed it was a home filled with sadness, a home no longer filled with life.

The back door's light shone bright and made it easy to unload his tools and supplies needed to temporarily replace the door's knob and locking system. He'd secure it enough so Madison could sleep more soundly, at least until he could fix the doorframe properly in the light of day.

He laid the last two-by-four on the ground near the base of the steps when the dilapidated door opened. Madison stood at the opening. Her eyes appeared puffy and tired, but she attempted to mask her sorrow with a weak smile.

"Hi, Vincent."

"Hello, Madison. Are you all settled in?"

Madison nodded and gave him a shrug of her shoulders. "As settled as I can be for now. I'd offer you something to drink, but…"

"Oh, I'm good. You don't have to worry about me. Besides, I won't be too long anyway, and I can get out of your hair."

"You're not bothering me in the least."

Madison wrapped her arms around herself and gave a sigh as she watched him struggle to open the new lock.

"This darn plastic packaging is enough to make a grown man have a temper tantrum and give up." He dug a box cutter out of his makeshift tool bag. "But I shall overcome this intrusion into my childish need to throw the packaging across the lawn and persevere in my endeavor." He was happy that Madison gave a genuine smile at his struggle. "There, you see, I won!"

"You sure did." She stepped back, giving him more space to work. "I hope your wife won't mind you being gone so long. I'd imagine she'll be waiting for you for dinner by now."

"Nope, I'm on my own for dinner." He pulled a screwdriver out of his bag. "No need to worry about that."

Vincent quietly worked on the door, and Madison withdrew into the house. He wondered what could have caused a rift between this mother and daughter. He and Cheryl had always wanted children, but it wasn't meant to be. It seemed a waste that Janice and her daughter were at odds when they were given the gift of having each other.

He opened and shut the door a few times, then stood back to examine his work. *Good enough for now.* He was about to open the door one last time to say good night when Madison appeared.

"Thank you," she said with a tap of her palm to her heart. "It's not many people who'd go out of their way to do what you did."

"The way I see it—I broke it—I should fix it." He stuffed his tools back into his tool bag and picked up the shopping bag and jagged-cut plastic packaging. "I'll be back tomorrow, if it's okay with you. I'd like to get the frame replaced before the rains come."

"Of course. I'll be heading out to check on my mother in the morning anyway, so make yourself at home, and do what you need to do."

He shoved the packaging into the shopping bag and, and with that simple thrust, slit his finger with the plastic. "Sounds good." He grimaced, not wanting to show the pain that shot through his index finger and shoved his hand in his pocket. "Okay then, have a good rest of your night."

Madison clicked the lock, and he backed away.

The moon cast its light over the small barn, and he remembered the pain on Janice's face. What must it have been like trapped inside on that moonlit night? His finger throbbed, but in the grand scheme of things, his pain was nothing.

He grabbed a rag out of his bag and wrapped his finger, then his gaze turned to the big old house before him. The door frame was just a tip of the iceberg. Even in the moon's cast, he could see how much it had fallen into disrepair. *It must have been a beaut in its heyday.*

Another light in the upstairs window clicked on. He laughed, as he didn't see how it was possible for there to be another light to turn on.

Madison's shadowy figure swept past, then disappeared. He thought of what a lonely place this must have been for Janice, then chuckled to himself. Now he, too, was alone in a big old house. However, Cheryl's presence was all around him, still.

Vincent climbed into his truck and pulled the door shut. He was grateful that he had a home to go to, not just a house.

"Well, my dear, I hope you're happy," he said into the empty space beside him. "It wasn't my best work, but it will suffice for now." Vincent imagined Cheryl would be pleased, but still reprimand him for procrastinating once again with his writing. He could feel her sideways glance of disapproval. "I know," he said, "I need to write again. I just need a little more time."

eighteen

Clutching the walker with white knuckles, Janice took her first painful step.

"That's it," the occupational therapist said, standing too close for comfort, walking in lock-step by her side. "Take your time. Nice and slow."

"Well, I'm certainly not going to run now, am I?" Janice snapped. She could see the woman's micro wince, and for some reason, it made her feel empowered instead of completely inadequate at the task at hand. She took ten more steps before the young woman guided her to turn back toward her room. Janice noted the swirly green laminate tiled floor that seemed to go on to infinity. How far had she walked? Beads of sweat broke out across her forehead.

She came to a stop. *Is my room two doors down, three, or ten?* "I need to sit."

"A few more steps and I'll grab you a chair. Okay?"

"I said, I need to sit—now!" Just then, Madison's face appeared in the hall in front of her. She'd be damned if she'd let her daughter see her weak. "Never mind. I could probably walk faster than you could get me a chair, anyway." She grimaced with each quickened step to prove she didn't need anyone's help, especially Madison's. "Well, which room is it?"

"Two more doors, Ms. Gable. You're doing great."

Janice thrust the walker forward a bit too far, and her legs couldn't seem to make up the distance. She teetered, and as she did, her feet tangled together. Her weight pitched to the side, and there was nothing she could do about it. She was going down on the damn green floor. In that split second, an arm grabbed her on each side.

"We've got you," said the woman to her right.

We? Janice jerked her head to the left. Madison's wide-eyed face stared back at hers. "You can let go now."

"Mother," she said.

"I don't need your help." Janice gripped the walker and looked at her daughter's pleading expression. "What?"

Madison shook her head and let go. She stepped back and held her hands up in surrender. "Never mind. Forget it."

Janice once again let her frustration spill out, just as she'd always done around Madison. *What is it with that kid?* "No, Madison." She shook with exhaustion. "Spit it out."

"I was just going to tell you how glad I was seeing you up and walking."

"Oh—well then, how about you seeing me getting into the damn bed?" A slight grin grew across Madison's face. Janice didn't see any humor in the situation, but Madison was there, so she could grin if she must.

"Okay, I'll let your daughter take it from here, Mrs. Gable."

"For the last time, it's Ms. I haven't been Mrs. Gable in a dog's age." Janice caught Madison mouthing the word *sorry* to the woman. "Sometime today would be nice, Madison."

Madison guided her toward the second door. Weary from the exertion, blood ran from her face, and her body grew heavy. She looked up at Madison. "Madison."

"Yes, Mother."

"I think I'm going to pass out."

Madison shifted, and before Janice could comprehend what was happening, she was in Madison's arms. "I've got you."

Madison sat in the hard vinyl chair at her mother's hospital bedside, staring at her mom while she slept. She was a wisp of the woman she remembered. The once dominating presence of the Mrs. Janice Gable, was no more. So why did she still allow her mother to get under her skin? Why did she continue to feel the need to play defense in every face-to-face encounter? And what was it about her that made her mother hate her so?

Her mother's rhythmic breathing made Madison dozy, and her eyes struggled to stay open. She lay her head on the side of the bed and tucked her arms beneath its weight, then breathed a sigh of relaxation. Madison no sooner began to drift off to sleep when she felt her mother's hand upon her forehead. With a stroke of her mother's fingers through her hair, Madison's tired eyes filled with tears. *I've missed you, Mom.*

nineteen

ang, bang, bang went the hammer, and the saw sang out with a *zip, zip, zip* of each cut of lumber. Vincent whistled while he worked, which prompted Madison to make a mental note to finally call Nathan as soon as she finished her breakfast.

She sipped her coffee as she sifted through the pile of mail, making judgment calls on what was junk and what she guessed was important. One envelope caught her attention. She flipped the clear-windowed, addressed envelope over. It looked official. *Should I open it?*

Madison chewed on her fingernail while she tapped the envelope on the edge of the kitchen counter. *Why would Mother be getting mail from the Law Offices of Halle and Cline Esq.?*

She was just about to lift the envelope up to the window to try to peek through the paper when she noticed the faint word *foreclosure* and Vincent pushed the door open. Startled, Madison nearly dropped the envelope, then collected herself long enough to place it back on the stack.

"I'm sorry, Madison. I didn't mean to make you jump."

"No. I—um. It's fine, really." She cleared her throat as guilt coursed through her bones. The letter wasn't any of her business, but her curiosity was getting the best of her.

"Good. That's good," he said with a brush of his hands. Bits of sawdust floated to the floor. "You're all set now. It wasn't quite as bad as I first thought."

"That's great news," she said with a little too much enthusiasm. *Pull yourself together. You're jumping to conclusions.* The letter could be something quite different from her mother getting foreclosed on. She was embarrassed for her mother, and she sensed her cheeks turn pink. "What do I owe you?"

"You know what?" He tugged on his tool belt. "Call this a welcome home gift from me to you."

"Oh, please. That's really kind of you, but I couldn't possibly accept. It's too much." Madison shook off the prickly feeling that his gesture welcomed. She, or her mother, for that matter, barely knew this man. Fixing it was one thing, but offering to do it for free, well, that was just too much and it didn't sit well with her. "I must insist I pay."

Vincent shook his head and mumbled incoherently as he stepped outside. "I'll get you the receipts." Vincent shuffled to his truck and swung open the door. His stocky frame caused him to stand on his tiptoes as he leaned in to retrieve a slip from the dashboard, then trudged back. "Here you go."

Madison snatched the receipt from his firm hand. "Thanks." She took notice of the amount owed. "What about your labor?"

"I said I'd fix it. Besides, I enjoy doing projects. It keeps me busy."

"But…"

"No buts about it. You can pay for the supplies. I'll give you that, but I've got the labor." With that, he spun on his heels toward his pickup.

Madison thought of the envelope from the attorney. She didn't want to ask her mother to foot the bill. "I'll go grab some cash," she yelled.

"That's fine." He slammed the truck door shut and turned on the ignition. The rumble of his engine and exhaust kicked in, and he rolled away.

Madison chased him down the driveway. "But I don't even know where you live!"

Madison stood in her stocking feet and threw her arms in the air as she watched the pickup get farther down the driveway and out of view. She was just about to go back inside when another vehicle approached from a distance. She squinted her eyes to see who it was, but the glare of the sun prevented her from seeing much of anything. Then she caught a glimpse of an arm waving out the window with gusto.

"It's Franky!" Madison's excitement soared and she ran through the yard to meet Franky at her car. "What are you doing here?"

"That's the most ridiculous question I've ever heard." She lumbered out the car door to wrap her arms around Madison, then leaned back to take all of her in. "For someone who looks like they just rolled out of bed, you look great!"

Madison curled her stockinged toes and tucked her hair behind her ears. "Oh my gosh, Franky, you haven't changed a bit." Madison gave Franky a hug in return. "It's so good to see you, my friend."

Franky stepped back and placed her hands on Madison's cheeks. "It's great to see you, too. So, how's your mom doing?" she asked as they walked arm in arm toward the back of the house.

"All things considered, she could be a lot worse."

Madison opened the door to the kitchen, and Franky stepped inside, with Madison following behind.

"Hasn't changed a bit, has it? Well, except for the—um. Well—what I mean to say is…"

"Don't bother saying it. I know. The place is pretty sad."

Franky pulled out one of the chrome-legged chairs and took a seat. "When do you expect her to get to come home?"

"Not sure. Want some coffee?" Madison held up the pot. "It's fresh."

"I'm already on a caffeine overload, and I've got the shakes, but hey, why not?"

Madison reached for a cup out of the cupboard. "A girl only lives once."

"Are you kidding me? I swear I'm on my third life, and the day's still young." She took the coffee. "Seriously, now, how are you holding up?"

Madison plopped into the adjacent chair. "As well as can be expected, I guess."

"That's good." She took a sip of her black coffee. "So, I suppose that means you have no idea how long you'll be staying?"

"That pretty much sums it up. Mom wasn't exactly thrilled to see me. Not sure why I bothered."

Franky leaned in. "How does Nate feel about you possibly being away for a long time?"

Guilt flooded in. Madison stood up and walked toward the fridge. "I'm not sure?" She moved a few items around on the shelves. "Man. There really isn't anything to eat in here." She shut the door. "What do you say I go take a quick shower and then we can grab brunch somewhere?"

"Mads?" Franky cocked her head and gave her a side-eye. "You didn't answer my question."

"I didn't? Oops."

Franky stood up and squared off in front of her. "Is something going on with you and Nathan?"

Madison couldn't pull anything over on Franky, but she thought she'd give it a try. "Nothing. Why would you think something was going on?"

"You haven't talked to him since you've been here, have you?"

Madison considered moving to the chair but thought better of it. She'd take Franky's inquisition standing up. "How is it possible you could know that, Franky? Honestly, it's kind of creepy."

Franky's sturdy stance hadn't changed, and Madison now wished she could crawl into a hole. "Seriously? You're still avoiding the question."

"I texted him to let him know I got here safely, but *no*, I haven't actually *spoken* to him. Okay?" Madison thrust her hands onto her hips and stared Franky down. "Are you happy now?"

Franky rolled her eyes. "Now you're acting like a teenager, and like I'm your mother. What gives, Mads?"

"Honestly, I don't know." A lump formed in her throat, and she had the urge to cry. "I really don't know. When I came…I thought…I'd miss him." She chewed on her fingernail. "But I don't. Not even a little."

Franky took Madison's hand and led her back to the table. "Did you have a fight before you left?"

"No." Madison paced the floor. "He was actually pretty great about my having to leave."

Franky took a sip, then set her mug down, but didn't say

a word. Their eyes met and Madison had to turn away. Franky knew her too well, and could read her like a book.

"Has he called you?"

"A couple of times, but I let it go to voicemail."

"He's probably worried sick, Mads. Help me understand."

Madison collapsed back into the chair and slumped her shoulders. "He's been distant—he's been that way for quite some time now, and I don't know, it seemed like when I was on my way here, and the physical distance grew between us, it occurred to me I didn't miss him as much as I thought I would. The sad thing is, I miss my horses more than I miss him. That's a terrible thing to say, I know, but it got me thinking. Maybe it's good that we're away from one another for a while." As she spoke the words aloud, the sense of angst dissipated and relief filled its place. Here, she discovered, she didn't feel on edge, as if he'd snap into one of his depressions at any given moment, and it was liberating.

Franky's hand rested on her thigh, settling her thoughts. "Don't get me wrong. I still love him—I do—but I don't think I'm *in* love with him, at least not in the way I had been before. He's changed, Franky." Madison leaned back. "Do you know what I mean?"

"I think so." She shrugged. "Do you feel like he's become more of a brother than a lover?"

Madison spun her ring while she considered Franky's analogy. "Maybe—sometimes, but when he's himself—his old self, I go back to feeling like we'll be okay, and then the cycle continues. I guess I'm tired of feeling like a hamster, caught in the wheel."

"So—what are you going to do about it?"

"I can't do anything about it right now because I need to focus on getting my mother back home and deal with this." Madison pulled the attorney's letter from the stack of mail and handed it to Franky.

She read who it was from, then shook her head. "I don't understand."

"Hold it up to the light."

Franky walked toward the overhead light above the sink and held it up. "It's a foreclosure notice. Sorry, my friend, that's not good."

"Not good at all."

twenty

Giddiness had bubbled to the surface as Vincent watched Madison running behind him from the rearview mirror. Being satisfied he'd pulled a fast one over on Madison gave him a sense of gratification. He wasn't about to let her pay for the small repair. Vincent loved helping people without asking for anything in return. Those moments filled him up more than anything else he could think of, which was why when he cared for his dear Cheryl at the end of her life, it had never become a burden. The people around him didn't seem to understand that, especially Zach, his publicist.

Zach did a great job. He went above and beyond, and it paid off. Vincent had become a success in the literary world and lacked nothing in the financial sense. Which bolstered Zach's career as well. So, when Cheryl became ill, and Vincent wanted to step away to care for her, Zach declared war.

It took a team of lawyers to try to convince Zach to drop the case and release Vincent from the contract, but it ended in a stalemate. It wasn't until Zach showed up on Vincent's doorstep that he'd backed off. Cheryl had gotten the strength to answer the door that day. Her bald head, wrapped in a floral silk scarf, and wearing a bright smile, despite her pain, won him over. Vincent presumed Cheryl made Zach see the error of his ways, and by the end of the visit, he and Zach shook hands on having had a great run and Zach left on his way to pursue his future success.

Cheryl had a way about her he couldn't explain. She simply put folks at ease and made them feel as though they were the most important person on the planet. So, when she'd see someone downtrodden, sour, or difficult, she'd figure they had reason enough to be in such a disposition. She found the good in people and inspired them to reach their full potential.

Vincent supposed, over the years, she'd rubbed off on him, and so he made it his mission to do the same, even though being social didn't come natural to him. He had to work at it. On those rare occasions he succeeded, doing good lifted him up, and while that giddy feeling stirred inside of him, he'd thank his Cheryl for the gift she'd given him. Yes, he thought, he would continue to reach out to both of the Gable ladies, as it's what Cheryl would have wanted.

twenty-one

"Nice, Janice," the therapist said. "Very good. You've made significant progress over the past two weeks."

Physical therapy was wearing Janice down, but she pushed through. She would do anything to leave the constraints of the rehabilitation center. She wanted to be in her own bed. Even having to ask for Madison's help to get around would be better than this.

Janice thought of the last time Madison had visited the rehab center. Madison had gone on and on about Vincent fixing this and Vincent doing that, but all that came to her mind was the price of this and the cost of that. She didn't like owing anyone for anything.

Janice had to leave this place, and now, because there was no telling when the other shoe would drop. And the cost of her medical bills was quickly adding up. She needed every dime she had left to beat the impending foreclosure that was coming.

Janice couldn't help but think Madison knew something was going on with her financially, as she'd been too nice when she'd visited. She'd offered to pay for her utility bills, and giving excuses why she should, saying it was just easier that way. But Janice feared she'd then end up in debt to one of her kids as well. Besides, she didn't want to give Madison the satisfaction of being correct. Perhaps Janice was just being paranoid, but she seriously doubted it.

"One last time, Janice, and you'll be done for today."

"For today? I want to go home *today*. I don't want to be in this miserable place anymore!"

"That's the goal we have now, isn't it?" the therapist said in her typical patronizing voice.

Janice rubbed her tender thigh. "Well, why else would I be here if it wasn't for me to go home? You do realize I'm not an idiot?"

"Of course—I know that," she stuttered, "I don't think..."

Janice thrust her open hand in front of the therapist's face. "Just get me back to my room."

"Sure thing, Janice."

She thought if she heard her name one more time, she'd scream at the top of her lungs and they'd have to reassign her to the psychiatric ward.

As they turned the corner in the hall, Vincent stood outside her doorway, holding a vase of lilacs. His face lit up when he saw her coming. Janice adjusted the tunic Madison had given her, and she stood taller, focusing on her every step so as not to stumble and humiliate herself in front of him again.

"Aren't you a sight for sore eyes!" he said and opened the door for her.

Janice glanced around to see who he was talking to. To her surprise, Vincent stepped closer. The room was tidy, and she breathed a sigh of relief at realizing the staff had straightened it up while she'd been in her rehab session. The last thing she wanted was for him to see her unmentionables lying about.

Her gaze shifted to the lilacs. "Are those for me?" *Good*

heavens, I've turned into one of them. Of course, they're for me. Who else would he be bringing them to? She gave a nod. "Thank you, Vincent."

"They're from your yard." He smiled. "I thought you might like something from home. Madison said you've always loved the scent." He brought the flowers to his nose and took in their aroma. "Mm, me too. I just wish they lasted longer."

"She, Madison, that is, would be correct." It surprised her that Madison would remember that. In fact, it shocked her to know Madison had ever taken notice of any of her likes and dislikes.

Vincent eased Janice into her bed. "I hope you don't mind, but I've taken the liberty of cleaning up the gardens around the rest of the house. I like to finish what I start, otherwise, it makes me…" he hesitated. "It makes it hard for me to sleep at night."

Janice knew that feeling. She used to be that way, too, until Charlie ended his life. After that, it didn't seem to matter if something was left undone. After all, what was the point? He was no longer around to try and please. "It's alright, Vincent. Madison told me. I don't mind."

Still, all she could think about was that his efforts would be in vain. She'd more likely than not lose the house to foreclosure anyway. But there wasn't a chance in hell she'd tell him that.

Vincent set the vase on her nightstand and motioned to the chair that sat in the corner. "Mind if I sit with you?"

Janice nodded, and he slid the chair closer to the bed and took a seat. What were his motives? No one did anything for nothing.

"Flowers, and a sitting visit. Are you sure your wife won't mind?"

"No worries there. She'd be fine with it," he said just as Jodie, Janice's nurse, entered the room.

"Hello, Janice," Jodie said as her outstretched arms and portly frame neared the bed. "Looks like you're stuck with me tonight."

Janice held back a laugh. "I'd say it's more like you're stuck with me." She could be a difficult patient, but she liked Jodie, and so she'd tried hard to be kind to her.

"It's my pleasure," Jodie said, then turned toward Vincent. "Hi, Mr. Clark. It's always good to see you."

"Hello, Jodie. It's good to see you, too."

Always the polite one, he is, Janice thought as she eyed their exchange. Jodie had said *always* when referring to his visits, as if he made it a practice to come to the hospital.

Jodie wrapped the blood pressure cuff around Janice's arm. "I've been hoping to see you again, Mr. Clark, but I kept missing you." She gave the cuff's ball a few squeezes. Janice flinched. "Will you be here much longer?"

Vincent glanced at Janice, as if to ask why Jodie would want to see him. "Well, I guess that all depends on how long Janice will have me."

The pressure finally released and Jodie tossed her stethoscope over her shoulders. Janice's curiosity peaked. "Do you have some need to have Vincent stay?"

"Oh, my gosh, I'm sorry. It's just that when I realized who Mr. Clark was, I couldn't resist asking if he'd sign one of my books. I know it's not very professional of me." Jodie's face pinked as she turned to Vincent. "I just love your books, Mr. Clark. I guess you could call me one of your biggest fans."

Janice's mind reeled with this realization. *He's an author?*

"My book club read your last book, *Clipped Wings*, a few years ago. If you'd be willing to sign it for me, the girls will be so jealous."

"Vincent, it seems to me you should stick around and sign that book." Janice took notice that Vincent didn't appear too thrilled with the idea.

He bit his lip and wrung his hands together, then put on a thin smile. "I can do that for you, Jodie."

"Super! I'll go get it in a few minutes, when I'm on break." She spun on the heels of her Dansko shoes and flitted out the door in a flurry. A faint celebratory squeal echoed in the distance.

"Seems you've made Jodie's day."

"Yep. Seems so," Vincent said as he gazed out the window.

Janice took in his strained face. He looked as if he was recalling something painful. "Why didn't you tell me you're an author?"

"Because I'm not." He stiffened. "Not anymore." Still, he didn't look her way.

"I don't understand. Isn't it like—once an author, always an author?"

He shrugged. "I stand corrected."

Vincent pushed up from the chair and walked closer to the window as if he were in search of something far off in the distance. He stood in silence, and Janice squelched her need to interpret his thoughts as rejection. Charlie would give her the silent treatment when she'd said something to upset him. Either that, or shout in bursts of anger or belittlement that verged on his version of humor. But getting the silent treatment was one of his specialties. A knot built heavy in her chest.

Vincent shrugged and gave a sigh. "I'm no longer a writer."

It wasn't me he was upset with. Even with that knowledge, Janice was still on edge. *Maybe,* she thought, *it's because I'm tired.* "I see."

Vincent clamped his hands together and withdrew from the window. "Looks like your physical therapy is going well. That must make you feel pretty good, right?"

"It makes me feel rather stupid, actually."

Vincent gave her a sideways look. "Didn't expect to hear that, but then again, your responses typically do tend to surprise me. Why does it make you feel—stupid?"

"Because I can't do the most ridiculously basic things!"

"Like…"

"Like putting on my socks."

Vincent chuckled. "The weather's turning warmer anyway. Before long, you won't need to wear your…stupid…socks, and by the time you do need to, you'll be much better."

"How on earth does your wife put up with all the rainbows and teddy bears that come out of your mouth?"

Vincent let out a belly laugh. "Practice, Janice. Many, many years of practice."

"Seems to me," she said with a yawn, "you married a saint."

"I prefer the term angel, but yes, I did."

Janice let out another yawn. "There you go with the puppies and unicorns again."

"Yeah, she brings out the best in me," he said as he watched Janice fight to keep her eyes open. He wished Cheryl were with him. He'd love to see how she'd react with the likes of Janice Gable. Who was he kidding? Cheryl would have Janice eating out of the palm of her hand by now.

twenty-two

Franky had no sooner dropped Madison off after their much-needed girls' day out, when Madison's phone buzzed. She picked the phone up and saw Nathan's image filling the screen. Madison paced in the living room cradling her phone in her hands. She had the urge to let it ring until it stopped, but she had to answer this time. Madison slid the screen to answer and took a seat.

"Hi, Nathan." There was a long pause on the other end, and Madison wondered if she'd missed the call.

"Hey," he said, clearing his throat. "It's good to hear your voice. How's your mom doing?"

Madison shifted in her father's tattered recliner and it squeaked. Her mind drifted to its squeaking in the past. Her dad's broad grin and sparkling eyes smiled at her as he slapped his thigh, after telling one of his corny jokes. Madison, more often than not, rolled her eyes, not admitting that the joke was rather witty, but not wanting to give her dad the satisfaction of knowing she thought so.

"Madison, are you there?" Nathan's raspy voice broke her drifting thoughts.

"Sorry. Yes, I'm here."

"Good, and your mother? How's she doing?"

Madison didn't know where to begin. She sighed and

blurted out the first thing that came into her mind. "She's still a pathetically miserable woman, but she's healing up and should be back home any day now."

"That's good—I guess." He chuckled. "Sounds to me, considering what happened, she's still the same old Janice you talk about. I would have thought such a bad accident might have changed her."

"You'd think so, right? But nope, not even a little bit. Honestly, I can't begin to imagine what was going through her mind in that barn. It's as if she thinks she's the victim, and she wanted some kind of revenge. But she wasn't the victim. My father was!" Madison threw her head back in the chair. "Mom has to make everything about her, even my father's death. Especially since she was the one that drove him to it." Madison stood and paced over the worn carpet. "You should see this place now, Nathan."

She flung her hand in the air, waving it about. "I mean, it was never a castle, but it's literally falling apart around me. On top of that, she's going to end up losing it, and end up God knows where. And I can't talk to her. I mean, that hasn't changed either. It's maddening."

"Then why don't you just come home? I miss you."

"Because I can't. Not now." She plunked down on the couch and rested her head in her hand. "I need to figure out a way to save this place—it's my home." She blurted it out without thinking, and the statement took her aback. *It's my home.* She paused and closed her eyes as her heart rate slowed. "How are Lily and Journey doing?"

"Lily's being an obliging mother. Journey's nursing well and scampering about the corral like he owns the place."

Madison smiled as she imagined her sweet Journey's skinny little legs jumping around. "Please send me a video. I'd love to see him."

"Sure thing. Is there anything else I can do?"

Madison gave a quick thought before answering. "Thanks, but no. I'm good." She wanted to want something from him, anything at all, but she didn't. And that realization broke her heart. "You know what, Nathan. I've gotta go."

"Please keep in touch, Maddy."

"Sure thing," she said, as the need to hang up became urgent. "Bye."

She stared at the blank screen. "What is happening to me—to us?" *Has there really ever been an us?* Not for a long while, she thought. Nathan did his thing, and she did hers. They gave each other that freedom, but they had nothing they did together, not like they used to. Chores and daily life things, yes, but the companionship that they'd had was long gone. And Nathan wasn't the attentive man he used to be. She felt alone, even when he sat right next to her. And, no matter how much she tried, he wouldn't let her in, and so she'd given up trying. *Now, who's the one who's being closed off?*

Madison's phone buzzed in her hand. Her mother's name scrolled on the screen. She shook her head and answered.

"Hello, Mother."

"I'm getting out of this hellhole. I need you to come and get me. All the discharge paperwork should be done by noon, so don't keep me waiting." With that, the ever-endearing woman disconnected the call.

"Unbelievable!" Madison gripped her phone and shoved it into the couch cushion, then ground it in with a heavy hand.

It was that or throw it across the room. She took a few deep breaths to expel her anger, but her effort was futile. Madison couldn't relax her clenched jaw.

"Why must you do this to me, Mother?" she yelled into the musty aired house. Then she marched out the door to breathe in some cleansing fresh air. Thick fog blanketed the yard, and a mist fell upon her bare arms, but she welcomed the sensation. She trudged down the drive until the York River came into view.

The salty air, the distant foghorns sounding, and the sight of moored boats rocking in the water calmed her anger. She should be happy, she thought. Her mother had recovered and was coming home. Which was a step in the right direction. She sighed. But why did her mother have to go and make a joyous time become such a bitter moment?

Madison scooched down on the bank and took a seat. Ground water soaked through her jeans, but she didn't care. This was her time. A time where she could be alone with her thoughts. A time to put things in their proper perspective. She had to make a change—a paradigm shift, if you will—to help her cope with her mother's return home. *At least I can make an effort to try to please her.*

Madison glanced down at her watch. "Okay, Madison Gable, you can do this." With that, she stood, brushed herself off, and took the walk back.

The exterior of the house seemed extraordinarily dim in the fog, not welcoming at all. When she got inside, she opened some curtains and turned on the lights. She found a radio station on her mother's FM radio, sitting on the end table next to her mom's living room chair. Easy listening played softly while she proceeded to her mother's bedroom. She stripped the bed and tossed the sheets into the washer and grabbed fresh sheets out of the hallway linen closet, then cracked the window open to bring in some fresh air.

Madison glanced at her watch again, then scrambled out the door to her car so she'd be sure to arrive by noon sharp.

As she made her way along the river, the fog lifted. She hoped it was a sign of good things to come. To her surprise, she found a convenient parking spot at the rehab center wing of the hospital. One that would afford her the ability to retrieve her car quickly when her mother got wheeled through the exit doors.

She hustled through the corridors and stood outside her mother's room at promptly twelve o'clock. Madison grinned with satisfaction and opened the door to find her mother dressed, holding a vase of lilacs, and waiting in her wheelchair.

"It's about time, Madison. I was beginning to wonder if you'd ever show."

Madison's chest tightened, and she turned to look at the clock. "It's noon, Mother. That's when you demanded I be here by."

"I said no such thing. I said I should be out by noon. Which would imply that I should be *out* by noon, not sitting in this damnable wheelchair!"

"Then why are you sitting there arguing with me?" she said through gritted teeth. "Let's go."

Madison grabbed the wheelchair handles with white knuckles and thrust it out the door into the hall. Neither spoke until they reached the hospital's exit.

"You'll have to wait right here while I get the car," Madison snapped. She took a step toward the parking lot, and her mother yelled.

"Put on the damn break, Madison. What are you trying to do, kill me?"

Madison closed her eyes and slowly counted to three. *If only.* "Sorry, Mother. I'm not yet proficient with wheelchairs."

She pressed on the brakes and scurried to the car.

By the time they made it to the house, the sun was shining. The temperature had turned chillier than Madison had expected with a strong breeze off the water cooling the air. She pulled the folding walker out of the back seat, then eased her mother out of the car and they carefully took each step until they reached the front entrance.

Madison smiled as she opened the door. It looked bright and inviting. A nice welcome home.

"Why on earth is every light on in this house? Don't you have any concept of how much electricity costs?"

"Yes, Mother, I do realize. I just thought…" She'd wanted to make the old house feel warm and inviting. But nothing ever pleased her mother. Why had she bothered?

"You just thought what? That money grows on trees?"

"You're right." At that, Madison left her mother to stand in the entry, while she turned off every light, then walked out the back door and slammed the door shut. "Enjoy your gloom!"

The front door banged. Janice sighed. She'd caused Madison to leave again, in her usual fashion—in anger. Why had she resorted to ridicule instead of gratitude? Madison had gone out of her way to make the house look nice. And she'd come to bring her home. Something Janice hadn't really expected.

She's trying, Janice thought. *I have to find a way, too.* They'd already wasted too many years.

Janice had stood for as long as she could. She hobbled with her walker to her chair and sunk into the cushion, taking in the gloom of her surroundings. Even with the sun out, the room appeared depressed, as if it were unhappy with her return. She leaned over the arm of the chair and snapped on the floor lamp. Its glow cast across the space, giving it almost a hint of welcome.

Her chest grew heavy. Madison had turned on all the lights to welcome her home.

twenty-three

Vincent's eyebrows furrowed together as he scowled at his computer screen. After leaving Janice's home the night before, he'd jotted a few words down. A poem, perhaps. Just a little something to force his mind back to writing.

He could sense his deceased wife standing behind him. If only she'd give him the words, as she used to. But his muse was gone. Still, he hoped her spirit would continue to speak to him. He waited, yet nothing came.

Vincent typed a word or two, then backspaced them all. He repeated this madness for quite some time, and his patience grew thin. He rocked back in his chair and lowered his gaze to the Nubble Lighthouse that stood as a monument of strength and perseverance through storms far worse than any he had endured. He thought of long-ago ships that sailed by in bad weather. The bright beacon of the lighthouse guided them to safety. But where was his safety now? And who would guide his path with his Cheryl gone?

Vincent mourned at his tremendous loss, and as much as he tried to move on, his sorrow was too great.

A shiver coursed through him, forcing him to snap back to the present. He crossed his arms against his chest until the shiver dissipated. He recalled Janice had the same protective stance when he'd had the audacity to show up at her doorstep the evening of their accident. Here he was, nothing more than a stranger showing up at her home. And yet, she'd invited him in.

Vincent, once again, looked at his blank computer screen, and clarity broke through his conscience. Words spilled across the page. He'd found his muse. His fingers flew over the keyboard as inspiration poured out with prose that seemed not of his own making. A childlike giddiness grew until he could barely contain his excitement and sheer exhaustion took its place. He closed his eyes and tears rolled down his cheeks and moistened his collar.

He pushed his seat away from his desk and spun it toward the window. The Nubble's light blinked as if giving him a wink of approval. He wiped his cheeks with the palms of his hands and made the decision to give Janice a call.

Vincent regretted not getting her direct line and dialed the number of the nurse's station. Discovering she'd been discharged didn't take long. He nearly jumped out of his seat. He realized that his inspiration to write had come back the same time they'd released Janice from the hospital. He couldn't wait a moment more before grabbing his jacket to take a drive.

As he took the turn onto Lilac Lane, Madison's car sped toward him. She whizzed by without taking notice of him. He grew concerned. Has something happened?

Vincent drove the expanse over the York River, and within moments, his tires rolled along Janice's gravel driveway. He leapt out of the truck and took the stairs two at a time. As he approached the front door, he collected himself. Cheryl would tell him to be a gentleman and not some crazed lunatic, ready to pounce. He knocked firmly on the door and awaited a response, knowing Janice would need some time to answer.

Then it occurred to him, she could be resting, and Madison wasn't there to answer on her behalf. He was just about to give up when the door creaked ajar. Janice's sullen face caused him to question his intrusion.

"Hello, Janice. I heard you were home, and I had to come by and wish you a happy homecoming."

Janice opened the door wider while shifting her walker, and yet her dour expression didn't change.

"Is everything alright?" he asked, shifting from one foot to the other. "I saw Madison flying by…"

"It's fine. Everything is fine. I set her off, is all." Janice shrugged. "Seems I'm pretty good at that."

Vincent shut the door behind them. Janice gingerly walked toward a chair in the living room. "Please, Vincent, have a seat. I'd offer to get you something to drink, but I have no idea what I might have in the fridge, and, well"—she patted the walker—"it's a little hard to get around."

"Then allow me to get you something. Madison usually offers me iced tea or coffee when I'm here, and at times, a beer. Would you like me to see what there might be?"

Janice sighed and gave him a weak grin. "That would be nice, Vincent, and if you could check to see if there's any Biscoff biscuits in the cupboard, that would be great."

"Of course." He stood, then scooted by her chair toward the kitchen. He tried to make an educated guess where the biscuits could be, but his instincts were incorrect. "Any chance you could direct me to where these biscuits you speak of might be?"

"Sorry. Try the tall cabinet to the right of the fridge. Hopefully, Madison didn't already scoff them down."

He opened the sticking door and ran his fingers over the top to see how much it rubbed the frame and made a mental note to fix it the next time he came by. Which, in his mind, would probably be the next day. He slid a box of Cheerios to the side, moved a container of Quaker oats, a jar of peanut butter, and a variety of teas before his eye caught sight of the Biscoff crackers. "Found 'em!"

"Terrific! The plates are to the left of the window," she hollered.

Vincent opened the package, and placed the two biscuits on a plate, then made his way back to Janice. "What did you decide on to drink? I saw some English tea. Would you like me to make you some?"

"That would be kind of you, Vincent."

He gave her a quick bow and headed back to the kitchen, then went about adding water from the faucet into the kettle he'd found on one of the stove burners. Madison bounded through the back door, then froze. Her eyes widened at seeing him, and her mouth gaped open.

"Hello, Madison. I'm just fixing your mother some tea. Would you like some?"

Madison blinked, then narrowed her eyes as if trying to sum up what was happening.

"I found she has quite the selection in the cupboard." He waited for her to respond before turning on the burner.

"I—um—" She shook her head. "No. I'm good, but thanks." Madison peered toward the living room, then glanced back at him before shaking her head again. "So, she just welcomed you in to make her some tea, just like that?"

She rolled her eyes and threw her arms in the air, then slogged off to the living room and lowered herself on the couch.

Vincent could hear murmuring, but couldn't make out what the two of them were saying until the voices grew louder. As the clarity of words seemed to reach a crescendo, he wasn't sure if he should intervene. When Madison dashed out of the room and up the stairs, he dared to return to the living room, tea in hand. He quietly set the cup on Janice's side table. "I'm sorry. I didn't mean to cause any upset. Perhaps it's best I leave."

"Don't be ridiculous. You caused nothing. It's just the way it is around here with us."

"I see," he said, but he couldn't truly comprehend it.

"We've never seen eye to eye." Janice's lips pressed in a straight line. "You know what it's like when you try to touch the north pole of a magnet to the south pole of another, and they repel each other? Well, that's us, and that was even before her father's death."

"Speaking of Madison's father—do you mind my asking what happened?"

Janice rolled her eyes. "As if you don't already know." She waved him off, then retrieved her tea and took a sip.

"No, Janice, I don't know."

She set her cup down. "Well, I don't think you're being honest with me. I saw the way you looked at the barn."

Vincent strained to think of what she could be referring to, but nothing came to mind. The only thing that he could gather was she saw something in him the day she'd screamed at him to leave. "The barn?"

"Surely you know. Unless you've lived under a rock for the past nine years."

Madison bounded down the stairs. "My mother seems to think the world revolves around her. And, God forbid, anyone shows an ounce of concern, because that would mean they are out to get her or want something from her."

"Shut up, Madison!"

In an instant, with her mother's reprimand, he imagined Madison must have felt transported back in time, as if she were a teenager again. She looked tense, her nostrils flared, her tight jaw showed her fury growing. She clenched her fists so tightly he feared she'd strike at any moment. Vincent didn't know how Madison held back, but she did, and he was grateful. He had to stop this madness.

"Ladies," he said, but they didn't hear him and they carried on with their barrage of daggers.

"Well, don't you think you know everything, Madison?" Janice's bitter tongue continued. "The all-knowing, self-righteous one in the family. But you know what? You don't know everything!"

Vincent clasped his hands together and looked on as the two women continued to throw accusations, insults, and hatred toward one another. He wasn't sure if he should intervene, slip out the door, or simply stay the course. He stayed because regardless of the outcome, as sure as he was sitting there, Janice would still need some help.

"You know what I do know, Mother?"

"No, Madison," she snapped back. "What is it you think you know?"

"I know that you're the reason my dad is dead!"

"How dare you!" Janice attempted to lurch out of her chair, but her injury prevented her from doing so. She picked up her walker and threw it to the side, which caused her to shift to the edge of the chair. Her eyes bore into Madison's, and she raised a fist, then thrust a pointed finger toward the front door, causing her to slip off the edge of her seat. "Get out!"

Madison stood there, staring down at her mother with such disdain, Vincent shivered. He leaned over Janice and lifted her to her feet.

"She has no idea, Vincent," Janice cried out. Her lip quivered as he sat her back in the chair. And Madison hadn't moved.

Vincent took a breath to try to comprehend how two people could have such hatred toward one another, never mind a mother and daughter. Sure, he'd seen Janice's burst of anger upon their first meeting, but never in his wildest imagination did he expect to witness this.

He calmly turned to Madison. "It has been a long day, and it's obvious you both have much to work through, but now is not the time. Perhaps it's best to *talk* through this once your mother has adjusted to being home and feels better."

Vincent could almost feel the darts Madison was throwing his way, but determined to help them, nonetheless.

"So, now you're my father?" She snorted.

"No. I'm just a man who's trying to be a friend."

Madison stormed out of the room, and Janice turned her gaze to the window. *What have I gotten myself into?* Walking away from the dysfunction would be the easiest thing to do, and yet, something inside him begged to stay the course.

twenty-four

Madison's blood boiled as she shoved her belongings into her suitcase. She'd be damned if she'd stay in the house one more minute. As she fought to zip the suitcase shut, the zipper's pull broke off in her grasp. She threw the silver tab across the room, then launched herself onto the bed and buried her face in the pillow. She was too angry to cry and too sad to scream, so she lay there, thinking how best to move forward. "I'm not a child anymore. I'm a grown woman! Why do I let her do this to me?"

A familiar voice drifted up the stairs. *Franky's here.* Madison didn't bother to go down to greet her. Her friend would make her way up the stairs soon enough. Her mind drifted to their childhood. Madison and her father had planned to take his fourteen-foot aluminum boat down the York River and out to the harbor, and she'd looked forward to it for days.

The day was calm, with blue skies. A perfect day to drop a line in the water. So she'd hastily fed Lily and did the rest of her morning chores, then gathered her gear and waited on the front steps for her dad to get home. Time had ticked on well past the time they should have been gone, but there was still plenty of time to fish.

Her father pulled up in his truck and lumbered out of the driver's seat. He'd greeted her with a big smile and said he'd be ready lickety-split, then bounded inside. Within moments, her mother said they couldn't go. Dad had answered that they were going whether she liked it or not. That's when Madison heard glass shattering in the kitchen. Her dad burst out the front door. He swung the truck's door open and climbed into the seat. He revved the engine and peeled out, flipping gravel into the air.

There would be no fishing that day or any day after.

Madison took off her fishing vest and hat before marching down the drive toward Franky's house, a safe place. She could still remember her mother's angry shouts as she walked farther and farther away.

A knock on Madison's door snapped her out of memory lane. "Come on in, Franky." Her face was still on her pillow.

Franky sat on the edge of the bed, then reached down and stroked her hair, pulling it away from the side of her face. "I brought you and your mom some clam chowder. Thought I'd save you from having to cook."

"Thanks," she muffled into the pillow.

Franky continued to sit, leg swinging back and forth, brushing the floor with her foot. "What's she done this time?"

Madison pushed the pillow over her ears.

"Okay then, what did you do this time?" Franky said. Her soothing voice didn't help Madison feel comfort. If anything, it caused her to feel guilty.

Madison pushed herself up, then shifted to sit cross-legged. "I opened my big mouth."

"You do tend to do that, don't you?" Franky chuckled. "What am I going to do with you?"

Madison reached over and plucked the pillow from the

bed and laid it across her lap. "I wish I knew. It seems I bring out the worst in people—Nathan, my mom…"

"Is that a pity party I'm hearing?" She raised her hand to her ear and cocked her head as if to listen more closely. "Yep, I do believe it is."

That's when Madison shoved the pillow into Franky's face, knocking her over onto the bed. Laughter filled the room.

"What do you say we leave your mom, and that guy she'd down there with, to eat the chowder, and you and I get outta here?"

Madison nodded.

She didn't look her mother's way as they left, but told Vincent to enjoy the chowder.

"Since you've been away for *so* long, what sounds good to you?" Franky started her car.

Madison thought for a minute. "You know what I really miss? Brick oven pizza from the Portsmouth Gas Light."

"You got it, my friend!"

Franky drove them the twenty minutes to Market Street in downtown Portsmouth. Even though it was too early in the season for the tourists to flood in, Portsmouth boasted a flurry of activity. Madison's mouth gaped open at the changes. "This is insane! I wouldn't know my way around here."

"It's a Millennial and Gen Z's mecca." Franky glanced over at Madison and scanned what she was wearing. "I guess I should have had you change. You take the chic out of shabby."

Madison spread her arms wide and examined her wardrobe. "Okay, you may have a point."

"Do I ever!" She laughed. "Seriously, I don't know what you were thinking when you got dressed this morning. You even make frumpy look bad, and orange is not your color—at all."

Madison smiled at the chiding. "It's a good thing I love you, or I'd…"

"What? Hit me in the face with a pillow—again?"

Franky came to a crawl as they approached the parking garage on Hanover Street. "Outside or in?" she asked as she pulled into a spot and exited the car.

Madison rubbed her arm. "I didn't grab a jacket, so how about inside? Besides, it'll be like old times."

"Sorry, but back then, we weren't old enough to drink, and I want a beer—or two, or maybe even three."

"What a lush." Madison grabbed Franky's hand while they walked around the corner to the Gas Light.

The pub smelled of garlic and wood burning in the oven, as if the brick and stone walls breathed history and aroma. They sat at one of the wooden tables in the corner. Chatter and clinking glasses had a rhythm of their own. The place was alive with laughter, and Madison's shoulders relaxed. "Thanks for this, Franky."

"Of course." She cocked her head and gave Madison a grin. "It's what friends do."

They got their beer and placed their pizza order. Franky wanted the classic Gas Light for her half and Madison's mouth watered for the Memorial Bridge Pizza of house sauce, fresh mozzarella, fresh basil, Romano cheese, and olive oil.

Madison took a swig of her icy-cold beer. "Isn't it crazy how our sense of taste and smell bring out long-forgotten memories?"

Franky greedily rubbed her hands together. "Oh, I'm intrigued." She gave Madison a mischievous-looking grin. "What memories just popped into your sweet little head?"

"Well, if you must know," she said, then batted her eyelashes. "Or maybe you already do. But if not, I'll enlighten you." She held her finger up while she took another gulp of her beer. "When your brother first got his license, he brought me here on a date."

"No frickin' way! Ryan asked you out on a date? A real live date!"

Madison leaned back in her chair to take in Franky's wide eyes and disbelief.

"How am I now just hearing this?"

"I made him swear never to tell," she said and gave a satisfying shrug. "Seems he can keep a secret."

Franky slammed her hands on the table. "Mads! Are you kidding me right now?" She lunged forward and about knocked her beer off the table, sloshing some of its contents over the edge of the glass. "Why would you keep that a secret? I thought we told each other everything?"

"Sit back and take a drink, Franky. You're getting yourself all worked up." She laughed.

Franky shook her head. "I may need something stronger than a dang beer after hearing this." She teasingly reached across and slapped Madison on the shoulder. "Seriously, why did you want it to be a secret? Did you think I'd get mad at you or something?"

"It was an, *or something*."

"For Pete's sake, spit it out! You're killing me here."

Madison motioned toward the approaching server. "Our pizza's coming. I can't wait to dig in!" They looked on as the server placed the pizza in front of them and served them their first slices. All the while, Franky didn't take her eyes off

Madison, for which Madison was most pleased. She loved getting under Franky's skin.

"Honest to God, Mads, I will take your plate away from you until you tell me all the juicy details."

"Well, that's kinda creepy, don't you think?"

"You know what I mean."

"Okay, ya big baby. The date was a complete and total disaster. I felt like I was dating a brother and he a sister. We didn't know how to act or what to say to one another, so—we talked about you."

"You didn't?"

"Yep. The whole time. And when he took me home, I made him make the promise, then I jumped out of the car and ran into my house." She stuffed a slice of pizza into her mouth while Franky sat there looking dumbfounded. "I don't think we ever looked each other in the eyes after that."

They both had a good laugh, but the laughter soon enough turned to a more serious vibe.

"Mads? Who was the guy hanging out at your house?"

"That's Vincent." Madison circled the rim of her near empty glass with her finger. "You know, the man that found my mother in the barn. I'm sure I've mentioned him."

Franky shook her head. "Nope. I think I'd have remembered if you told me she had a man friend."

"He's not a *man* friend. He's a man that happens to be a friend—I guess. Although, I must admit how strange it was to see him standing in the kitchen making tea for my mother. I mean, odd jobs around the house are one thing, but seeing him inside, making himself at home is another."

twenty-five

Vincent warmed up the chowder and guided Janice to the dining table, as she thought it would be easier to manage her walker there than in the cramped kitchen. "Have they told you when you'll be switching to a cane?"

"Not really. A therapist is supposed to come by a couple of days a week to check on my progress, so I guess it all depends on that." Janice took a spoonful of chowder and, out of the corner of her eye, watched Vincent do the same. She hadn't realized until now that he was left-handed. His worn wedding band caught her attention. "There should be enough chowder left, if you'd like to bring it home for your wife."

"That's kind of you to suggest," he said, as he stared down at his bowl. "I love clam chowder." He smoothed his goatee. "But, Cheryl's—um… She's never been a fan of seafood."

"I can't imagine that! Especially given you live on the coast of Maine."

They sat in silence. The only sounds were a clinking spoon against the bowl, or a slurp now and again, until Vincent broke the quiet by clearing his throat. She could tell he'd had something on his mind.

"Janice, now I know this is none of my business, so please don't feel you have to tell me, but—why would Madison accuse you of being the reason for your husband's death?"

Janice gave a half-hearted laugh under her breath and set her spoon down. She paused as she tried her best to collect her thoughts. "Truth is, Vincent, I honestly couldn't tell you whether or not it was because of me. It's a question I've asked myself for nine years."

"I assumed natural causes, but I sense it was something more."

"Oh yes, it was definitely something more, but if you don't mind, I'd like to leave it at that." Janice pushed her empty bowl to the side. "I suppose I should get myself to bed and get my leg up."

"Absolutely. Yes, indeed, you should. But, before I head out, is there anything else I can do for you?"

"If you'd grab my bag, I have my meds in there, and I'm overdue to take them."

Vincent jogged to the living room, and handed her the white plastic bag full of hospital supplies. "Let me get you a glass of water."

He filled a juice-sized glass while she popped the top off the pain meds, and dropped a tablet into her palm. Vincent was at the ready with the glass. She gulped the pill down with the tip of her head.

"I should be all set now. Thank you for your company and your help."

With that, he bid her a good night and made his retreat.

Janice came to a stand and headed to the downstairs bathroom. She breathed a sigh of relief that she'd moved her bedroom downstairs. Since Charlie's death, and after the girls left, there wasn't any need to heat the upstairs. Everything she needed was on the main floor. She took small steps down the hall and turned to the bathroom. The room was tiny compared to what she used at the hospital, but she managed just the same, then crossed the hall and opened her bedroom door. A gust of cold air greeted her. "You've got to be kidding me!" She flipped on the light switch to see her window was open. "What would possess you to open the damn window, Madison?"

Janice shivered, which made her body rigid, which caused her leg to ache even more. That's when she remembered she was supposed to ice her leg. She hoped the meds would kick in soon, so she could avoid it for tonight.

Janice noticed the turned down bed. An extra blanket laid at the foot of the bed, so she shifted the walker out of her way, unfolded the blanket, and tossed it on top of the comforter. Good enough, she thought. With her efforts, she'd worked up a sweat, so she sat on the edge of the bed to rest before realizing she'd never shut the window. Without thinking, she took a step. Janice's leg went out from under her, which pushed her walker out of her reach. As she fell, her back scraped along the sideboard of her metal bed frame. Her skin stung and her butt hit the floor hard. The shock of having fallen again sent her on a downward spiral of self-loathing, a feeling she knew too well. Determined not to give into her despair, Janice tried to come to a stand, but she couldn't find any leverage. This effort continued until she grew too angry and frustrated to attempt it again.

She reached behind her and pulled her pillow to the floor, then grabbed the corner of her blankets and dragged them to the floor as well. "So be it!" she said, as she made herself as comfortable as possible, flat on the hardwood. She stared at the water-stained ceiling, recalling the time Charlie had let the tub overflow. "Damn you, Charlie Gable."

As the clock ticked on, she succumbed to her exhaustion, but awoke sometime in the night by the sound of Madison opening her bedroom door. The hall light shone through the room, and Madison's silhouette approached the bed.

"Stop!" Janice said, and Madison froze mid-stride.

"Mother! What are you doing on the floor?" Madison ran to the wall switch, and the room burst with light. Janice squinted at its brightness and covered her eyes as Madison scooched to her level.

"Did you fall?" she asked without malice, but with tenderness.

Janice's first instinct was to make a snide remark, but Madison's concern for her stripped the response from her lips. "Unfortunately, yes."

"Let me help you get into bed." Madison retrieved the walker and brought Janice to a stand. "I'm sorry. I should have been here to help you."

"What's done is done. All things considered, I slept pretty well." Janice shifted on the edge of the bed and lifted her leg to rest it on the mattress while Madison collected the bedding that lay strewn across the floor. "I could use some ice, too."

"Sure, I'll get you some. But first, I have to shut that window." She pulled the sash down and closed the curtains. "It was stuffy in here earlier, so I opened it up, but I'd intended to close it when you got home. You must be freezing?"

Janice looked on as Madison doted on her and flitted about the room. Once again, her throat grew tight. "I'm glad you're here."

"I'm glad I can help."

twenty-six

Vincent tossed and turned through the night, as thoughts of Janice and Madison's blowup weighed heavy on his mind. At last glance, the time was about 5:00 in the morning, so he decided to give up on the idea of sleep.

Vincent threw off his covers and slipped on his shearling-lined scuffs. He grabbed his navy plaid robe off the hook, a robe Cheryl had given him on their last Christmas together. He pulled the robe over his shoulders and looped the belt around his waist, then padded down the hall toward the grand staircase. He paused at the landing and took in the Nubble's light, which beamed through the vast Palladian second-story window, before setting his feet to the stair treads.

Vincent popped a latte pod into his espresso machine. The countertop felt cool to his touch as he watched the cup fill. The aroma of mocha was enough to relax his mind. He removed the cup and considered going to his writing desk, but his hesitancy caused him to waiver. Instead, he picked up a book he'd been reading, strolled over to Cheryl's swivel rocker, snapped on the lamp, and slipped on his reading glasses. As he read, the words blurred, and he found himself rereading the same sentences over and over without comprehension. And so, he closed the book to await the sunrise.

Echoes of Cheryl's voice flooded through his mind. If he

128

closed his eyes, he could almost hear her puttering around the kitchen. He imagined her pulling a pan out of the drawer and placing it on the stove. She'd crack an egg and flip the frying bacon over in the skillet. He'd see her snipping her blue hydrangea cuttings and placing them just so in the vase. She'd be humming a tune at her delight with the morning. This vision—this memory—her presence surrounded him with love and an enveloping comfort.

I hear you, my darling. Vincent wiped his damp cheeks.

Cheryl's spirit remained, and for that, he was most grateful. "What am I to do for them?" He set the book on the side table and strolled to the atrium door that looked over the Atlantic. A distant boat sat on the horizon, making its way to some unknown destination. "I can't help but feel that I'm like that boat, my dear. I'm drifting in the sea, and I can see the lighthouse that's telling me to stay clear of the hazards ahead, and yet, it calls me to its shore, just the same."

Vincent took a sip. The warmth ran down his throat, and he savored the feeling. He gazed at the Nubble's beacon, just as the sun began its assent. Colors of brilliant pink, orange, and yellow slowly filled the sky, as if God were creating a painting for Vincent's pleasure. "I see it, my darling."

This new day, and the beauty of the morning, stirred a sense of hope in him. He could feel Cheryl's touch—a nudge, perhaps toward a future of unlimited beauty. There was a reason he and Janice's paths had crossed. He could feel it. And this reassurance, be it from his beloved, or from his maker, couldn't be pushed aside. He'd stay the course, just as the boat that cut through the waters, where rough seas could roll, where storms could blow, where unforeseen hazards lay in the distant unknown.

He wouldn't walk away from Janice and Madison, and he lifted a prayer that he'd be the bridge to bringing them to a place of forgiveness. Now, if he could only figure out how.

Vincent placed his empty cup on the bookshelf that stood to his right and continued taking in the sunrise while rolling his gold wedding band around his finger. He recalled Madison had the same habit. He smiled as he reflected on the day they'd first met. Madison's fury with the broken door lock wasn't that much different from Janice's anger at their first meeting in the parking lot. "I do believe, my love, that those two ladies aren't oil and water as they seem to think. I trust they are two of a kind."

twenty - seven

Janice's leg throbbed as she lay in bed. To her relief, she noticed Madison had placed her pill bottles and a glass of water on her nightstand. She took the meds and, as she lay back, the stained ceiling mocked her. It hadn't bothered her in the years since Charlie's passing, so why now? Maybe having Madison home finally opened her eyes. But what could she have done to prevent the house from falling into disrepair? It was all she could do to keep the house, let alone maintain it. Charlie's recklessness had far-reaching consequences, and she had no clue how to save the home she'd grown up in. She was lucky to have held onto it this long.

Janice had wisely stashed her inheritance money away when Charlie was alive, or he'd have spent every last dime to their name. But now, all that was pretty much gone, and creditors nipped at her heels, and their bark was getting louder and harder to ignore. She could have kept her head above water if she held a job, but time and time again her panic attacks squelched that idea. Janice sighed, then sat up and pulled the blankets back. She set her feet to the floor and gripped the handles on her walker, came to a stand, then shuffled to the bathroom.

Janice was once again grateful she'd chosen to sleep in one of the downstairs bedrooms. In the beginning, it had been an adjustment, but she simply couldn't see herself sleeping in the same room she and Charlie had shared. She'd closed that door and hadn't stepped foot in it for years.

She sat down to relieve herself when she heard Madison's distinctive stride approaching. "I'm in here!"

Madison stopped just outside the door. "Are you good?"

Janice wanted to say that nothing was good, but knew that was a waste of her breath. "Yep."

"I made you some coffee and some oatmeal with blueberries and strawberries. Do you want me to put it in your room, or would you rather eat at the table?"

Janice sat there in awe of the turn of events. Never had she imagined one of her daughters would be standing in the hallway asking where she'd like to have her breakfast. The fact that it was Madison, and not Hannah, made the event even more unreal. "I'll take it out there—at the table."

She washed up and took the slow walk to the kitchen.

Madison clung to her mug as if to keep it from escaping. Madison's pale face stared back at hers. She knew that look well. "You're not eating?"

"Nah, I'm not feeling so great. Coffee's good for now. Maybe I'll have a slice of toast later."

"I take it you and Francine had a good time last night?"

"You could say that."

Janice managed to get to her chair and pick up her spoon. "I haven't had this since you were a kid." She slid the spoon into the oatmeal and mixed the fruit in. "Sorry I lost my temper with you last night, but…"

Madison held her head with one hand and picked up the other to wave off her mother so she wouldn't continue. "Please, Mother, no buts. Let's just drink our coffee."

Janice opened her mouth to speak, but snapped it shut, and went about eating her oatmeal and berries. They sat in silence, coexisting. Janice picked up on every sound the house made: the refrigerator humming, the click of the heat running through the pipes, the kitchen clock ticking, and her own stomach growling while it digested her breakfast. But even though the house was quiet, she wasn't alone, and that made it okay. She looked over her spoon in Madison's direction. She was home. At long last, her baby girl was home within her reach, and that revelation was an answer to her prayers.

A peck at the kitchen door broke their quiet. "Sounds like Vincent," Madison said. "Door's open."

Vincent cracked the door open a sliver before fully entering. He held a corrugated tray with three coffee cups in hand. "I see you beat me to it."

Madison glanced in his direction as if this were a common occurrence. "I'll take all I can get." She held her hand out, and Vincent pulled one coffee out and handed it to her. Madison examined the label. "Perfect, just the way I like it. Thanks, Vincent."

"Janice, I'm not sure how you drink yours, so it's black. Figured you could add what you like." He set the cup in front of her and retrieved his own. "Well, better get back to it."

"Back to what?" Janice picked up her half-empty mug of coffee.

"I've been tackling the overgrowth in the front yard, along the roadside. Seems a shame to obscure the view of the river."

So, now he's judging me, too. "I see no point in doing that. Besides, it seems to me, you should spend your time with your wife, and not wasting time traipsing and digging around my property."

"Mother…"

"Madison, it's not for you to say."

"It's just that we thought you'd like…"

"How could either of you possibly know what I'd like?" *It's just as before with her father.* "It's not like you've asked me, is it?" She sighed with the weight of this revelation.

Madison glanced at Vincent and turned back. "You weren't here to ask, and why on earth wouldn't you like the grounds to look nice? We thought…"

"There you go again. *You* thought, so that makes everything all right now. Doesn't it? Well, what about what I want, Madison?"

"Fine." Madison threw her hands up in defeat. "What do you want, Mother?"

Janice's anger subsided, and an overwhelming sense of sadness filled its place. "I'm embarrassed, and I don't want people driving by to see the house the way it is."

Vincent pulled a chair out next to her and sat down, turning to face her. "Janice," he said as he took her hand. "I'm sorry. I won't do another thing without asking you first. Better yet, how about you write me a list of what you'd like, and I'll work off that?"

"But why would you do this, Vincent?" She couldn't fathom what was in it for him.

"Because it gives me purpose and brings me joy."

The word *joy* hit her. Janice wasn't sure she knew the meaning of it anymore. She had to admit it would be nice to see the river again, but to what end? Odds are, she'd end up losing the house to foreclosure anyway, but how could she deny him joy? Nausea, in the pit of her stomach, grew. If Charlie wasn't already dead, she'd kill him for the position he left her in. "Do as you will, but understand that I can't pay you, and make sure your wife doesn't get upset with me because you're spending too much time here."

Vincent smiled, and his eyes lit up. "Terrific!" He patted her on the shoulder and stood. "I can't wait to see the view from your front porch."

He grabbed his coffee and scampered out the door like a little kid.

Janice turned her attention to Madison, who was staring at the door Vincent left through. Concern rested on her face. "What is it, Madison?"

Madison bit her lip.

"If you're worried about having to take care of me, don't," Janice said. "I'll be fine."

"It's nothing," Madison said and slowly adjusted her seat and turned to face her.

"You know, I could always tell when you're lying, just like your father. You could pull just about anything over on him, but not me."

"I never lied to my father. I didn't have to."

Janice held back the urge to laugh. "Seems to me I remember you blaming Hannah for a multitude of mishaps, and poor Hannah ended up paying the price."

"Poor Hannah?" Madison raised her eyebrows to the ceiling, then turned away and huffed. "After all this time, you're still taking her side. You've *never* believed me about anything."

Janice had to admit she did tend to take Hannah's side, but she had good reason to. Madison was a hothead, and Madison followed in her father's footsteps and blamed everyone but herself for anything that befell her. "Let's just get back to what's troubling you, because if you're worried about having to stay here with me, you don't have to. I've managed quite well on my own all these years."

"Now look who's lying." Madison tossed her head back and laughed. "You nearly killed yourself, Mother."

"Well, that was an unfortunate accident. It could have happened to anyone."

Madison's mouth about dropped to the floor. "Do you hear yourself?" She shook her head. "The barn couldn't have been in that bad a shape to topple over because you *mistakenly* ran into a beam with the tractor. I'm not an idiot, you know."

"It was an accident! I never, ever tried to hurt myself. I would never do that!"

"Yeah, well, I didn't think Dad would either."

The bite of Madison's words cut to her core. "I didn't mean to drag all that up. I simply wanted to know what might be on your mind."

"Don't you see?" Her glassy eyes stared back. "My worry has everything to do with the past. I've lived every day of my life thinking about that day and everything that might have led up to it. I can't escape it, Mom. No matter how much I've tried, I can't escape it."

Madison's confession tore at her soul. She'd spoken those same words to herself, day in and day out since that horrific day. They were both broken. "I understand."

"Do you? Because the way I see it, you lost a husband you despised and a daughter you couldn't care less for. And even though your other daughter left you to join the service, at least that gave you something to brag about. I lost a father who adored me. I lost my sister, my home, and I lost my beautiful Lily. That horse was the only thing that kept me alive, and you took her from me! Don't you see? I had to leave for my sanity. I needed a new life!"

Madison's bitter words stung.

Janice pulled her walker closer and shoved the chair back. She braced herself to come to a stand, then took a tender step. She hesitated as she stood next to Madison. There were no words right now that could take away her daughter's pain. No, she thought, there were no words that either could voice without causing more heartbreak. So, she continued toward her bedroom and shut the door behind her.

Janice gripped the doorknob to steady herself, as her legs trembled. Her physical pain was nothing compared to the emotional pain she was experiencing. Regret poured over her like a raging storm, battering her, and tearing her apart. Janice was harder on Madison. She knew that to be true. Madison had a fire that burned inside of her she admired. Janice pushed hard to fan the flames, not to break her but to make her even stronger, because Janice did have a favorite daughter, but it wasn't Hannah. *What have I done?*

twenty-eight

Vincent heard every word. He hadn't intended to listen in, but one of his work gloves had fallen out of his sweatshirt pocket, and when he'd approached the kitchen door to see if he'd dropped it inside, their raised voices spilled through the door. He couldn't pull himself away. Now he wasn't sure how to proceed until the front door slammed shut. *Madison left.*

Vincent, knowing Madison was no longer in the house, and recognizing he shouldn't be intruding, opened the kitchen door and stepped inside. He eyed his glove on the floor near the counter, and as he reached down to scoop it up, Janice's muffled cries came from a room down the hall. Vincent took a step toward the hall, then stepped back, thinking better of it.

Janice's weeping stirred his heart. He hated to think of her all alone, especially after enduring an injury she was still recovering from. Thoughts of Cheryl and her days of suffering and crying flitted through his mind. Vincent never backed away when she needed a shoulder, and he wouldn't back away from Janice now. *Thanks for the nudge, my dear.*

Vincent removed his muddy boots and strode down the hall. He came to a halt outside Janice's room and cleared his throat to announce himself before knocking on the door. She shuffled about as if she were preparing for him to enter.

"Come on in, Vincent."

Janice's red nose and swollen eye greeted him. "Are you alright?"

"Sure—I'm just dandy," she said as tears rolled down her cheeks.

He hesitantly approached her side. "Mind if I sit with you?"

Janice's shoulders sagged as she nodded her okay, so he sat on the bed next to her and retrieved a couple of tissues from her nightstand. He wrapped the tissue over his finger and dabbed her cheeks, then handed her one to take care of her nose, and didn't say a word. Vincent learned long ago that sometimes, no words were the best way to communicate.

Vincent reached for her hand, and they sat in silence. If she needed to talk, he thought, she would when she was ready.

In the quiet, he took in the room. Wallpaper hung on all four walls. He smiled at seeing the pattern. Clusters of lilac of various sizes adorned the room. Yes, it was rather worn, and the colors dulled over time, but the room held a certain charm. Built-in bookshelves inset on either side of the rather large window, and a small, brick hearth shared the space of another wall with what he reasoned to be a closet. He guessed the room may have been a den at one point. His gaze turned back toward the window. A roll of front lawn, which abutted Lilac Lane, had an overgrowth of brush and gangly trees blocking the view of the river. Vincent imagined what the house and grounds would have been like back when they were maintained. He was sure the York River would have added a stunning backdrop to Janice's view when she'd once looked out the window. He was anxious to begin the work.

"Thank you, Vincent."

He gave her hand a squeeze, but remained silent.

"I've only tried to protect her, you know." Janice leaned into his shoulder and wiped a lasting tear. "I didn't mind taking the brunt of the wrath." She pulled her hand away and sat up to face him. "She was just a kid, and it was worth it."

Vincent nodded his head, but he wondered whose wrath she was referring to. He spun his ring around his finger as he tried to make sense of her words.

"But now, after all these years, she comes back here and…" She bit her lip, then gave a heavy sigh. "You know what?" She patted his thigh. "You don't need to hear any more about our dirty laundry. But I do thank you for caring enough to check in on me."

Vincent gently took hold of her chin and turned her head so he could peer into her green eyes. "Alright, I'll go, but please know I can be here for you anytime—anytime at all."

"I'll keep that in mind, Vincent." A tender smile brightened her face ever so slightly. "Now get out of here."

Vincent stood, and out of habit, bent over and kissed the crown of her head, then walked away.

twenty-nine

Janice eased herself down on the bed and sank into the pillow. The memory of Vincent's kiss on her head overwhelmed her. The last time Charlie had kissed her with any kind of tenderness and care was about five or six years before his death.

Janice rubbed her lips. Charlie's last kiss was forced upon her. She remembered specifically the smell of alcohol on his breath. He'd been blubbering on about some get-rich scheme that he *knew* this time would pay off. Charlie's words had slurred as he'd spoken about how they'd do something special together and emphasized it with a sloppy kiss while squeezing her butt cheek. She recalled pulling away just as Madison got home from school. He was none too pleased about her pulling away, and his voice grew louder. Janice could clearly remember his hurtful words: *All I try to do is make things better for us, and this is the thanks I get? You push me away!* He'd stormed past Madison in a rage and left. Janice didn't see him again until the next evening.

Janice touched where Vincent had kissed her. Yes, she thought, she needed to forget the past, and try to move on. Her hand lingered where his lips had lain. Oh, how she'd wanted him to stay. She wished she could have placed her head on his lap as he caressed her hair. She'd wanted him to wrap his arms around her and hold her tight, telling her everything would be okay. Janice had felt something with Vincent—a feeling she'd forgotten she'd ever had. Even in her sorrow, she'd felt it. Janice's heart fluttered in her chest. Or was it butterflies? She rested her hand under her breast, closed her eyes, and took a deep breath, envisioning Vincent kissing her lips, and recalled his strong hand holding hers.

It was then that the spell broke. *He's a married man!*

thirty

Vincent yanked and tugged the bittersweet vines engulfing a mature lilac tree by the handful and laid the vines atop the ever-growing pile of unwelcomed tree saplings, dead branches, and various other undergrowth. Next, he'd fire up his chainsaw to remove the larger brush and trees that took root. He was careful to leave the lilac tree that sat at the corner boundary, along with many clusters of lavender, and a variety of other perennials that sat on the banking, then raked what remained to help bring the lawn back to its former self.

As Vincent went about his task, he couldn't help but compare his own life to that of the land he now pruned and shaped. There was something profound about cutting back the old to make room for new growth, and keeping what was healthy, so what lived could flourish.

Vincent's thoughts turned to Janice. Hearing her cry just about ripped his heart out, but witnessing her tender side was good, too. She wore a tough façade, that was certain, but he had to believe that beneath the exterior was a kind woman who simply needed to be loved, much like a school-yard bully who lashed out at others.

Janice gave him a peek at who she really was. Just as the lilac exposed its splendor once the bittersweet released its hold over it. Yes, he thought, little by little, she'd be able to grow stronger, and that strength would be something to behold. In a way, he envied how Janice's façade was carefully breaking away. His own protective armor was securely fastened.

Vincent held on tight to his losses. Cheryl's death still didn't seem real, as her spirit stayed with him, spoke to him, teased him, and comforted him. And yet, even with her presence, and his recent divine exception, he couldn't write. That part of him—the part where he could write of his innermost thoughts and spill his heart out on the page—escaped him. Vincent had hoped his passion for writing had returned, but no, as with everything else, it wasn't meant to be. Perhaps, Cheryl's loss had been the final straw.

He put the chainsaw down, removed his work gloves, and took several gulps from his water bottle. Since the clearing exposed more of the water view, he sat down to take it in. The sun had reached its apex. He tipped his head back and shut his eyes to receive its rays upon his face. Sloshing water caressed the moored boats, and seagulls called into the breeze. Vincent welcomed the symphony.

A wisp of hair blew across his cheek. He smiled at the memory of Cheryl's once long hair. "I'm glad for your visit, my beloved," he whispered. "I've needed you today, more than you could ever know, but I guess you already knew that, or you wouldn't be here."

"Excuse me?" Madison said as she came to a stand.

Vincent's eyes popped open in bewilderment as Madison's incredulous expression stared down at him.

"I'm so sorry. I thought you were—I thought…" Vincent covered his mouth with his hand. He felt a fool and scrambled to his feet. "Please forgive me. I didn't realize it was you."

"I should think not."

"So—um—what do you think?" he said, trying to change the subject. "Looks better, doesn't it?"

Madison surveyed the changes by walking along the sloped embankment. "I'd forgotten we'd had such a beautiful view of the river." She crossed her arms with a broad stance. "I guess I'd taken it for granted all those years ago." Madison pointed to a section of the river just up the road from the driveway. "My dad used to tie our fishing boat near that big rock up there. We used to moor it over there." She waved a hand in the other direction.

Vincent enjoyed casting a line or two, but he'd always thrown whatever he caught back in, especially since Cheryl didn't eat fish. "Did you like fishing?"

"Are you kidding me? I loved it. My dad and I would catch bluefish, flounder, and an occasional striper, oh, and eels. I hated catching those. They creeped me out, but he said they were good in chowder." Madison grimaced as if repulsed by the thought.

Vincent laughed. He hadn't taken her for the squeamish type. "Sounds like you and your father shared some memorable times together."

She smiled and rocked on her feet. "We sure did." Madison's smile faded. "I wonder whatever happened to that boat?"

Vincent enjoyed the small talk, and was happy she shared some memories with him, especially after the death stare she'd given him when she and Janice had their blowup. *Progress is good.*

"Well, I suppose I better get back to it," he said as he slapped his gloves together. "I plan to finish another section before I head home." He gave his stomach a pat. "I've got a roast beef sandwich calling my name."

"Sure thing. You get back to it. I have groceries to get in the fridge, and I really should check on the broom-carrying witch." Madison thrust her hand to her mouth. "Yikes, did I say that out loud?"

She gave a chuckle and walked away.

As she padded her way toward the house, he shook his head and hoped their afternoon would go better than their morning.

He traipsed over to a stump that was giving him trouble earlier. He considered the best way to remove it, but opted to try digging it out with a shovel before having to resort to heavy equipment. Vincent shrugged, wishing he could use the tractor that had been in the barn, but that was out of the question. Janice's accident had destroyed it. He put one of his rawhide gloves on, and as he went to slide the other on, he'd noticed his wedding band was gone. Vincent's heart sank. He tipped the glove upside down and gave it a shake, hoping the ring would fall into his hand. It did not.

Vincent's pulse quickened, and he couldn't take air into his lungs. Panic tore through him like a tornado to his gut. He'd seen Cheryl experience panic attacks before, but he'd never had one until this moment. *Breathe*, he told himself, while recalling how he'd coached Cheryl. He sat down on the grass and closed his eyes. *Breath in—one, two, three, four, five. Breath out—one, two, three, four, five.* He continued this pattern until his lungs expanded enough that he no longer felt dizzy, then tried his best to keep his composure while he searched for the ring. He was at his wit's end when he remembered taking his gloves off to take a drink from his water bottle. "It must be near the chainsaw!"

He ran to where the chainsaw sat and frantically ran his hand along the blades of grass searching. *What's that?* His heart leapt with hope. *Nothing.* His every nerve heightened and frayed. Vincent's hand felt something. *Is it?* "Yes!" There it was, lying with the sun glimmering off the gold. He couldn't grab hold of the ring fast enough, as if it were a drowning child, precious, and nearly lost for good. Vincent gripped the ring in his grasp and sobbed for another loss that might have been. He slid the ring onto his finger and rubbed the smooth surface. He could finally breathe.

thirty-one

Madison left Vincent to his work, then remembered her initial intention was to apologize for lashing out at him earlier. But when she sat down next to him, and he rambled off *my beloved* and whatnot, it threw her.

Madison grabbed a handful of groceries out of the car's passenger seat and turned the corner toward the back of the house. The dilapidated barn that barely held on to what was left of its supports stared back at her. A vision of her father flooded her mind, and she pressed her temple to push the image away. She'd never find closure with him; it was her mother, trapped inside, that she needed to understand. This was a mystery she could solve. She came so close to losing them both in there. The barn had once been her salvation, her sanctuary, her life. But now, it brought her nothing but pain and anguish. Madison turned away and took the uneven path toward the house, hoping she might try to understand her mother a bit more. *She almost died in there, too.* She shook her head and with her free hand pulled the door open.

Madison placed a container of almond milk in the refrigerator and took a bite out of a Gala apple she'd picked up at the store. Some juice ran down her pinky and palm, and she slurped the apple to prevent more of the juices from escaping when her phone rang in her pocket. Madison set the apple down on the counter and wiped her hand on the nearby dish towel, then slid her phone out. Nathan's smiling face stared back at her; she answered. "Hi, Nathan."

"Oh, good—it's you. I figured I'd end up going to your voicemail."

"Nope, it's me. How are Lily and her sweet baby doing?"

"Yeah, I'm doing great. So good of you to ask. It's good to know you've been thinking about me, too." His sarcasm wasn't wasted on her.

"I'm sorry, Nathan. How are you?"

"Super. Besides the fact that you're not here, and I rarely hear from you," he said, taking a more light-hearted tone. "I'm just ducky. How about you?"

Madison took a second to process how she was doing. "Besides it being a shit show around here, I'm doing okay."

"Sorry to hear that."

"Thanks."

"Oh, my dad was asking about you."

Madison chuckled. "He just misses me at work. Please let him know I've not dropped the ball on anything."

"He knows that. He actually said he misses seeing you around this place. So does my mother, by the way."

"I miss her, too. Especially after spending time with my mom. I guess, over time, I'd forgotten how ridiculous she can be." Madison pulled Chapstick out of the bag and tore open the packaging. "After all these years, I kinda hoped things would be different, you know? Like, maybe she'd actually be happy to see me or something. I mean, you would think after having a near-death experience, she might have softened a little."

"Then why are you bothering to stay?"

Madison stopped short with her application of the Chapstick and leaned into the counter. "Good question." *Why am I?* "I guess it's because since I've been here, I realized how much I've missed it—not my mother, but the area and my home." She rolled the stick across her lips and gave them a smack. "You wouldn't believe this house…it's so sad to see it run-down like this. But it's my childhood home, and I feel like it needs me. Crazy, I know." Madison hopped up on the kitchen counter and dangled her legs just as she had a hundred times before. "She got a letter from an attorney—a *notice of foreclosure*, Nathan. I think she's gotten herself into a lot of financial trouble."

"I guess that's a pretty good reason to stick around a while longer then."

"Yeah, I think so, too. I'm not exactly sure what I can do, though." Madison heard voices shout Nathan's name and telling him they don't have all day.

"In a minute! I'm on the phone," he said, before turning his attention back to Madison. "You'll think of something. So, I hate to go, but I gotta…"

"No need to explain. Go and please give my love to your parents for me."

"Sure thing, Maddy," he said, then hesitated. "Love ya," and ended the call.

Maddison held the phone and stared at the screen. *Love ya?* She shrugged off the sentiment before hopping off the counter. Her stomach was growling, and she imagined her mother was hungry as well, so she plucked some deli chicken salad and a jar of pickles out of the fridge, and made them both a sandwich, finishing the plates off with a few chips. Madison arranged it all on a tray she'd dug out from the cabinet and carried it to her mother's room. She shifted the tray and pecked on the door.

A tired sounding "Come in" came from the room.

Knowing she'd be broaching the subject of the foreclosure letter, Madison prepared herself for another potential battle, then opened the door. "I brought you some lunch. I hope you like chicken salad?"

"I'm not hungry," Janice said, staring at the ceiling.

"That may be the case, but you need to eat something." Madison set the tray on the bed and sat with it between them. "I'll stay and we can eat together. What do you say?"

Her mother's puffy eyes narrowed as she took in the tray of food. "I suppose I'll have a bite or two, since you went to all the trouble." She scooched up to a sitting position, and Madison reached to help her adjust her pillow.

"I made us chocolate milk, too. It's in the kitchen." Madison got off the bed and headed to the door. "Remember when you, me, and Hannah used to drink it together after school?" Her mother's thin-lipped smile reassured her she'd remembered. "Be back in a sec."

A knot formed in her stomach as she slid the foreclosure letter into her back pocket, scooped up the two glasses, and headed back to her mother's room. Madison figured no time would be good to approach the subject, but every day that went by was a day wasted, and they needed as much time as possible to remedy the situation.

Janice was already devouring the sandwich when Madison set the glasses on the tray. "Seems you were hungry, after all?"

"Seems so," she said with her cheeks puffed out like a chipmunk's.

Madison sat on the bed with one leg dangling over the side, then brought her plate to her lap and popped a chip into her mouth while her mother washed down her sandwich with a drink of the chocolate milk.

"Food tastes better when other people make it, don't you think?"

Madison considered her question. She pictured all the meals her mom has eaten alone over the years. No one to cook for, no one to share it with, no reason to experiment. There wasn't much joy in only cooking for one. Back in the day, her mother had luncheons with her lady friends. They'd usually take turns at each other's homes, or they'd go to dinner or lunch at a few of their favorite spots: the Union Bluff, York Harbor Inn, or the Stage Neck Inn. Come to think of it, her mother had stopped going to the restaurants long before her father's death. She recalled her mother making one excuse after another for not being able to join her friends, and she'd stopped offering to host altogether.

"Madison?"

Madison's walk down memory lane scattered like a flock of birds at the clap of thunder. "Sorry. I guess I was in my own little world there," she said as she picked up a pickle. "Do you ever see the friends you used to have dinner with? Beth—Betty—Betsy." She waved off her forgetfulness, and continued, "Susan, and the lady with the long black hair." Madison snapped her fingers, trying to think of her name.

"It was Barb, Susan, and Claire, and no, I haven't seen them in years. Why do you ask?"

Madison adjusted her legs. "I remembered how you used to have your weekly get-togethers, and thought, once you're all healed up, maybe you could start back up—like old times." She snapped off a bite of the pickle, while her mother dropped hers back on the plate.

"I don't think so." She paused. "We've drifted apart, since your dad…" She cleared her throat. "Let's just say they weren't too comfortable being around me." She rolled her eyes. "As if our situation were contagious."

Or maybe it's because you are difficult to be around. But she had to admit, there could be some truth to her mother's statement. She, too, had experienced the looks some of her own friends had given her and the parents that didn't think it a good idea to hang out with her, let alone ever coming over to her place. There were, however, some "friends" who had a morbid curiosity, but Madison shut them down. That's when she discovered Franky was her truest friend. She couldn't have imagined what her life would have been like had Franky not been there for her.

Madison looked at her mother, and for the briefest of moments, felt sorry for her. Or was it pity? She wasn't sure. "It sure seems as though Vincent is comfortable being around you." Madison didn't miss her mother's cheeks turn pink, which was a pleasant contrast from the pasty complexion she'd had.

Janice dabbed her mouth with the paper towel she'd removed from the tray. "Well, I could say the same about the two of you now, couldn't I?" she said in an accusatory tone without looking in Madison's direction.

"Seriously?" Madison considered the term of endearment Vincent had used earlier. "Why would you think that?" Madison's stomach churned. "He's your friend. I'm only being polite."

"We're acquaintances—we hardly know each other."

"He saved your life, Mother."

"It was fortunate for me that he happened to come by."

"Ya think?" Madison shook her head. "I don't know. I'm not so sure I believe in fortune, coincidence, or whatever else you'd like to call it. I'm just glad he found you. And you can balk all you want, but I can't help feeling like there's more to him than meets the eye." Madison once again noticed how her mother's cheeks and neck blushed at the mention of his name and recalled Vincent's, *my beloved* comment. *He'd said he thought I was someone else.* It clicked. *Oh, my Lord, that's why he's always here, poking about and seeming to have one excuse after another for being here? Had Vincent thought I was my mother? Is his beloved my mother?* She shuddered at the thought.

"He's a married man, Madison. I'm sure he's just being kind."

"Are you sure that's all it is? Because I find him being here all the time a bit odd."

"For crying out loud, Madison. You're the one that's had him here all the time, not me. I've been in the hospital." She pointed to her thigh. "Remember?"

"Yes, but…"

"I'll not hear another thing about it. He's a kind man that—well—likes being helpful. Now, why don't you get this tray off my bed so I can get some sleep."

Madison figured there wasn't any point in pushing the issue of Vincent. Maybe she was reading into things, or maybe, she considered, Vincent might have thought she was his wife coming for a visit. Yes, that made perfect sense. She slid off the bed and picked up the tray. "Can I get you anything else?"

"Not that I can think of," she said as Madison opened the door. "Thank you for the lunch. It was nice."

She nodded and stepped into the hallway, closing the door behind her. In an instant, she was overcome with emotion. Her mother had thanked her. Madison couldn't remember those words ever leaving her lips, unless stated in a bitter, back-handed way, and usually that was directed toward her father.

Madison placed the tray of dirty dishes on the counter and proceeded to clean up the mess. Her mind rolled with possibility. She pictured her and her mom having more mother-daughter talks, the kind of conversations she'd seen on television, or read in books. The kind she'd experienced seeing with Franky and her mom, and with Nathan and Val. Sure, she had to admit, hearing *thank you* come from her mother's mouth was most likely a one and done, but she had an inkling of hope. With those two words said in gratitude, she finally felt seen and valued, if only for a moment.

thirty-two

*J*anice's need to sleep dissipated just as Madison's footsteps had. She glanced out the window at the sun getting low on the horizon. The water glistened and moored boats teetered with the tide. Janice hadn't realized what she was seeing right away, similar to not recognizing when a man has shaved off his beard after having had one for years. She pressed her hand to her stomach in utter astonishment. There it was, right before her eyes. Vincent had done it. Janice's once cherished waterfront view was back, and she no longer cared who could see her house from the road. She was already judged for far worse than a house in disrepair. For once, Janice considered her own desires and needs. She'd spent too many years dwelling on what others thought of her. It was high time she enjoyed some simple pleasures in this world. *My beautiful view is back.* Janice couldn't wait to see Vincent and thank him.

She hobbled to her closet and chose a comfortable rose-colored sheath dress and an ivory-colored, close-knit cardigan, and placed them on the foot of her bed, then went about changing to go outside so she could see Vincent's work up close. Janice ran a comb through her snarled, bed-head hair and vowed to ask for Madison's help with a shower before she'd call it a night. For now, she'd settle for a floral cap that hung on a hook in the washroom, near the back door. The last thing she had to do before heading out was the laborious task of putting on socks, but she'd mastered it in rehab, so she could manage it on her own. After her battle with the socks, and having worked up a sweat, she sank into the foot of the bed to catch her breath. "Okay. I did it." She smiled at her accomplishment. "Wasn't my finest attempt, but I'll take it."

Janice pushed herself up from the bed, with a groan. Her hand brushed something foreign on the unkept bedspread. She slid her hand behind her again to locate it. An envelope? She wondered if it might be a get-well card. Madison must have brought it in and forgotten to give it to her. She smiled at the prospect of receiving a card, and yet, it didn't look like a card. Janice flipped the envelope over. The Law Offices of Halle and Cline screamed out at her, and in a flash, a multitude of thoughts rushed through her mind: foreclosure. Madison saw this, losing the house, another humiliation, something else Madison would blame her for, and the never-ending reminders of the devastation Charlie's choices had caused.

Janice crunched the envelope into a ball and threw it at the window, but the balled-up notice revolted and ricocheted off the glass, landing at her feet. Her previous joy shattered into heartache, and so she did what she'd always done. She burrowed under her covers to shut out the world.

She lay tucked under her blankets, but the world and the letter didn't go away. They persisted with their taunting and nagging. She gave in, tossed the blanket to the side with a huff, then retrieved the crinkled-up correspondence. She smoothed out the envelope as best she could across her thigh, then slid the tightly tucked letter from the folds of the envelope, causing no further damage, and read its contents.

Janice read and reread the letter. She found it hard to breathe as scary words of condemnation jumped off the page: mortgage in default, breach of contract, demand to pay, made multiple attempts, all blurred together. No sooner did she blink to clear her eyes, new tears would well up. *I'm going to lose my family home.* She thought of all the times she'd ignored her bills. Of course, the mortgage company would catch up with her, but after the whole barn fiasco and ending up in the hospital, and having Madison here, she'd focused on healing, and she'd pushed the mortgage aside. *I'm so stupid!* Janice wiped the tears off the letter with her blanket. *How could I have let this get so bad?*

Janice flopped back on the bed, letter in hand, and stared at the ceiling's watermark. She had hoped to handle this financial debacle on her own, but who was she kidding? She couldn't even hold down a job, never mind make mortgage payments. *I'm a fool.* With each step, she'd become increasingly aware it would be an impossible feat. She needed help, and fast, as the letter had deadlines upon deadlines for this, that, and the other thing, which she did not understand.

Janice couldn't bury the foreclosure under the rug any longer, especially knowing the foreclosure date was fast approaching. Humility wasn't her strong suit, by any stretch of the imagination, but she needed to talk to Madison. After all, Madison had seen the letter. Clearly, Madison had intended to give it to her, but had forgotten. Or had she? Was it Madison's way of saying she knew, but was kind enough to leave it at that? Janice let out a laugh at realizing her daughter would use any means to stick it to her, given the chance. Being kind to her wasn't in Madison's playbook. No, Madison would choose the right moment to lash out and use it against her.

"I'm so angry with you, Charlie!" she wailed, but more importantly, she hated herself.

Janice played the reel of her past repeatedly over the years. She'd tried to keep Charlie from blowing their money on gambling, and on one get-rich-quick scheme after another to try to recover his losses. He thought he'd hid his addiction from her, but when he drank, his lips were loose. And anytime she'd confronted him about it, his temper would flair. He was careful at first, as the bruising he had caused didn't show, but little by little, the angry grip of her arm, or a shove, made it harder and harder to cover up. The one thing, the most important thing, was they did a good job hiding it from the girls. In those times she'd preferred the silent treatment.

Janice's anger toward him grew with each passing day. He'd depleted their savings and drained his retirement account. He'd piled on debt upon debt to the point they had no means to pay it back, and so, she did the only thing there was left to do. She mortgaged the house and depleted its equity to pay off his creditors, only for him to do it all over again, until he did the unthinkable; he killed himself. Which left her without his life insurance.

He'd destroyed everything, and Janice's world had continued to collapse around her. She'd withdrawn from her friends, she'd lost her daughters, her standing in the community erased, and the small nest egg she'd used to make ends meet, along with her will to move forward, vanished with time.

Janice dreamed of passing on the family home to the next generation, just as her father before her, and his father before him. Now, that dream had become a nightmare. There would be no home in which to live in or pass on. She'd have nowhere to go, and this frightened her more than anything else. So, she crawled back under the covers and prayed for sleep to come.

Janice didn't see the brilliant sunset. She missed the seagulls swooping gracefully with the wind. She didn't witness Vincent taking in the scope of his accomplishment, and she didn't see the day turn to night and night turn to day. Only when she smelled coffee brewing did she stir, and in her groggy state, she wondered why Charlie would be up this early. *Charlie?*

A tap on her door jostled Janice from her confusion. She opened her eyes and gave them a rub. "Come in," she said with a yawn. Madison's smiling face entered the room, and as much as Janice wanted to rejoice in seeing her daughter's happy face, she knew it wouldn't be long before they had to face the elephant in the room, the dreaded letter. She didn't want to face that time, not now, not ever.

thirty-three

Vincent grimaced as he climbed out of bed. His back and shoulders ached from clearing Janice's overgrowth, but he didn't care. His pain was a good hurt—the kind of hurt that made him feel as though he'd accomplished something. He welcomed the feeling. Today, he hoped to bring Janice outside so she could see the progress for herself.

Vincent thought of the many times Cheryl had stroked his ego. He relished receiving her admiration for a job well done; it made him want to do more—please her more.

As he drank his coffee, the sight of his computer grabbed his attention. He could sense Cheryl pushing him to go to it—to write. He'd rarely told her no, but today he needed to stay the course.

Vincent twirled his wedding band around his finger. "Well, my love, should I bring some sweets to Janice's today?" His mouth could almost taste the blueberry muffins Cheryl used to bake for him, and this gave him an idea. *I'll bake them myself.*

He pulled the cookbook Cheryl used most often off the shelf. "Do I have the right one, my girl?" He nodded as if she'd answered, for he was sure she had, then flipped to the index: muffins. "Success."

Vincent checked to make sure he had all the ingredients, then followed the directions. He'd shower while they baked, so they would still be warm when he arrived at Janice's.

The heat of the shower dulled his aching muscles. He relaxed his head and allowed the water to run over his shoulders while he whistled "Blueberry Hill," then stopped short as he thought of the words. He envisioned Cheryl's teasing grin at the seductive lyrics. Oh, how he missed her touch, the smell of her hair, and the taste of her mouth. He missed the sound of her footsteps and the brush of her hand, but more than anything, he missed the sound of her voice, as she whispered *I love you* into his ear while they'd made love. Yes, her voice permeated his every waking thought, as if she were right there with him today. He'd heard her voice in the wind as he woke, when he'd needed her, and yet, he couldn't touch her. He couldn't feel her touch. *Oh, my love, how I miss you so.*

Vincent turned off the water that had grown cool, and stepped out into the steamy room. He sighed, then threw on his clothes and hurried to the kitchen just as the timer for the muffins rang out. "Yikes, I cut that close," he said as panic hit, thinking the timer might have gone off earlier.

He opened the oven door, and the aroma filled his senses. Not burned, he thought, then placed each blueberry muffin on the cooling rack. Vincent grinned with pride. He'd learned something else about himself: he could bake.

He packed the muffins in a paper bag, then headed to Lilac Lane. Seeing Madison's car in the driveway pleased him. He didn't hear any yelling as he got out of his truck, so that was a plus. He retrieved the bagged muffins and traipsed across the damp grass to the kitchen door. His heart skipped a beat when Janice's eyes lit up at seeing him. She waved for him to come on in.

"Well, aren't you a sight for sore eyes?" Vincent said.

Janice grinned at the compliment.

"You know, I never really understood that expression, do you?" he asked as he pulled a muffin out of the bag and placed it in front of her.

"I guess I never gave it a thought, but I'll take it as the compliment it was intended to be." She leaned into the muffin and took a big sniff. "So, kind of you, Vincent. These smell scrumptious. Where did you get these, Hannaford's?"

"Nope. You, my dear, are looking at a world-class baker." He laughed and pulled a muffin out for himself. "Mind if I sit with you?"

"Sorry, yes, please sit." She gestured toward the chair, then removed a chunk off the top of the muffin, popped it into her mouth, and chewed. Suddenly her mouth contorted into a question, which turned into an expression of revulsion.

"What? What is it?" He could clearly see she'd worked hard to swallow the muffin down. "It's that awful, isn't it?"

Janice yanked a napkin out of the holder that sat on the table and wiped her mouth. "Well, what do they say? Hmm, yes, it's the thought that counts."

"No!" Vincent had to see for himself. He took a bite of the muffin top and believed he realized his error. "I forgot the sugar, didn't I?"

"Or, more likely, you used flour in place of sugar." A broad grin caused her laugh lines to show, and that made his error worth it.

"I see what you mean." He followed Janice's lead and grabbed a napkin, but spat the muffin into it instead. "Sorry. It's pretty dang dense, too."

Janice's smile grew bigger. "I think that makes two of you."

"Well, now, aren't you the clever one?" He joined in her laughter. "Okay, smarty-pants, do you feel up to going for a ride so we can find an edible blueberry muffin?"

Janice's demeanor changed. She seemed pensive and fidgeted with her hair. "I don't like going out." She looked toward the door as if it were the boogie man. He thought of her the first time they'd met; she'd been *out*.

"I tell you what. Why don't you come along for the ride, and if you decide to not get out of the car, I'll run in and get the muffins myself, then I'll bring you right back home?" Janice chewed the inside of her cheek, and she thumped her thumb repeatedly on the table, considering his idea.

"I suppose I could do that, so long as you promise to bring me home, right away, if I ask you to."

Vincent stuck out his pinky finger. "I pinky promise."

Janice chuckled, and her wall appeared to come down as she lifted her pinky to his. "Maybe you should warn your wife before we go out. I'd hate to have her eat one of your muffins because you're not home to give her the Heimlich. You know—because they're so dry?"

"Aw, gotcha. Fortunately, the whole dang batch is in this bag, so there's no chance of that." He spoke before he could think. It wasn't a lie. He brought the whole batch, but he couldn't bring himself to tell her the truth about Cheryl, not yet, anyway. Speaking the words aloud would cause Cheryl to disappear completely, and he couldn't imagine that. He still needed her.

"It's good to know there won't be any medical emergencies then." Janice let out a shy giggle but cut herself short.

"Speaking of medical—well, not an emergency, but my physical therapist called this morning and said I've graduated to using a cane. Is there any chance we could swing by so I can pick one up?"

"That's terrific news, Janice. It would be my pleasure. How about we leave the walker here, and you can take my arm instead?" He propped his elbow out for her to take, and it pleased him when she took it. "Off we go?"

"Just a minute, okay?" she said, then jotted down a note on the back-of-the-envelope she'd received from the attorney's office. It said, *I've gone out with Vincent and I'm not sure when I'll be back.* She left it on the kitchen table, grabbed her purse, and took his arm. He could feel her body shaking.

"Off we go." Her nervous expression, however, turned into a smile when she tossed the muffins in the trash. He adored her smile, but seeing her arm in his warmed his heart.

They took the short trek to his truck, and Janice ran her free hand along the hood. "I see you got your truck fixed. I still can't believe I backed into you the way I did." She shook her head and her shoulders slumped.

"Hey, there is no beating yourself up today. No, ma'am, today is a new day full of possibilities. The sun's shining, birds are singing, and you, my dear, have graduated to a cane, but..." He pointed toward the sky. "The icing on the cake is we're getting ourselves some edible muffins."

He opened the passenger door and helped her get inside. By the time he reached his door, it dawned on him the last time he'd closed his truck's passenger door for anyone was for Cheryl. She'd been frail, so much so that he had to lift her to her seat, and then reminded himself it was a new day and hopped in.

Vincent glanced over at Janice. Her clasped hands on her lap appeared restless, and she shifted one hand over the other and back again.

She cleared her throat. "The therapist's office is on Long Sands Road."

She stared straight ahead at the road. Her hair lay softly against her cheek and rested on her shoulders. To his relief, she seemed to look healthier than before. He took the left onto York Street toward the village, and the traffic moved along nicely.

"What do you say we head to Short Sands afterward?" he said. "There's a bakery along the way, and then we could either sit on one of the benches by the beach, or if you'd prefer, we could head to the Nubble Lighthouse and take in the view from the car?"

"It's been a long time since I've sat near the beach." A grin raised her cheekbones. "And that way, I could practice with my cane and get some exercise because we could walk to Whispering Sands from there—it's one of my favorite gift shops."

With that simple request, he was even more convinced that he was doing the right thing. Janice felt safe with him. And why wouldn't she? Cheryl had never steered him wrong before, and so he gave a little thank-you toward the heavens.

"That sounds like a great idea." Vincent wondered if she wanted to look for something in particular or just wanted to browse, but he secretly hoped Janice's intention was to buy a gift for Madison.

He pulled into the parking lot of the therapy office and escorted Janice inside. An hour later they had muffins in hand and were on their way toward Short Sands Beach. "Mind if I roll the windows down to take in some of the warmth?"

"Oh, please do," she said. "I've been waiting for the weather to turn. Seems to have taken forever."

"Sure has, but you know what that means, don't you?" he asked as Janice flopped her arm out the window and allowed the wind to sway her open hand.

"All the tourists will be showing up?"

"Yep, tis the season," he said. "Gotta love vacation land."

They drove along as the view of the sea opened before them. The beach stretched out with the tide. The rocky coast boasted seagulls diving and splashing about in search of crabs. And even though he lived next to the Atlantic, he never grew tired of the fresh scent of sea air. It filled his senses with pleasure and helped him escape the gnawing ache of losing Cheryl.

Janice leaned her head out the window, and he watched her hair blow in the wind. "Isn't it the most perfect day, Vincent?"

"It is, indeed."

A few more minutes went by, and they pulled into the parking lot for Short Sands. "Would you look at us?" Vincent said. "We have the pleasure of a premium parking spot and a bench to ourselves." He stepped around the truck and opened her door.

Janice gave him a grin and stepped out, cane in hand, and took a step. "I think I've got this." She smiled with satisfaction. "Let's go sit first because I don't know about you, but I'm famished. Then, when we're done, we can head over to Whispering Sands Gifts. Okay?"

"Your wish is my command." Vincent hovered near Janice as she attempted to master her new apparatus. "You're a natural. Does it hurt?"

"Yes, but nothing like it did just a few days ago."

She made a small grimace and paused before stepping onto the boardwalk. "Are you sure you'll be up for the walk?"

"Absolutely! Especially after I eat my muffin." She grasped the back of the bench and took a seat. Vincent did the same. He opened the bag and handed her a delectable looking muffin and watched her devour it as the tide rolled in.

"Is there anything special you'll be looking for at the gift shop?" he asked, then stuffed a gratifying morsel into his mouth.

"I'm not sure. Something that expresses my gratitude, I guess."

He washed down his muffin with a swig out of his water bottle. "Well, let's see. I'd imagine it could be hard knowing what she likes, since she'd been gone for so long, but I can't imagine it would be hard to find something appropriate."

Janice cocked her head in his direction. "I'm not sure I'm following." Janice shook her head and looked at him as if he'd lost his mind. "You know her. What do you think she'd like?"

Vincent considered her and Madison's relationship, but had to guess she'd have some inkling of what she might like. "Let's see. Is there anything that you can think of that would be sentimental to her?"

Janice shrugged. "Beats me," she said, as if it was the most ridiculous question she'd ever heard. "Maybe we just need to look around and see if something speaks to us." She folded up the paper from the muffin and rolled her napkin around it. "Ready to see what they've got?"

"Absolutely. I'm sure we'll find something suitable." With that, he helped her come to a stand and tossed their rubbish into the trash barrel, then strolled toward the gift shop.

Janice's grip on his arm tightened as her gait stuttered. "Did you know the shop's been around for over seventy years?"

"I guess I never thought about it. Makes sense though, because it's been around since I vacationed here as a kid, roller skating where the Fun-O-Rama is, and I'm no spring chicken."

"I used to skate there too!" She paused to catch her breath. "I wonder if we were there at the same time?"

"Wouldn't surprise me."

Janice continued around the corner, and Whispering Sands was just ahead on the right. "I used to bring the girls to the shop when they were young. Madison's request was always getting a piece of walnut fudge, but Hannah wasn't much of a chocolate lover. Can you imagine that?" she said, shaking her head. "She preferred rock candy or saltwater taffy."

"Seems to me you've answered your own question?" Vincent said at his epiphany.

"Come again?"

"Since Madison likes their fudge so much, and since it's been years since she's had any, it sounds like the perfect gift."

Janice came to a stop. She placed her hand over her eyes to shade them from the sun and looked up to at him. "I can do that. I'm sure Madison would appreciate it, but I'm shopping for Cheryl, your wife, because she's been kind enough to share her time with you for me."

His heart nearly jumped out of his throat. It hadn't occurred to him one iota that she'd think of giving Cheryl a gift. His knees grew weak, and he felt lightheaded. "I um—I'm—a…"

"What's wrong, Vincent? You look like you've just seen a ghost. Do you need to sit down?"

"No. Yes. No," he said, as he pressed a hand to his chest, willing himself to breathe.

"You're scaring me. Is it your heart?" She grabbed his arm. "Should I call 911?"

"No. I'm fine. I'm just, well—it's just that…"

Janice groped into her purse that hung over her shoulder. "I think I should call."

"No, really, I'm okay. Maybe I just had a sugar rush, but I'm fine now." He took in a deep breath and let it out. "Seriously, I'm good. Let's go find that gift."

He didn't know what to do. No matter what he said, it would be a lose/lose. Janice would be upset that he'd never told her Cheryl had passed away and led her astray, but if he persisted with the illusion that Cheryl was still alive, he'd continue to lie to Janice.

By the time they entered the doors of Whispering Sands, he'd made a decision. "You know what? For today, why don't you go ahead and get Madison her fudge? It would certainly be a wonderful gesture, since she's come home to be with you. In the meantime, I'll think about a gift and it would give us another excuse to go shopping together again."

Janice didn't seem too convinced, but resigned to the suggestion. "Okay, but let me at least pay for the muffins, and you can bring them home for her to enjoy."

"Deal."

Janice selected a quarter-pound of walnut fudge for Madison and Vincent indulged in a slice of plain fudge for her and Vincent to share. They enjoyed it together on the ride back to the house.

"I've had a wonderful time this morning, Vincent. Thank you."

"As did I." He helped her out of his truck and escorted her up the walkway. "You've got Madison's fudge, right?"

She patted her purse. "I do."

"I'm sure she'll enjoy it and recognize your thoughtful gesture." As they approached the door. Madison greeted them, but her sour expression didn't give him the warm fuzzies. Janice squeezed his arm so much so, he thought he'd gain a bruise.

"What is it now, Madison?"

"Well, let's see," she said as she stood in the doorway. "I woke up to find you've been out gallivanting together, and you didn't care enough for yourself to take your walker. Then, you got a phone call from your mortgage company, but all they would tell me is that it was imperative that you call them back and that it was urgent. I'm here to help you, Mother, but I can't help you if you're running around and keeping secrets from me."

Vincent cleared his throat. "Madison, perhaps it's best if we get your mother inside so she can sit down."

"Oh, really? And who are you to tell me what she should do? You know what, Vincent? Maybe you should go home and take care of your own wife and leave my mother alone." Her steely glare bore through him like a drill into sheetrock.

"Madison Marie Gable! Who do you think you are to tell either of us what *we* should do? Now, let me in my damn house. I need to sit down."

Vincent steadied himself at Janice's side as she forced her way through the door and slammed her purse onto the kitchen table, shaking the table's legs. She tore into her purse and pulled out the Whispering Sands gift bag, shoving it into Madison's chest. "Thank you for your help, but it's time for you to go back to your own life. I've survived this long without you, and I can damn well do it again!"

Madison's mouth dropped open as she clung to the gift bag. "No! I'm not going anywhere. I've had to leave my home once because of you, and I'm not doing it again until I can be sure I'll even have a home to come back to." She turned her attention to Vincent. "And I'd strongly advise you to keep your distance from my mother. She does nothing but destroy anything and anyone that is good, and I have no doubt she'll make your life a living hell as well. So, go home to your wife, Vincent."

Vincent wanted to interject, but he was at a loss for words. He recognized that Madison's anger was stemming from fear, and fear was a great catalyst for overreaction. He wanted desperately to see her break free from those fears. He'd seen glimpses from time to time, and that was encouraging. She and Janice needed to resolve their differences, no question, or they'd never find peace. All he could do was be available to listen, even if that meant he'd be the one taking the arrows. He'd grown too fond of them to let them down.

Janice slapped her cane across the table, getting Vincent's and Madison's attention.

"Your concern for me and this house is noted, Madison. Now shut your mouth and eat your damn fudge."

thirty-four

Madison glanced down at the bag in her grasp. *Whispering Sands?* She opened the bag and peered inside. She could smell the fudge immediately, and it thrust her back in time. Going to Short Sands Beach with her sister and mother held a special place in her heart. It brought on wonderful memories of her youth, a time when her mother smiled, and they laughed together. Going to the gift shop and buying fudge was the one extravagance her mother granted her, and it made her feel loved.

Madison swallowed the lump forming in her throat and directed her attention to her mother. "I'm sorry. I overreacted, but I'm concerned, and…" She bit her tongue. "Thank you for the thoughtful gift."

Her mother nodded.

Vincent was stoic. His hand rested on the back of her mother's chair. Clearly Vincent had taken her mother's side, but she had to tell him how she felt. Her mother destroyed people's lives, and he would become another one of her victims. What also bothered her was his constant presence. Vincent's wife must wonder why he'd been spending so much time with another woman. She found the whole thing unsettling, but it wasn't any of her business, and yet, her need to express her opinion on the matter had to be said.

Madison inched her way out of the kitchen toward the living and dining room. "I'm going to go for a walk," she said, then pointed to the table. "I wrote the phone number for the bank on the note you left me. You really have to call them back, right now." Madison glanced at Vincent and bit her tongue. She didn't want to spill more dirty laundry. "You can't put this off anymore. Please call."

Madison eyed Vincent again. He didn't turn away. He peered into her eyes without flinching. *I'm watching you, mister.* She wanted answers from him, but her mother didn't need the distraction or the argument. She had a phone call to make. With that, she turned tail and hurried through the dining and living room, grabbed the sweatshirt that lay on the back of the couch, and left through the front door.

The day was gorgeous. The sky was robin's egg blue without a cloud. The warmth of the air was just right, so she tied her sweatshirt's sleeves around her waist and bounded down the stairs toward the river. Her intended destination was the Wiggly Bridge. Madison retrieved the wrapped treat out of the bag and peeled back the wrapping to expose the walnut fudge. She took a bite of the decadent chocolate and allowed it to melt in her mouth. Between her mother and Vincent's antics, and the mortgage situation, the sheer act of eating the fudge calmed her nerves.

Madison glanced up at Franky's childhood home and noticed her car was in the driveway. She debated for a moment, as she wasn't sure if she wanted some alone time, or to spend it with her friend. Madison tore off another chunk of the fudge and popped it into her mouth.

She rolled up the top of the bag and stuffed it between

the knotted sleeves and her waistband, then trudged up the stairs and knocked on the door. As she waited for a response, nostalgia hit her like a ton of bricks. She could practically hear Franky yelling to her mother that she was going to hang out with her. Madison also thought about all the times she'd walked up these stairs and didn't knock before opening the door. It had been her home for nearly a year.

The curtain on the door slid open, and bright eyes smiled back at her. Franky's mom threw open the door in grand style. "Well, I'll be! If it isn't Maddy Gable."

"Hi, Mrs. Murphy."

"Come in! Come in! Franky told me you were back, and I hoped to see you, but I didn't want to bother you. I'm so sorry to hear about your mom," she said in a hushed tone. "How's she doing?"

"Thanks. It has been a roller coaster ride, but she'll be okay."

"Well, please let me know if there is anything I can do." She swung her head around. "Franky," she yelled, "Maddy's here to see you!" Mrs. Murphy pivoted back to Madison and planted a kiss on her forehead. "Sit, sit. Can I get you some iced tea or a soda?"

"No thanks. I'm good."

Franky practically limped down the stairs with a cardboard box in her arms. "Hey, Mads. What's up?"

"I was walking by, on my way to the Wiggly, and I thought maybe you'd come with?"

"Sure." Franky cocked her head and gave her the side-eye, then set the box on the floor near the front door. She brushed her hands together as if to wipe away dirt and dust.

"Mom, don't be picking that up. It's heavy. I'll take care of it when I get back." Franky opened the door.

"It was good to see you, Mrs. Murphy." And the two of them bounded down the stairs like a pair of school kids, going on an adventure.

"It was nice to see you, too, dear!" She waved and watched them until they were out of view.

"Your mom is the sweetest."

"And let me guess," she said, tapping her finger to her lips, "yours is not?" Franky gave a chuckle and grabbed the distinctive bag from Madison's waist. "I knew it! It's fudge, isn't it?" The gleam in her eyes meant she was up to no good.

"One bite," she said, as she jabbed Franky in the chest. "I know you. You can have one small bite and that's it, Franky Murphy."

"We'll see about that." She fondled the white paper bag greedily, then took off in a sprint, laughing along the way.

"You are a brat, Franky! An incorrigible brat!" Madison caught up as Franky slowed her pace. They were both sucking in air, and Madison rested her hands on her knees to catch her breath, while Franky laughed between gasps. As soon as they collected themselves, Franky tore off a morsel of fudge, and they continued their way toward the bridge.

Madison was the first to break the silence. "My mom got that for me."

She snatched the bag back and took a piece for herself.

"That was nice of her."

"It was, but Vincent took her to get it. Don't you find that odd?"

"He's married, right?"

"Yep. He sure is, but I swear he's at my mother's house every day doing this, that, and the other thing. I think he has a crush on my mother."

"No way!"

"Yes way."

"Well, I guess that does make it rather odd then, doesn't it?" Franky picked up a rock and threw it into the river. "Maybe he and his wife are on the outs. Have you ever seen her?"

"Not even a glimpse. But I don't think they're on the outs. He talks highly of her." Madison swatted at a mosquito. "You'd think she'd at least ride over with him to see what he's been doing and to meet us, but he's always by himself." Madison kicked a small rock, and it bounced a few feet in front of her, then she repeated the kick. "Vincent says it makes him happy when he helps people, but I think there's something more to it."

"So, you think he's hiding something?" Franky stuffed her hands in her jeans' pockets.

"I think so." She kicked the rock. "On top of that, I think my mother is smitten. I mean, why else would she ask him to Whispering Sands and not me? Plus, I've discovered she's using a cane. I gotta tell ya, it kinda bugs me that I've come all the way here to help her, and she calls Vincent instead of asking me, and I'm right there."

"I hate to break it to you, my friend, but I'm sensing a wee bit of jealousy."

Madison stopped in her tracks. "I am not in the least bit jealous. Honestly, I can't believe you just said that."

"I call it how I see it." She smacked her lips and gave Madison's rock a big kick, sending it into the river.

"Thanks for that, Franky."

"It's a rock. Look around you, Mads. There's a bazillion more where that came from."

They'd approached the bridge, and Madison was happy to

see no one else around. "Race ya!" They took off across the wobbling bridge that swayed with each thunderous step.

"I win!" Madison declared with a triumphant Rocky pose.

"Because you cheated." Franky snatched the fudge from Madison's waistband and played keep-away until she successfully took a bite. At which point, she sat down on the edge of the island's path and gazed out at the water. "There's a pair of bald eagles that nest here. Have you seen them?"

"Nope, but I'd like to." Madison looked toward the sky and the tops of the surrounding trees, hoping to catch a glimpse.

Franky plucked a twig off the ground and dragged its tip across a sandy patch, squiggling doodles. "They mate for life, you know."

"I've heard that," she said, as she lay back on her elbows and closed her eyes, allowing the sun's rays to penetrate. "I can't imagine it."

"Why is that?" Franky asked.

Madison considered the question. Visions of her parents flooded her mind: the arguments, the disrespect they had for one another, her father's death. *I suppose it was death till they parted, but that was not the intended vow or sentiment.* "I guess it's because nothing ever lasts—not really."

"Aren't you the pessimist?"

"It's true." Madison sat up and faced Franky. "I know more divorced couples than married couples, and most of those married couples probably wished they divorced."

Franky tossed her twig to the side. "Do you hear yourself right now?"

"Yes," she said, then laid back down. "It seems to me that relationships are built on trust, and how much can anyone really know about one another?"

"Isn't that the point of trusting?"

"But how can two people profess to love one another and say they trust each other, but still keep secrets?" Madison shifted onto her elbows. "And I mean, big secrets."

"Do you and Nate keep secrets? Is that why you haven't married after all these years?"

"I'm pretty sure he does. I mean, he's troubled, and I don't know if it's me, work, or something else altogether. He never talks to me about it, and I don't want our relationship to end up like my parents'. I feel like I'm walking on eggshells all the time."

"Have you talked with him about how you're feeling?"

"Yes, but he just shuts me out. I know he loves me, and he's even asked me to marry him—many times, but I think he only does that because it seems like the logical next step. But I don't think either of us is truly happy. We keep going through the motions, like my parents, and you see where that got them?"

"Oh, Mads, you can't live your life in fear of that. What your dad did was a tragedy, but it's a huge exception. Please don't allow what he did to skew all that is good in love and marriage."

"I hear you, but you didn't live it the way I did. You didn't see them the way I did, and you certainly didn't experience what I saw when he did what he did."

"You're right. I didn't. But, Madison, you are not your father."

Tears welled up in Madison's eyes, and she fought to keep them from falling. "No, but I could be like my mother, and that scares me more than anything."

Just then, two bald eagles swooped overhead, circling in tandem, then soared away together. All she could think about were those two beautiful creatures soaring by. They'd found their soulmates. And here she was, leaving what she thought was once hers behind. She came here to help her mother heal, but now she felt like she was the broken one. Her tears fell uncontrollably.

thirty-five

Vincent's truck pulled away. Janice's gaze turned toward the view of the river. A small mast of a boat tipped back and forth with the swell of the river. The tide was turning, in more ways than one.

Vincent's presence was the first act of honest-to-goodness kindness she'd experienced since Charlie's death. He touched her heart in ways she thought were impossible. Somehow, Vincent was able to reach in and help it beat once again. She just hoped Cheryl appreciated him.

Janice couldn't believe the anxiety she usually felt when going out. But with Vincent's encouragement, her anxiety took a back seat. She didn't have the sense that all eyes were on her—judging her. Perhaps they were, but she hadn't noticed. She'd had a great day until she got home. A part of her was furious with Madison's outbursts, but Madison's concern for her also touched her. And as much as she hated to admit it, maybe, just maybe, she had a point. She was relying too much on Vincent, and that couldn't be good for his marriage.

Janice thought of the muffins. At first, it pleased her to know he'd thought enough of her to bring them to her. That he baked them himself, was over the top. Not to mention, he hadn't so much as left one for Cheryl to enjoy. She had to wonder if he'd baked them for her out of pity. Still, his demeanor didn't come across as pity, for pity's sake. He seemed genuine in his care.

Janice rubbed her thigh. The throbbing and gnawing ache remained, as did her curiosity about Cheryl Clark. She knew absolutely nothing about her, but now that she thought of it, she hadn't thought to ask, and perhaps Cheryl hadn't thought to ask where Vincent was spending his time. For all Janice knew, Cheryl might not even know she existed. Janice considered sending Cheryl a note of thanks, but thought better of it. The last thing she wanted to do was stick her nose in where it didn't belong, and cause trouble for Vincent. Still, it was unsettling. Janice had to admit, the fact he'd shut down her idea to purchase a thank-you gift for his wife was unexpected. She thought he'd be thrilled to know she was thinking of his beloved Cheryl.

Janice's attention drifted to a pair of bald eagles flying over the water. The majestic birds soared with grace and beauty, like a dance between lovers, as if no one were watching. The sight took her breath away. Oh, to be loved like that. Visions of Vincent pressed upon her mind, leaving an indelible mark. If she'd had a husband as gentle and kind as him, she could have been happy.

The throbbing of her leg deepened, and she needed to take her medication. As she reached for her cane, the envelope with the bank's number caught her attention. Janice pressed her palm against the tabletop and came to a stand. Right now, however, her leg needed her attention, she'd call the bank later. Besides, she knew what they wanted—money, and she didn't have any to spare. Maybe she could tell the bank about her medical situation, and that could bide her more time. She thought of the cost of the fudge, but she hadn't purchased a gift for Madison in eight years, and she wasn't about to feel guilty about it.

Janice opened her pill bottle and washed the capsule down with a glass of water. Once again, she thought of Vincent, and the more she thought of him, the angrier she got. She had no business thinking about him at all, and yet, something compelled her to do just that.

An uncomfortable feeling in the pit of her stomach gripped her when she thought of Cheryl sitting home alone. She knew too well what that was like. At least Charlie was no longer among the living, and it made sense she'd be alone. Cheryl's husband was very much alive, and having him away so much had to hurt. So, she pledged she'd let Vincent do his thing around her yard, but she would not go out on more jaunts with him, even if their motives had been pure. Still, she wished circumstances were different because he brought new life in her, a hopeful life where she could laugh again.

Janice gripped her cane and limped toward the living room, then flopped down on the couch. She massaged her shoulder and rubbed her palm. The prolonged use of the cane had caused tenderness. Janice welcomed the discomfort. It meant she was one step closer to being independent, and, as much as it killed her, she would no longer have to depend on Madison.

Madison didn't want to be here with her; she'd made that abundantly clear. But having her home took away the empty spot Janice had carried with her from the day Madison had walked away. Janice loved Madison's passion for life. Even her rebellious nature was admirable. Madison adored her father. With all his faults, Madison could see past them, whereas she could not. Madison was no longer the lanky kid that walked away; she was a grown woman with a life of her own. Janice wouldn't begrudge Madison going back, even though Janice wished she'd stay.

A shadow moved across the front yard, and she realized her prodigal daughter had returned home again. She ached to have a relationship with Madison, but as things were, she had little hope that would change. *I need to try harder.*

thirty-six

Vincent poured a glass of red wine and carried it outside onto the veranda, which overlooked Short Sands Beach. A pair of wicker chairs sat on a hydrangea-printed rug. The soft blue of the print matched the hue of the sky. He sank into the chair while the classical sound of Debussy's "Claire de Lune" played softly in the background and whitecaps rolled along the shore. He sipped his wine.

"Well, my dearest, how did I do today with Janice?" he asked, hoping Cheryl would speak to him. A gentle breeze caressed his skin, and he stilled in anticipation of her answer. He whispered, "Are you here?"

Vincent sighed with her silence and turned his gaze in the direction of a couple walking on the beach. He guessed them to be about his age. They held hands as they strolled together. A flock of seagulls flew overhead, and a sandpiper teetered across their path. He thought of the sandpiper's meaning: compassion and staying focused, but with a playfulness that brings lightness in the here-and-now.

A smile washed across his face. Vincent wasn't sure if Cheryl had directed his gaze to the sandpiper, or if it was of his own volition, but he sensed it was Cheryl. He remembered having a discussion with her long ago about the busy little birds that danced on the waves. *Thank you, my love. I will stay the course.*

Vincent pondered the bird's meaning once again; *the here-and-now*. He took another sip of his wine and replayed his morning with Janice. They'd had a lovely morning, even though he'd royally messed up the blueberry muffin recipe, but because of his error, it had given him the opportunity to take Janice out. She'd seemed more relaxed than he'd ever seen her—softer and more approachable. Janice had somehow turned a corner. Vincent just wasn't sure if her demeanor changed because of him or because her daughter was home. Either way, it pleased him.

Janice's smile came to his memory. He hadn't noticed it before, perhaps, because she'd rarely smiled. She wore the smile well, and he'd also taken notice of her deep-green eyes, that she shared with Madison. He wished he could see a photo of Janice in her youth. He bet mother and daughter were the spitting image of each other. Vincent chuckled. He was confident they wouldn't find the similarity particularly pleasant.

As Vincent consumed the last of his wine, his thoughts drifted to his writing, or lack-thereof. He padded back to the kitchen and poured himself another glass, then sliced a few pieces of cheddar cheese, grabbed a cluster of green grapes, and threw a handful of pretzels onto a plate for good measure. Vincent's itch to write grew the closer he got to his desk. However, not knowing what to write hindered him. He contemplated his dilemma, then he decided to follow his own rule—just type: the words would come.

An hour went by in a flash, and when Vincent noted what he'd written, it surprised him to see it wasn't part of the story he'd initially intended—but in columns of text. Each column was a means to an end, with a common goal of helping to patch Janice and Madison's relationship, as well as progressing his and Janice's friendship.

Vincent was tired of being alone in his big house, and he was tired of being alone with his thoughts. He'd missed having Cheryl as a sounding board, companion, and lover. Vincent missed waking up to a smile. He missed the aroma of dinner cooking and being surprised to find his favorite dishes prepared especially for him on a special day. He missed hearing happy birthday from someone that deeply loved him and blowing out candles on his cake.

Vincent closed his laptop and raised his glass as if to make a toast and wished himself a happy birthday. He then lifted a prayer: that it would be the last birthday he'd spend alone.

thirty-seven

Madison thanked Franky for keeping her company and gave her a hug goodbye. She looked on as Franky entered her mother's home, then strolled along Lilac Lane toward her own. Madison passed by elegant historical estates, and impressive, mid-century, cottage-style homes, some abutting the York River, and others sat across the street with a view. The well-maintained and manicured homes were worth at least a million and a half or more.

She thought of the house she'd grown up in. It had, at one time, been comparable to those she walked by, but the disrepair since her father's death, nine years ago, made their house appear anything but majestic. Despite the work Vincent had done to the property, the house desperately needed cosmetic help.

Madison stopped at the end of the driveway and shoved her hands into her sweatshirt's pouch. Her hands landed on the crunched up, empty bag of fudge, and she snickered at the memory of Franky's playful way of snagging her treat. Madison examined the view of her childhood home and considered how they could possibly save it from going to foreclosure. She needed her mother to open up and talk to her, but wasn't looking forward to another fight. Try as she may, she found it difficult to bite her tongue where her mother was concerned.

She slow-walked up the drive and noticed her mother watching her from the living room window. Madison waved, and Janice gave her a smile and waved in return. As she took the steps, her mother greeted her at the door, much like Franky's mother had. Somehow, she doubted she'd get the same warm welcome.

Madison cleared her throat, a nervous habit Nathan said she'd developed. "Hi, Mom."

"Did you have a—nice walk?" Janice asked, as she limped to a swivel rocking chair that had belonged to her grandmother. As she sat, it squeaked. The sound instantly brought her to a flash from the past. Her mother was snuggled up with Hannah and rocking while reading from a picture book. Hannah was around four and she was about nine. Even way back then, Madison wished she'd had that same attention from her mother. *Squeak, squeak, squeak* went the chair.

"Madison?"

"Yeah. I stopped at Franky's. Mrs. Murphy says hello, and asked how you were doing."

Janice rolled her eyes, and with sarcasm said, "That's nice of her."

"I take it the two of you drifted apart?"

Janice quieted the chair and rubbed her thigh. "You could say that."

Madison sat on the couch and pulled her legs up and rested her arm on an overstuffed pillow. "If it makes you feel any better, she seemed genuinely concerned." She shifted her legs and stuffed her toes between the couch cushions. Her mother pursed her lips and rocked. "I know you don't want to talk about it, but you can't ignore the letter from the attorney's office anymore. Did you at least call the bank back?"

Janice puffed out a sigh. "Vincent was here and by the time he left, I figured the bank would already be closed. Besides, I wouldn't even know what to say."

"How long have they been calling you?" Madison asked as she got up from the couch and walked to the kitchen to retrieve the letter. She hollered, "I'm guessing quite a while, seeing you got the notice of foreclosure!"

Madison clomped back in and plopped onto the couch. She slid the letter out of the envelope and skimmed through the content. "It says you have to make a payment within…" She pulled her phone out of her pocket and counted out the days on the calendar. "You have forty-five days to catch up on a payment, or they'll start the foreclosure process. It's not an astronomical amount. You can surely do that." Madison looked at her mother and she hadn't seen her this pale since she'd been in the hospital. "You can, right?"

"Don't you think if I could have, I would have?"

"Well, I don't know," she said in exasperation. "I thought you might have forgotten to pay it or something. People can do that when they're—um—going through stuff."

"I don't have it. Plain and simple."

Madison collected her thoughts. She set the letter on the coffee table and clasped her hands. "Please help me understand." Madison looked at her mother, who rocked in her chair and avoided her gaze. "How can this happen?"

"I didn't get any life insurance because…"

Madison dropped her head. "Because dad's death wasn't an accident."

"Yes."

"Surely you must have had money from his social security, a pension, or some savings?"

"I did, as well as the money I inherited, but it's gone, Madison. All I have is his social security." She threw her arms up in defeat. "The rest is all gone."

A trickle of tears ran down her mother's cheeks.

Madison crept up to her mom and scooched next to her chair. "I don't understand. You inherited this house, too. Wasn't it free and clear?" Her mom nodded her head. "I see. You mortgaged it to live off of, didn't you?"

Janice wiped her cheeks with her hands and shifted in the rocker. "Yes, kind of, but not exactly."

Madison sat on the floor at her mother's side and rested her head in her hands. "What do you mean, kind of? Is there any equity left at all?"

Her mother shook her head and tears fell upon her cheeks once again.

"Where did it all go, Mom?"

Janice turned to face her. She reached out and cupped Madison's chin. Her expression was that of deep sadness before setting her jaw with determination. "It went to pay back debt, and that's all I'm going to say."

Madison wasn't sure how to respond. She certainly didn't want to have another blowup, seeing her mother like this, but she needed answers. Her mother wiped away her tears and sat back in her chair.

"Well, you'll need to make at least one payment until we can figure out a long-term solution. I can do that for you, but you can't keep burying your head in the sand any longer. This isn't going away, and I know how much this house means to you. Eventually, they will foreclose."

Janice nodded, and Madison stood up. "I'm going to get something cold to drink. Can I get you something?"

"No—no thank you."

Madison's heart felt heavy with the weight of her mother's predicament, but she couldn't fathom where all that money had gone. Her mother certainly didn't use the money for the house's upkeep, and her mom should have had enough to live on for the past nine years, so why the equity line? What bothered her more was how the bank could have given her mother the loan in the first place. Her mother had never worked, and she had no means to pay it back. Madison chewed her lip. Unless the loan was taken out before her father's death. That was the only possible explanation, but why had her parents done that?

Madison shoved the question aside. *What's done is done.* She would make the payment per the letter, but they had to come up with some sort of plan to save their family's home. As much as living in it brought her pain, it also brought her joy, and she would be damned if she'd allow the bank to take it.

• • •

Janice desperately wanted to tell Madison the truth about her father. He was a heavy gambler, and his addiction cost them everything, including his own life. But how would that help anything now? Madison was right, she'd lost a lot, and Janice didn't want Madison losing more of her father than she already had. As much as it pained her, she would continue keeping Charlie's gambling problem to herself, and allow Madison to continue to blame her for his death. Taking the blame was the least she could do. Looking back now, Janice recognized why Madison had favored her father. Charlie made an effort to be a part of Madison's world, and she had not. The fact that they rarely saw eye-to-eye was not an excuse. She was the mother, and she should have tried more. Janice laughed. But Madison sure hadn't made having a relationship easy.

Janice picked up the letter Madison had dropped and read it. Never in her wildest imagination would she think she'd be holding a *notice of foreclosure* letter. She should have seen the possibility the day she'd signed the mortgage note, but she'd ignored her gut instincts. It hadn't been Charlie's fault, after all. She could have said no to his requests to take out a loan on the house. She should have seen the risk, but she'd agreed to mortgage her family home anyway. A decision she'd have to live with for the rest of her life. Janice bowed her head and wept.

thirty-eight

Vincent, wrapped in a towel around his waist, stood at the bathroom sink, and wiped the remnants of shaving cream off his chin. He ran a comb through his thinning hair and nodded with satisfaction that he still evaded having a bald spot. "Not too shabby for a fifty-six-year-old."

The chilly morning caused him to shiver, so he grabbed a pair of jeans off a shelf in the closet, then hunted for his favorite heather-gray, zippered, pullover sweater.

"Success," he said, then pulled the sweater over his head, messing up his hair all over again. Vincent peered into the mirror and ran his fingers through it. "Good enough."

He trotted down the stairs toward the kitchen. He poured himself another cup of coffee, then opened the front door to retrieve the Sunday paper from the porch. The rolled-up paper was stuffed into a clear plastic bag to protect it from the pouring rain. He picked it up and gave it a shake, then went inside.

Vincent sat back in his soft leather chair and put his feet up on the matching burgundy-colored footrest, and gazed out the window. The sea swelled with the rain. There would be no yard work today. He opened the paper and folded it a couple of times to better handle it. Vincent smiled as he recalled Cheryl teasing him about reading from a printed paper while she'd stared at her computer or phone screen, but he couldn't be swayed from his routine, or by the changing times. Most might think reading a physical paper is archaic, but he enjoyed holding the paper in his hands. He didn't even mind getting ink-smudged fingers. Inked fingers were part of the charm. There was something special and nostalgic about the sound of a rustling paper, and it brought him comfort. Some things were perfectly fine just the way they were.

Vincent turned the page of the paper, and a headline grabbed his attention. "Turning the Page on Grief." Vincent read about letting go, moving beyond loss, but the one that hit him the most was, setting your loved ones free. Vincent pressed his fists to his chest. His heart grieved in an immeasurable sorrow. He hadn't let Cheryl go. He hadn't let her go as she slipped closer to her death. He'd refused to. And he hadn't let her go since her passing. Vincent now recognized his beloved Cheryl actively spoke to him so she could be set free. Only then could he also turn the page and be free to fully live life again.

Tears dropped onto the pages of the paper on his lap, and ink smeared across the page, just like the rain ran down the window panes. Divine intervention was cleansing everything in him and around him. Vincent bowed his head and asked Cheryl to forgive him. He could no longer feel her presence or hear her voice. All was quiet; the rain had stopped. Vincent opened his eyes and a double rainbow filled the sky.

Cheryl is free.

Vincent got up from his chair, clutching the paper, and moved toward the open floor-plan kitchen area. He spread the newspaper on the marble countertop, then searched for a pair of scissors in the junk drawer. Vincent snipped the article out.

He'd need the reminders from time to time because living without Cheryl wouldn't be easy.

The house, he thought, was too quiet. Vincent strolled over to his vintage record player and removed a record from the shelving. He slid the vinyl from its sleeve and placed it on the turntable. The needle scratched as he lay the arm in place, then the music rang out with the sound of violins, cellos, bass, saxophones, and piccolos, and his soul took flight. Vincent swayed and dipped as the music soared, and with each crescendo, his passion for life grew.

He'd made a promise when he set Cheryl free that he would write again, dance again. He'd not only bring the soil and plants back to life, but he'd find new life in himself to fully live again—to love again. *I am free.* The music pierced his unconscious mind and awakened his body as he played conductor to each symphonic tempo and modulation. Tears of joy rolled down his cheeks. At last, his strength was gone, the song came to a celebratory end, and Vincent sank to the floor in utter exhaustion. *I can live again, and that's okay.*

thirty-nine

Madison sat on her bed and held the phone to her ear as it rang. Nathan's raspy voice answered. "Hey there."

"Wow, you sound tired. Did I wake you up?"

"Nah, you didn't wake me up. I am tired though—didn't sleep very well last night. I think I've come down with something."

"I'm sorry to hear that. Be sure to drink plenty of water and get some rest."

Nathan muffled a cough as he tried to speak. "Sorry about that," he said, then cleared his throat. "You've been heavy on my mind. I thought about coming to see you, but with this cold, I don't think it's such a good idea."

Madison was relieved he wasn't coming, which tugged at her heart. After their long relationship over the past eight-plus years, she thought she should feel happy about the prospect of him coming to visit. But Madison was glad he wasn't. Just the same, she was glad Nathan was thinking of her. "Is everything going well for you at work?"

"Yeah, it's okay. My dad's psyched, though. Our profit margins are fantastic, and I suspect we'll both get raises."

"That's fantastic." A sense of relief came over her. Having the need to help with her mom's finances was manageable, but she welcomed the idea of having extra money. "So, I have something I need to talk with you about." She cleared her throat. "Remember when I told you about my mom's finances and how bad the house is?"

"Yes—I take it you've talked with her and found out more about her situation?"

"Sure have, and I can't believe it, Nathan. She's going to be foreclosed on unless I figure out a way to help her." Madison's heart rate went up as she thought about how to approach the subject and how it would affect hers and Nathan's relationship. *Just rip off the Band-Aid.* "I'd like to see if my mother would be willing to deed me the house."

Madison tensed up, and her pulse raced as she waited for his response. When Nathan remained quiet on the other end of the line, she continued. "I was thinking about just making the payments, but I know I'd never get that money back. So, I figured, if she deeds it to me, I could take over the note, and stop it from being foreclosed on. What do you think?"

Nathan sighed. "I don't want to be a downer, but you said the house was a disaster. It could be a money pit, and you wouldn't be around to take care of it."

Madison paced. "It is in shambles, yes, but it's mostly cosmetic and updating. And you know how we've tucked quite a bit away into our savings account, right?" She didn't wait for a response. "Well, I could use my share, and with that, and a raise, it would make it easier to cover the expenses."

"But that doesn't answer the question of distance. How could you manage it from so far away?"

Madison closed her eyes and tried to collect her thoughts. "I wouldn't, Nathan. I was thinking it might be best if I just stay here." Nathan's breathing quickened, but he didn't say anything.

"I know," she said, and flopped on the bed. "I just threw a lot out there, but you must admit, you haven't been happy—*we* haven't been happy. And honestly, if it wasn't for our work, Lily, and now Journey, I doubt we'd have stayed together as long as we have. We've become nothing more than roommates."

"You've given this a lot of thought, haven't you," he said in a monotone.

"Nathan, you've had to have felt us drifting further and further apart, too. Didn't you?"

"You know I love you."

"Of course, I do." She wanted to say she loved him back, but the words stuck in her throat. "We haven't been...*us* in a long, long time." She chewed on her lip. "We've been going through the motions for so long that we've forgotten what we were like when we were truly *in* love and happy together. We want different things—things I'm not willing to give you. And, maybe, just maybe, with me gone, you can find someone that can make you happy again, and give you the family you've craved."

"I hear you. I really do, but..."

"You know I'm right, Nathan."

"Maybe you are, but what happens if you stay there longer and you change your mind?"

I won't change my mind. She knew staying here was the right path for her. New England is her home. Ohio, on the other hand, had become her crutch—her escape. She hadn't an attachment to the life she was choosing to leave. Here, however, she had roots. As tangled and messed up as they were, this was home, and home is where she needed to stay.

"Besides," Nathan said, "for all you know, your mom wouldn't even go for your grand idea. And what happens if my father doesn't like you working remotely, long term?"

Madison hadn't considered this. "I guess I'll have to ask him, and if he's willing, then I think it's what's best."

"Best for you," he snapped.

"Best for both of us," she said calmly.

Silence fell over the conversation until Nathan went on a coughing binge. When he gained his composure, he said he hoped she'd reconsider, wished her luck with her mother, and his father, then said goodbye and hung up.

Madison stared at her phone as the finality of their relationship ending sank in. *Did I really just do that?* She didn't feel like crying or celebrating. She felt content with her decision.

As much as she hated to talk to him about breaking up over the phone, time was of the essence, and she didn't see another way around it. She checked her emotions. *Yes, this is for the best. I know it is.* Still, she'd just closed a large chapter in her life, but a new story was being written.

Now, she thought, the only pressing things she and Nathan had to discuss were her precious horse, Lily, and her foal, Journey. But she'd broach that subject later. Madison climbed off the bed, and felt lighter. She still needed to talk with her mother about her proposal, but first she had to make sure she still had a job. If not, she'd look for one immediately.

Madison loved Nathan's parents and appreciated everything they'd done for her. They thought of her as if she were their own daughter, and she realized the magnitude of the decision she was making. The home she and Nathan shared on the Hawkings' property had been a gift when she'd needed it the most. The cottage had become their home, even though most everything in it belonged to Nathan's parents. Madison thought of the barn and her beloved horses. Her heart ached with the knowledge she'd have to leave them behind. Those beautiful animals were like children to her. But with all she needed to do regarding her family home and her job, she wouldn't have the time to care for them the way she'd like. Plus, she didn't have a barn for them, anyway. Sadly, she'd miss Val and Winston Hawking more than Nathan. The realization cemented the idea that she was doing the right thing. She hoped and prayed Nathan would reach the same conclusion.

Madison picked up her phone and her hands shook and her underarms dampened. *Please be okay with this. Please understand.* She tapped the number for Winston Hawking.

forty

Janice fumbled around the kitchen at a slow pace. At the fridge, she teetered with her cane as she removed the salad makings Madison purchased that afternoon and placed them on the butcher block counter. She retrieved a large wooden bowl from the cabinet and was just about to set it down when her phone rang, startling her. The bowl slipped out of her hand, bounced off the counter, and rolled around on the floor underfoot. Janice took a moment to steady herself, then she picked up her phone from the kitchen table.

It's Vincent. Seeing his name sent butterflies off in her stomach. She had no right to him, but her feelings for him grew with each passing day.

Janice nearly let the call go to voicemail, but at the last second, she went against her better judgment and answered. Vincent's calming voice responded to her hello, soothed her trepidation, and she'd become putty in his hands. She was in trouble. She pulled out a chair and took a seat.

"What's up?" She nervously twirled a strand of her hair. After realizing she was acting like a schoolgirl, she sat on her hand. *For goodness sake, I'm a grown woman.* She rolled her eyes. After all, she was confident he'd only called to plan for the next day's project. Still, her heart thumped at a quicker pace.

"I was wondering if you had dinner plans?" Vincent said.

Janice glanced at the head of lettuce, tomato, and other salad fixings spread across the counter. She and Madison had planned to order a couple of subs to go with it. "Why do you ask?"

"I'd like to invite you to dinner—at my house."

"How nice of you," Janice said. She was finally going to meet Cheryl. As much as she wished Vincent were single, Cheryl sounded like a lovely woman, and she thought it would be great to make a friend. Madison would have to drive her, and she'd feel bad, since they were finally getting along well enough to share a meal. "I would like that, but I'd need a ride and…"

"Please don't worry about that. I'll come and get you," he said, cheerfully.

Janice was having a hard time saying no, but she figured Madison would be fine to eat on her own. She'd probably understand because they would finally solve the mystery of Cheryl. "What time are you thinking?"

"I have spaghetti sauce simmering on the stove. I hope you like spaghetti," he said with a touch of apprehension in his voice.

"I do."

"Great! How's about I pick you up in an hour?"

Janice thought about what she'd wear and how much time it would take her to look presentable when she met Cheryl. *I'm going to meet Cheryl—with Vincent. This is madness. Why did I say, yes?* She hadn't worn makeup in years. She didn't even know if any of her old stuff was usable. Janice told Vincent the timing worked, and they said their goodbyes. She no sooner hung up, when the hint of terror tore through her.

Madison stepped into the kitchen and stopped short. Janice was sure her fear showed.

Outside of getting groceries, running to doctor appointments, and the time going to Whispering Sands Gifts, she hadn't socialized in years. Janice's heart raced and her hands grew clammy. Soon, her anxiety would build to the point where she wouldn't be able to breathe comfortably. Janice clung to the edge of the table and tried to take in air.

"Mom? What's going on?" The look of concern on Madison's face didn't change her disposition.

"I—I just need a minute."

"Do you need some water?"

Janice shook her head.

"Should I call 911?"

Janice stared at the door frame, her focal point, and slowly breathed in, then let it out at the same pace. "I'm having an anxiety attack. It happens." She took another breath. "I'll be okay in a minute or two." Her anxiety slowly dissipated. When Janice finally felt more like herself, she turned and looked into Madison's worried eyes. "I've been invited to Vincent and Cheryl's home for dinner."

To Janice's delight, Madison gave her a broad smile.

"That's wonderful, Mom."

Janice's breath caught in her throat. *She called me Mom. Not Mother with a cutting edge to it. She said Mom.* All her earlier stress dissipated with that one word—*Mom.*

Janice looked on as Madison sifted through her closet to help her pick out an outfit. Madison told her mother about the conversation she and Franky had about Madison's poor fashion choices.

"All I care about is having something that fits. I have worn none of my dressy clothes since..." Janice stopped to think, then shrugged her shoulders. "Well, I don't remember when."

"I'm sure we'll find something. Let's stick with a casual dress. That way, you won't have to worry about a pair of slacks or a skirt sliding down to your ankles."

They shared a laugh.

"I guess that wouldn't make for a very good first impression." *What would Cheryl be wearing? I bet she's pretty.* "I'm not really up on the latest makeup trends, but you probably wore it when you were working. Right?"

Madison cocked her head to the side and gave a small grin. "Would you like me to help you with that?"

Janice thought she'd died and gone to heaven. Never in her wildest dreams did she think they'd be going through her closet and talking about makeup, let alone have Madison help her put it on. "If it's not too much to ask."

Madison grabbed a berry-colored, white pinstriped dress with three-quarter-length sleeves and a winged collar, and a stretchy matching belt, then laid the pieces across the bed and headed toward the door.

"I'll be right back." Madison dashed out of the room and was back, just as she finished slipping her arms through the dress sleeves. "Looks like it fits."

Janice leaned against her bureau and her hands shook as she buttoned the front, and adjusted the collar. Madison collected the belt and waited for her to finish her task. Janice took the belt and wrapped it around her waist, but she had trouble with hooking the latch.

"Let me help." Madison's slim fingers easily guided the hook, then Madison turned her gaze. Madison's emerald eyes drank her in just as they'd done when she was a child. Janice fought to keep her emotions down.

"Thank you," she said, then retrieved her cane and hobbled toward the full-length mirror to look at her reflection. *I can live with this.* She smiled. She ran her fingers through the length of her hair at her shoulders. It was soft to her touch, with a gentle wave to it, and her gray strands mixed well with her dark brown shades. *I actually look pretty.* Even without makeup, she felt giddy as she touched her cheek. "I don't think I want too much."

"Don't worry. I'll keep your face looking natural. I just want to brighten you up a bit."

"That sounds perfect." Janice sat down at her vanity and turned toward Madison as she did her magic. Her heart swelled as Madison hummed a tune while she applied the makeup. Janice recognized the song at once, as Charlie used to whistle it. "You remember."

"What's that?" Madison asked as she applied blush.

"Your father's favorite tune. You were humming it."

Madison's gaze drifted away, but a smile remained on her face. "I hadn't realized I was." She stopped applying the makeup. "Is that okay? My humming it, that is?"

"Oh, honey, of course it's okay."

Madison smiled, then dabbed lip balm to her lips. She stood back to admire her work. "Perfect. Take a looksee."

Janice swiveled in the seat. She gasped. "You've made me look—I look ten, no, twenty years younger."

"Okay then. Skedaddle." Madison motioned toward the bedroom door. "He's going to be here any minute."

As Janice sat in her heirloom swivel rocker, she realized this was the happiest day she'd had since Charlie's passing. If she were being honest with herself, she had to admit she hadn't been this happy since long before his death.

Madison wished her well, then took the freshly delivered pizza into the old library that sat just off the living room. Madison currently used the space as a temporary office. In the meantime, Janice literally twiddled her thumbs in anticipation of Vincent's arrival while trying to ignore her moist armpits. *Breathe. Just breathe.*

*V*incent's truck pulled up right on time, and Janice collected her purse off the back of the couch. She opened the door to greet him. He raised his eyebrows and wore a toothy smile.

"Wow, you look beautiful." He reached out to take her extended hand and helped her down the steps toward the truck.

Janice sat quietly in the passenger's seat and fixed her gaze on the road ahead. The farther they got from her home, the more anxious she became. She straightened her dress with a tug here and there, then fidgeted with the flap on her purse.

"Everything will be fine," Vincent said. "You don't have to worry."

I don't have to worry, he says. I have everything to worry about. She shook off her downward-spiraling thoughts and exhaled.

"What are we having for dinner?" she asked, then remembered they were having spaghetti. "Dumb question."

Janice glanced over, and Vincent gave her a wink. Heat rose from her neck to her cheeks, and she turned away with embarrassment.

"I'm sorry I didn't have a chance to get something to bring." She wished she'd thought to make the salad she'd originally planned to have for dinner.

"Your presence is all I need, but thank you for the thought."

Janice thought it curious that Vincent said *I* and not *we*, but she didn't bother to correct him. She gazed out the passenger window and watched the ocean waves crash along the breaker wall. "The tide's really high."

Again, Janice's embarrassment grew. She hated small talk. She might as well have said she heard the weather was going to be nice. "You said your home is near Short Sands Beach. We must have been close by when you took me to get my cane."

Vincent turned the wheel toward the Nubble Lighthouse and climbed the winding road along the water, then headed the back way to Short Sands. "We were within walking distance. A long walk, but a walk just the same. Sometime, when you're all healed up, perhaps you'll walk with me?"

Again, his use of the singular pronouns troubled her. "We must be getting close, then."

"We sure are." He put his blinker on, then pulled into a driveway three houses down.

The imposing two-story home was stunning, but with the windows lit up, it had a warm, welcoming elegance. As she peered through the front window from the truck, she could see all the way through to the back of the house. Its view overlooked the vast ocean, gleaming in the distance. The landscaping, as she expected, was manicured to perfection, and she wondered how he could maintain it and still find time for all the work at her place. Vincent left the truck in the driveway instead of pulling into the garage and stepped around to open her door.

"Your home is beautiful," she said in a near whisper as he escorted her to the front door, and unlocked it.

The aroma of garlic and tomatoes wafted through the

door. She placed her free hand on her stomach as it rumbled. She glanced around the large foyer area, to the rest of the open-concept living, dining, and kitchen areas. But she didn't see Cheryl, and assumed she must be in the bedroom or bath. Vincent took her purse and placed it on a hook near the door, then led her toward the kitchen. He reached over to turn on a burner under a large pot on the stove. Janice climbed up onto the high-top stool at the island's counter. A bottle of wine and two glasses sat in front of her, while classical music played lightly in the background.

Vincent poured the wine. "I'm glad you like it. We drew up the design together. It wasn't the easiest thing to do for a marriage, but Cheryl prevailed with the bulk of the decisions, and we were both happy with the outcome." He explained how the house used to look and all the improvements they'd made over the years.

"I can see why you love it so much," she said as she took in the room. "It truly is lovely. It's much bigger than it looks from the outside."

"Not as big as yours, by any stretch of the imagination, but it suits me." He turned the burner up on the stove. "I hope you're hungry because I've made enough to feed the summer crowd." He chuckled.

"You cooked our dinner?"

"Sure did."

"Is it safe to eat?" She laughed, remembering his attempt at muffins.

"I can assure you that I can cook. It's baking that escapes my mastery."

They sipped their wine, as he told her more about the

house. Soon the water reached a rolling boil. He grabbed a box of pasta, then dropped it into the pot.

"As soon as the pasta's ready, we can eat. Unless you'd like to start with our salads first. They're already made and in the fridge?"

Janice's feeling of unease was gaining speed. She listened for Cheryl, then stretched her head to the dining area. *Hmm, only two place settings.* "Vincent? Where *is* Cheryl? Won't she be joining us?"

Vincent's head dropped, and he picked up his glass of wine, then took a big swig. "She's not here. I should have told you that up front. I'm sorry." He shook his head and said, "I wasn't thinking."

Janice tucked her hair behind her ear and teetered back and forth on her seat. Feeling suddenly exposed, she had an overwhelming urge to cover her open neckline. "So, let me get this straight. Your wife isn't here, and you thought it would be a good idea to wine and dine me—alone—in your home?"

"Yes," he said with a look of panic.

"Yes? Your answer is yes!" Janice trembled as she climbed down from the stool. "I thought better of you, Vincent. I thought you were a gentleman!" She snatched her cane. "I thought you were trustworthy."

"I—uh—I didn't mean *yes* like that. I mean *no!*"

"Well, Mr. Clark, what is it then?"

"I—well, what I mean to say is—I…"

"You know what? It doesn't matter what you meant. Your seduction, while your wife is away, says it all." Janice thumped the cane with each hasty step and made it to the door. She tore her purse strap from its hook and opened the door. "Take me home, Mr. Clark. Take me home right now."

Vincent hurried to her, and his eyes glistened with dampness. "Please let me explain."

"Seriously? What is there to explain? You and I are here, and the woman you've spoken so kindly about isn't. So please don't tell me you're separated, Vincent, because I don't buy it!" She shook with anger. "Can't you see how humiliating this is for me? I thought I was being introduced to your wife!"

Vincent sank into the cushioned chair next to her. He rested his elbows on his thighs and bowed his head in his hands. And, like flood gates being opened, his shoulders sagged, and he shook with jagged tears. Janice froze as she looked down at Vincent in despair, and she did not know how to console this broken man.

The sound of water hissing and sizzling snapped her out of her frozen state. The pasta was boiling over, so she hobbled to the kitchen and turned down the burner with a flip of her wrist, then leaned against the counter to try to make sense of Vincent's behavior. Never had she considered getting this perplexed about a situation by anyone outside of her own dysfunctional family, but here she was.

Vincent's sobs grew weaker, so Janice made her way back to where he sat. He lifted his head and wiped his face with the back of his hands, sniffed, then hopped up from the chair and snagged a few tissues from a side table and blew his nose. By now, Janice had calmed down considerably. However, she needed to understand what was happening with Vincent. Was he feeling remorseful for acting unfaithful? Or was it something altogether different? She waited until he seemed more settled. "What's going on, Vincent?"

"I should have told you earlier. I wanted to, so many times, but I wasn't ready." He stuffed the used tissues in his pocket and looked in her direction. His puffy face and red nose caused her to feel sympathetic.

"What is it you're trying to tell me?" She watched him chew on his lower lip and saw another tear roll down his cheek. "I'll just listen, and I promise I'll keep an open mind to whatever it is you've been wanting to tell me."

He cleared his throat and peered into her eyes with such intensity that it caused her breath to hitch, and she waited for the shoe to fall.

"My beloved Cheryl died three years ago."

Janice tried to grasp what she'd just heard, but her mind swirled with their previous conversations. He'd spoken so many times of her in the present tense. She could swear she'd asked about Cheryl numerous times, and he never let on…

Vincent finally broke away from their locked eyes. "You must think me to be crazy. In all honesty, I thought I was for a while, too." He glanced toward the kitchen. "Do you mind?" he said as he took a few steps and gestured to the filled wine glasses that sat untouched. "I don't know about you, but I could really use a drink." Vincent didn't wait for a response as he retrieved the glasses, then stopped short. "I'm so sorry. You wanted to go home."

He turned to put the wine back on the counter.

"It's okay, Vincent. I'll stay," Janice said as she made her way to the kitchen. "I'll have one glass." She motioned toward her leg. "I'm still on medication, and I don't want to overdo it."

He nodded his head in understanding. "Are you still up for dinner?"

Janice could feel her stomach growl, and she doubted

Madison had any leftover pizza since she'd changed the order for a small. Besides, she thought, she wanted answers. "I suppose I could stay and eat."

Vincent's visibly tense shoulders relaxed. A tentative smile formed across his face. "I sure was hoping you'd say that."

forty-three

Madison's pizza was long gone. Its dried-up pieces of crust lay in the grease-soaked box on the top of her bed. She leaned into the pillowed headboard and closed her laptop that sat across her lap. She glanced at the time and peeked out the window, hoping to see headlights through the light rain. Her concern for her mother grew by the time another half hour passed by.

Madison set her laptop aside and slid off the bed. She folded the pizza box's cover closed and barefooted it to the kitchen. She stuffed the box into the trash and popped open a can of Pepsi. As she took a big gulp of the soda, the carbonated fizz tickled her nose, and she held back the pressing urge to sneeze. Madison couldn't remember the last time she'd had a Pepsi. When she was a kid, soda was pretty much her go-to drink.

The house creaked with each step she took. She thought about all the times she'd tried to sneak in after being out past her curfew. Now Madison understood her mother's worry. Too restless to sleep, she turned on the television and clicked through the limited channels on the outdated TV. With a sigh, she turned it off and set the remote down.

Outside, the rain's intensity picked up, and the boom of thunder filled the room. Madison thought about all the years her mother had sat in her chair, alone, in this big empty house. How had she got through the days? She certainly didn't pass the time cleaning it. She peered at the TV remote on the side table and presumed all she did was glue herself to the television. Or, more likely, her mother slept the lonely days away.

Madison glanced at the large bookshelf that stood against the wall. *Maybe she reads?* She skimmed the shelves packed full of books, magazines, leather-bound photo albums, and various sized shoe box containers. She perused through the shelves and tugged at one of the photo albums until it came free from the shelf. Then Madison curled up on the couch and opened the cover. As she flipped through the pages, its well-worn binding barely held together. The photos ranged from the time she was about fourteen to the time she left home, at nearly eighteen. A photo of Madison in her school play, several of her playing sports, and a few of her and Franky. She laughed as she examined the image of them wearing their first formal dresses. Neither one of them was comfortable in high heels, and it showed. Quite a few random images from around the house graced the album as well. One of her in her fishing gear, baking cookies, when she received her driver's license, but the one that grabbed her attention the most was the day her horse Lily arrived.

Madison stroked the photo with her finger as if to feel her sweet quarter horse's mane. The day she got Lily was one of the happiest days of her life. She sighed. Another photo depicted her and her father feeding Lily a bunch of carrots. This image made her realize that her mother had taken all the photos in the album, many she hadn't known were being taken. She scanned through the pages and noticed a few here and there with Hannah, but mostly, she was the focus.

She loved me.

The rain finally subsided, and she glanced at the time. It was nearing midnight and her mother still wasn't home. Madison picked up her phone to call, but thought better of it, and set it down. *Leave her alone. She's just having a good time.*

She sighed and flipped the worn album cover closed and squeezed it back into place. Headlights shone through the sheer window curtains. She breathed a sigh of relief. *Finally.* The truck doors shut and laughter filled the night. She considered running up the stairs, so she wouldn't appear as if she was up waiting, but she was eager to hear all about how her night went, and she wanted to learn what Vincent's wife was like. When they were taking so long to reach the house, she couldn't resist seeing what was keeping them.

Madison tiptoed to the window and pulled the edge of the curtain back. She was grateful for the front porch light, so she could better see Vincent and her mother standing at the base of the steps close together. Madison gulped as Vincent reached to tuck her mother's hair behind her ear. He rested his other hand on her shoulder and they continued to talk. Madison couldn't hear because their voices were low.

Then they embraced. Vincent tipped his head down and kissed the crown of her mother's head. They gave a long goodbye with her mother tracing Vincent's arm until their arms were fully extended with only their fingertips touched, then lingered. Her mother broke the intimate moment and turned toward the door.

Madison snapped shut the curtain and ran up the stairs, taking them two at a time, entered her bedroom, and shut the door behind her. Her heart pounded, and she shook with anger. *How dare they?* She paced around the room with her hands on her hips. *He's a married man! After all the kindness he's shone, he's nothing but a two-timing adulterer.* Madison didn't know who to be more angry with, Vincent, or her mother.

forty-four

Vincent lingered until Janice was safely inside her home. He turned the key just as a thunderous burst of rain pummeled his truck's windshield. *Not a moment too soon*, he thought, as he replayed their long goodbye over in his mind.

He'd thought the night would end up being a disaster after his emotional outburst, but Janice shared a side of her he hadn't seen coming. Yes, she was upset at first, and she should be; he'd deceived her. The grace and gentleness she'd shown afterward stirred his soul. She showed a kindness and warmth, one that he'd wished she'd show her daughter. Janice wasn't resentful or judgmental. She had put on her caregiver hat and allowed him to receive comfort and understanding. When they'd pulled into her driveway and walked her to the door, he wanted to kiss her and hold her in his arms, but he held back. Too soon, he'd thought. Just too soon.

Vincent maneuvered around a few rain-soaked potholes in Janice's driveway, then made the turn toward home. His wipers tossed the rain back and forth at a furious pace, and he found it hard to see the road clearly, especially in the dead of night. He leaned over the steering wheel and squinted to better see each turn, when his truck started to sputter and shake. Vincent only made it another fifty yards before making the decision to pull over onto the edge of Lilac Lane, just as his truck backfired and died. He tried the ignition and the only sound it made was *click, click, click.*

He rested his forehead on the top of the steering wheel to think. He was tired and his frustration grew. *I knew I should have driven the car.* Vincent pounded the dash, then sank into the seat, and turned over ideas for a solution to his problem. After a handful of minutes passed, he thought it best to call AAA to get a fix or a tow. Vincent soon learned he didn't have cell service. With great reluctance, he pushed the button for the hazards and stepped out of the truck into the deluge of water falling from the sky. Within seconds, he was drenched through and through. He turned on his phone's flashlight and trudged down the road toward Janice's, while cursing himself for not having an umbrella in the truck. *Some kind of Boy Scout I am.*

The silver lining in Vincent's cloud was that while he walked, he had additional time to reflect on his evening with Janice. After he got beyond his embarrassment and finally spilled his heart out to her, they'd found an understanding of each other's sorrow. Yes, he had lied. But in his defense, Cheryl seemed very much alive in his misguided sense of reality. He recognized that now. To Janice's credit and wisdom, she'd helped him acknowledge the truth and assured him it was okay to "talk" to his wife in the spiritual sense. Janice said she did the same from time to time with Charlie. He laughed when she confessed her words to Charlie weren't quite as loving as his talks with Cheryl were. He hadn't meant to laugh, but her demeanor and expressive delivery gave him no choice. He couldn't hold the laughter back, and to his delight, she'd joined in, which broke the tension and heaviness of the situation.

In the beginning, they'd sat side by side on the couch, but as evening went on, they'd faced one another. Oftentimes, they clutched each other's hands, and they shared the bittersweet times of their lives. Janice's smile became infectious, and the night filled with promise. For a moment here and there, Janice was all he could see, feel, and hear. Cheryl was gone, and that was okay—he was okay.

Vincent trudged on and Janice's house appeared up ahead. To his relief, the lights were still on. They weren't expecting him, so now his biggest concern was showing up on their doorstep in the middle of the night, in the pouring rain. He checked his phone for service, but he had zero bars, and the phone was wet. Would it work at all? Just in case he got lucky, he'd text his arrival, so he wouldn't scare Janice and Madison half to death. He punched in Janice's name to retrieve her number, and the phone slipped from his grasp. It fell into one of the potholes he'd steered around earlier, and he wanted to scream. He fished the phone out and stuffed it in his pants pocket, then sloshed to the front door and knocked. No answer. He knocked again and waited. Still no response, so he ventured toward the back of the house.

Vincent's feet sunk into the saturated soil with each step until he reached the kitchen door. He could see Janice through the door's window pane. She carried a glass of water in one hand, and was reaching for the light switch with the other, her cane hooked over her forearm. He pecked on the door and she jerked her head in his direction, but she didn't approach, so he knocked harder. Janice set the glass down, then withdrew a large knife from the butcher's block knife rack and cautiously stepped toward the door.

He stuck his face between the door and its frame and hollered. "It's me, Janice. It's just me."

He suspected the rain muffled his voice enough that she didn't hear him because she held the knife ear high, with its aim directed at him.

"Janice! It's Vincent!"

Still, she didn't lower the knife, so he knocked again and scrambled down the few stairs onto the ground. Janice opened the door with exceptional speed. She stood there looking like a woman scorned, and ready to destroy her adversary.

"It's me—Vincent!"

"What are you doing? I could have killed you!" She lowered the knife and doubled over, gasping for breath. "You—scared me—to death."

Vincent slipped on his way up the stairs and slammed his hands on the top step, trying to break his fall. "I'm so sorry." He came to a stand and Janice stepped back to give him room to enter. "My truck broke down, and my phone didn't work, and…"

"It's okay." Janice shut the door behind him, then put the knife down on the table. She gave him a double-take. "You're soaked. How far did you walk?"

"I—well—I'm not quite sure. It was dark and the rain…"

Janice brushed off his attempt to respond. "It doesn't matter. I'm glad you're here, safe and sound." She eyed him from head to toe and shook her head. "Stay right there. I'm going to get you a towel to sop up some of your…" Again, she shook her head, then headed toward the bathroom. She returned a few minutes later with a large towel and handed it to him.

"Thank you," he said with a shiver, and lifted the towel to his face and gave it a good rub.

"Take off your shoes and socks, then head to the bathroom. I've hung a robe in there for you to wear. So, get undressed, and throw your wet clothes outside the door, and I'll put them in the dryer. If you're done before I get back, help yourself to a cup of tea."

"Yes, ma'am."

He'd never seen Janice that decisive and in control of a situation. He got a kick out of it. She wasn't speaking out of fear, anger, or with a cutting edge. She was acting motherly, and he found that refreshing.

Vincent tugged on the robe's belt to tighten it and headed back to the kitchen. He picked up Janice's wall phone and called for roadside service, then selected a mug for his tea. He stood at the sink to fill it with water, wearing a thinning plaid cotton men's bathrobe and bare feet. His hair was askew and damp. He felt like he'd just rolled out of bed. He dropped a tea bag into his mug and placed it in the microwave just as Janice approached. She, too, wore a robe and appeared just as tired. She came up behind him and retrieved a mug for herself and gave him a weak grin.

"You don't have to wait up with me. If you show me where the dryer is, I can get my clothes in. I'm hoping by then, AAA should be with my truck."

"Don't be ridiculous. I don't mind waiting up with you." She shifted a few boxes of tea around in the cupboard and pulled out a tin of chai. "If you'd like, you're welcome to stay here overnight." Janice opened the tea packet. "You're all dried off, and it seems kind of silly to go back out in this mess. Surely, they can work on the truck without you there."

Vincent considered what she'd said. He had left his truck key on top of the front driver's side tire for that purpose, as he wasn't sure he'd get back in time once AAA arrived. "There's a good chance it might have to be towed anyway," he said. "And then I'd need to get a ride home. The last thing I'd want to do, at this hour, is trouble Madison for a ride."

"Exactly."

Vincent retrieved his mug and held the warmth in his hands. "I think you're right. It makes sense for me to take care of the trunk in the morning."

As they sat at the table together, wearing bathrobes, he didn't feel self-conscience, if anything, he felt content. A feeling that had eluded him for quite some time. He smiled over his tea mug, and Janice's tired eyes narrowed as she grinned in return.

forty-five

Madison awoke in the morning to sunshine. This normally made her happy and excited for the new day, but the storm in the night kept her tossing and turning. She rubbed the sleep from her eyes then squeezed her temples with her fingers. Her pounding headache and restless night made her feel agitated and irritable. This was a recipe for disaster while living here with her mother.

She'd intended to talk with her mom about the house and the intimate moment she witnessed between her mother and Vincent, but she wouldn't dream of approaching either subject until she had a strong cup of coffee and a couple of aspirin.

She slid out of bed in dramatic fashion, much like she used to do when her mother woke her for school. Only now, the aroma of French toast or pancakes wasn't coming from the kitchen like back then. Her stomach growled at the thought of breakfast.

Madison eyed her crumpled up robe on the floor but left it there. Instead, she remained in the oversized T-shirt she'd slept in and quietly padded to the kitchen for her jumbo-sized coffee. She crept down the squeaky back staircase so she wouldn't wake her mother, who'd been out so late. Madison wished she were still tucked in her bed, but she'd promised Winston Hawking she'd get some projections to him in short order. *Coffee. I must have coffee.*

Her foot hit the last step and rounded the tight corner to the kitchen. She gasped as she eyed Vincent opening a cabinet. He was wearing her dad's bathrobe, the one he'd worn every day for as long as she could remember until the day he'd died. Madison cleared her throat, and Vincent startled. He spun on his heels and his mouth gaped open.

"Good morning, Madison. I was just, um…"

"Making yourself at home? It seems the logical thing being you're in my mother's kitchen wearing my father's robe."

Vincent's face drained of its color. "It's not how it looks."

"Seems pretty self-explanatory to me." Madison nudged him aside and retrieved a cup. "You brought my widowed mother home and stayed the night with her."

"It rained and my clothes needed to dry—and…"

"And yet, you're still here—in his robe." She popped a K-cup into the coffee machine and pressed the button to start, then leaned her back against the counter and crossed her arms, waiting for him to explain the obvious, but all he did was avert his eyes and stay silent. She'd chalked it up to him feeling guilty, but that was until she remembered her own appearance. Her T-shirt barely covered her, and she increasingly felt exposed.

"I'll just get my coffee, and leave you," she said with a throw of her hand, "to do whatever it was you were doing."

Madison tapped her foot as she anxiously waited for the coffee to finish dripping, then hurried to the staircase while tugging the back of her T-shirt down to cover her backside. She turned back. "Maybe, while you're here, you could see what you can do about the dryer. Apparently, it doesn't seem to be working."

With that, she headed up the rest of the stairs to her room.

Madison's head was spinning. She couldn't understand how her mother could have had dinner at Vincent and Cheryl's home, then end up having Vincent staying the night. Unless Cheryl hadn't been home at all. She'd thought Vincent a gentleman, but her suspicions were wrong all along. Vincent Clark had a thing for her mother, and for the life of her, she couldn't figure out the appeal. She wasn't rolling in cash.

She paced back and forth as her mind reeled. Maybe he had an interest in her mother's property. He obviously knew the place was falling apart, and he probably looked at the public records. Maybe he was trying to get the house for a song. But the thing that threw a wrench into her thinking was that he was fixing it up. If he wanted it, at a discount, he wouldn't be doing that.

She put her nearly empty coffee cup on her bureau and collapsed back onto her bed and stared at the ceiling, as if it would give her some answers. Her mind drifted to seeing Vincent in her dad's bathrobe.

Her dad had never owned a robe, at least Madison had no recollection of him having one. She'd saved her allowance and took babysitting jobs to come up with enough money to purchase the plaid robe as a Christmas gift. Hannah had saved for a gift for their mother and they'd agreed to split the credit of the gifts between them. Madison beamed with pride when she'd handed the carefully wrapped package to her dad. The gift was the most expensive one she'd ever given without receiving money from her parents. He'd opened the present and pulled the robe out of the box, gathering it into his arms. She'd never forgotten the smile on his face, nor would she forget his embrace.

Tears dripped down Madison's temples and dampened her hair as she lay atop her bed. He'd been vibrant and had an abundance of energy. He'd tease and joke, he'd laugh, and she never, for a moment, doubted his love for her. She lay there, tears flowing. How could he have ruined it all? How could he have killed himself? How could he have left her? He'd been her rock, her constant presence, her daddy. Now the pain of seeing him in the barn was all she had left. The unfathomable image set firmly in her mind, and as much as she wished to forget—it remained.

A knock on her bedroom door snapped Madison out of the past and into the present.

"Madison. May I come in?" Janice said.

She wanted to shout *no*. She wanted to scream *how could you?* She wanted to throw the stupid stuffed bear Nathan had won for her so many years ago at the door. She wanted to pout and stomp her feet, but Madison restrained herself and said, "Come on in."

Her mother's unsteady limp crossed the floorboards, and she sat down on the edge of the bed. "I understand you saw Vincent in the kitchen this morning."

"Sure did."

"I'm also to understand you've misinterpreted the situation."

Madison came to a sitting position and wiped her damp temples. "Am I? Well, then, by all means, enlighten me."

"His truck broke down after dropping me off, so he came back here during the storm. I gave him something dry to put on…"

"That bathrobe was Dad's."

Her mother nodded and looked away. "The robe was all I could think of that would fit."

Despite her mother thinking of giving Vincent her father's robe to wear, it moved Madison to know her mother had kept it. She fiddled with the fringe on her blanket.

"I asked him to stay because I thought it was too late to ask you to take him back to his truck once it had been fixed." Her mother turned in her direction and set her hand on Madison's knee. "Not that it should concern you, but we talked for a while, then *I* went to bed. Alone." Her determined gaze remained. "And Vincent slept on the couch."

Madison remembered the intimate kiss on the outside steps. "You know what? You're right. It's none of my business, but don't you think his wife might see things differently?" Madison shifted and grasped her mother's hand. "He wants something from you, Mom. I'm not sure what it is, but I don't trust him anymore."

"I can assure you, he's a decent man, and I can take care of myself."

Madison's astonishment soared. "Can you? Can you really? Look around you, Mom. I hardly think you've shown how capable you are of caring for yourself."

"I will not argue with you about this. As you know, I have more important things to worry about than the likes of that kind and generous man." Her mother came to a stand. "Now, if you'd get over your distrust, for a moment, I'd like you to take him to his truck."

Directly below her bedroom window, the front door opened and shut. She jumped up and peered out. Vincent, now dressed, strode up their driveway toward the road. "It seems that won't be necessary. He's leaving."

Janice met her at the window. "Well, that's a shame. I was

thinking we could have all had breakfast together, then said our goodbyes."

Madison tried to bite her tongue, but the urge was too great. "Seems to me you already had the goodbye you were hoping for last night."

"Madison Marie Gable! I'll have you know that our good-bye last night was nothing but sweet and caring. It was the kind of goodbye that friends share with one another. And, even if it were what you are so rudely implying, it would still be none of your damn business." With that, her mother pounded her cane with each step she took, until she slammed the door behind her.

Madison grabbed the stuffed bear off her bed and threw it at the door. "Unbelievable!"

forty-six

Janice almost turned around to set the record straight regarding her and Vincent, but her temper took over, and she didn't want to say anything more because undoubtedly there would end up being something else to scream about, which would add to their already strained relationship.

Her head pounded, and she wondered if the wine from the night before, or the stress of everything else she'd experienced over the past few weeks was causing the headache. She laughed at the thought. The past two decades were nothing but stress.

Janice made it to the bottom of the staircase and rubbed her thigh. Her pain was lessened, but she had a way to go before she'd be back to herself. Again, she laughed. She didn't want to go back to her old self. She wanted to find joy. The kind of joy that comes from living a life unashamed of the past, free of fear, with acceptance. She wanted to embrace life to its fullest, to trust in people, but more than anything, she wanted the freedom to love and be loved.

Forgiving Charlie, however, was something altogether different. Janice wasn't ready for that.

Vincent Clark was a good man. He warranted compassion and understanding. He'd lost the love of his life, and yet, he still found it in his heart to help others. Vincent mourned his wife's passing with every fiber of his being, and she envied that kind of love.

Janice couldn't bring herself to mourn Charlie's death. She hated him for what he'd done, but she could mourn the loss of their marriage. She'd loved him once. He'd charmed her, and, as the saying went, he'd swept her off her feet. They'd lived comfortably. He'd worked hard and loved hard. Charlie was passionate, charismatic, and dashing. Then he began to change. Little by little, his downward spiral spun out of control. His drinking picked up and his gambling began. Janice just wasn't sure which came first. Either way, that combination was toxic. Charlie's manic episodes became more frequent, their arguments accelerated, and she fell into the trap of enabling him—becoming angry and bitter in the process. Then she'd enable him again, and again.

Janice sighed with the weight of the past. When the girls were young, she'd done her best to hide her anger. She'd wait until they were at a friend's house, at school, or in bed. She didn't want them to hear the fighting, but as time went on, her patience grew thin, and she could no longer hold it back. Charlie would act like everything was a joke. She supposed it was the alcohol talking. He'd laugh and relentlessly tease her—chide her. But what was happening in their home was no laughing matter. Their finances and marriage were taking on water and sinking fast, and no matter how much she tried to bail them out, they were destined for disaster. She would have to pick up the pieces, only she had no strength left to do so.

Janice remembered seeing Madison's red face streaked with tears at witnessing their arguments. She worshiped her father. In her eyes, he could do no wrong. She'd tell Madison to go to her room, but she wouldn't listen, and so she'd yell. Madison would run.

Janice sat in her chair and closed her eyes as the memories continued to flood her mind. Madison saw. Madison heard. Madison cried. Madison ran. Madison hid—in her sanctuary—her barn. *Madison saw.*

Tears flowed down Janice's cheeks, and her breath hitched with each intake of air. She'd failed her girls. There should be no joy in her life without her family in it. And there should be no forgiveness. She deserved every ounce of their anger and sorrow. She sobbed until there were no tears left to fall.

Sunshine burst through the front windows and floating dust particles grabbed Janice's attention, snapping her back to the present. She glanced around the living room and her eyes opened to her surroundings. It seemed as though her home was also in mourning for a life that could have been. Her home reeked of sadness and decay.

Janice stood and ran her finger along the shelf that held the school pictures of her girls. Layers of dust sat upon it. She focused on the corners of the ceiling where cobwebs collected. It was as if time had stood still since Charlie's passing, and her home was a reflection encased in the past. Her once lovely home appeared to cry out for attention. Its curtains hung in grief. The paisley-printed rug at her feet seemed to groan with each step. It ached to be seen anew, to once again show its vibrant color. Everything around her recoiled from her because she hadn't shown love, and the house could no longer trust her for its care.

The weight of neglect for her home and her daughters shouted in unison: *Please open your heart to us. Please love us again.*

Janice could no longer blame Madison for the harm she'd caused, regardless of the reason. She wanted to shout back at the feelings that now pressed upon her: *I've always loved you. But…* Janice choked on the realization that one word, *but*, stood in her way, both then and now.

Janice fixed her gaze on Madison's senior picture. The smile on her face appeared genuine. The photo was taken before her father's death. Madison's green eyes matched her own. However, unlike today, the shine in Madison's eyes was dull, much like her own. She removed the framed photo from the shelf and touched the glass. She didn't even know her daughter. She'd been so self-absorbed she hadn't asked a single question of what she'd done with her life. Come to think of it, she wasn't even sure where she lived. Janice shivered with this realization.

No wonder Madison hates me. She sank back into her chair and held the frame to her chest. *I'm sorry.*

The rickety railing sounded as Madison took each step of the staircase leading to the front entry. Janice's heartbeat nearly jumped out of her chest, but before Janice could say a word, Madison's long strides brought her to the front door and out the door, leaving Janice to watch her walk away, just as she'd done eight years ago.

Janice inhaled deeply and pushed the air out of her lungs with force, convincing herself not to dwell on the fact that Madison needed her space.

She slow-walked to the kitchen and poured what was left of the Cheerios into a bowl. She hoped Vincent had made it home with no further troubles. She imagined him sitting at his dining table and having his breakfast as he gazed out at the water. Janice wondered if he was thinking of her, just as she was thinking of him. She thought of their first meeting at the supermarket. The accident was as if it were ordained and not just by chance. Janice shuddered at the recollection of her behavior. *What must he have thought of me?* She couldn't imagine what possessed him to pursue her. Had his deceased wife really encouraged him, as he'd said, or was it simply out of pity? Either way, both options were unnerving.

Vincent and Cheryl have a gorgeous home, Janice thought.

She took in the space during her visit, she could tell the home was alive with the beautiful voices of the past, and the love that it shared with those occupants.

Janice pictured herself living in their house. She imagined cooking dinner for Vincent in his bright kitchen. Music would play, and he'd come close to her and whisper in her ear—*I love you*. They'd dance cheek to cheek, and he'd press his hand against the small of her back, bringing them closer while moving her to the rhythm of the tune. Their bodies would move in perfect harmony with each step, and at the end of the song, Vincent would bring his mouth to hers, his lips soft and tender.

Oh, how she wanted that life. She wanted him. Pity or destiny? And at that moment, she'd take pity, if that's all Vincent could offer her.

forty-seven

A half-eaten slice of French toast lay soaked with syrup in the middle of Vincent's plate while he thought about the past twenty-four hours he'd shared with Janice. As he sat in the chair at the table, the empty place next to him didn't have the same vacant feeling it had. His grief was less. Somehow, the empty space seemed as if it were waiting, as though the emptiness was expecting someone other than Cheryl.

When Janice joined him for dinner, his heart beat faster. He'd been nervous at first, but after everything about Cheryl had come out into the open, he finally felt free to fully be himself. No more secrets were left for him to hold close to his chest.

She looked lovely in her dress, and he'd noticed a brightness to her, as if she were beaming from the inside out. He'd never seen her like that, and it pleased him. Her deep-green eyes appeared to see right through him, to the deepest part of his soul. He felt as though he existed. He'd become a man again, and not just a wisp of a man that went throughout his days in a fog. Cheryl had been right—he'd needed Janice in his life. Not only that, but Madison still pressed upon his heart. She was hurting, and he didn't know how to break through her hardened façade.

Vincent picked up his plate and scraped the remnants of his French toast into the garbage disposal and washed his plate. He refilled his coffee cup and stepped outside onto his deck, overlooking Cape Neddick to his left and Short Sands Beach to his right. The sun gleamed and sparkled on the water, and the crashing waves pounded thunderously against the rocks. He took a seat in his white Adirondack chair, stretched his legs out, and crossed his ankles while he sipped his steaming cup of coffee. He wanted to share this moment with Janice. In time, he thought, in time.

Vincent's neighbor, Gayle Hines, bounded down her back deck stairs with Sissy, her happy, yet yappy, little Bichon. As soon as he saw her, he wished to duck inside, but he was too late; she'd seen him.

"Howdy hoady, Vinny," she said with a wave of her hand and a high-pitched voice. She was wearing a pair of navy leggings and an oversized white sweatshirt, its neckline draped over one shoulder, exposing a teal-colored sports bra underneath. She approached his deck railing and rested her hand on the gate, then lifted her sunglasses and set them on the top of her head. "I noticed you had a lady friend over last night." Even from a distance, he could see her flash a wink. "You should really close your curtains when you have—guests."

Vincent winced at being called Vinny, and he wanted to tell her she should really mind her own business and not peek into other people's homes, but he refrained. "Nothing gets by you, Gayle."

Gayle gave a gentle tug on the dog's leash, shushing Sissy. "I heard you leave, but unless my ears deceive me, I didn't hear you come home until this morning. Is everything alright?"

He could tell she was just aching to get the latest scoop, so she could blast any tidbit of information with her lady friends at her weekly Union Bluff luncheons. "All is well. You have a good day now."

His attempt at ridding himself of her was fruitless.

"Your lady friend seemed awfully familiar to me. Might I know her?"

"I wouldn't know."

She picked Sissy up and stroked her back. "Aren't you the coy one? She must be someone special." She flashed another wink. "I'm sure I must know her. You count my words, she'll come to mind, as I never forget a face." Gayle set the Bichon down. "Toodles, Vinny," she said with a flit of her hand, and strutted along the banking.

Mrs. Gayle Hines was part of the "upper crust," and she'd made that clear for the past thirty years. By all accounts he, too, would be considered one with financial means, but he and Cheryl hadn't often taken part in the activities in her circle of friends.

But, shortly after Cheryl's passing, Gayle's third husband, Wilfred, had died, and so she'd clung to Vincent, claiming her visits were the neighborly thing to do. She delivered meals, and she had no intention of allowing him to eat alone, but all he wanted was for her to leave him be. Fortunately, she turned her attention to a more affluent gentleman and left Vincent alone, except for butting in whenever she saw fit. Vincent just hoped Gayle didn't know Janice. Not because Vincent was embarrassed by Janice. He simply wanted to protect her from the likes of his haughty neighboring gossip.

He drank down the last of his coffee and stepped back inside, leaving the door wide open, taking in the salty air and warm breeze. His landscaping birthed late spring blooms of lilies, asters, coneflowers, daisies, a multitude of daffodils, and tulips. Soon, the scent of peonies, lily of the valley, and lavender would fill the air. But his most prized plants were his hydrangea bushes.

Vincent changed into a pair of work pants and a T-shirt, then pulled a shovel out of his tool shed and headed into his gardens. His plan was to separate a hefty batch of perennials so he could replant them in Janice's gardens. As the day went on, he shooed one of his neighbor's cats away, gave gardening advice to the new residents that moved across the street, and when he was finally ready to call it quits, Gayle once again graced him with her presence. Her ankle nipper circled around him and squatted in one of the beds. Gayle paid the dog no mind.

"You've been busy, Vinny. No more company?"

"Nope."

"Well, then, I guess that old saying is true."

Vincent didn't want to take the bait, so he put his head down and kept digging. She was chomping at the bit to share her profound wisdom. He decided to indulge her, hoping the sooner she spit it out, the sooner she'd leave. Vincent glanced up and a snickering face met his.

She slowly pulled her sunglasses off with an air of self-righteousness. "Busy hands keep the devil away."

Vincent tensed with the insinuation, and mumbled under his breath, "It didn't work this time." He came to a stand and faced her. "And, as Amit Kalantri once said, 'Busy hands are better than babbling mouths.'"

Gayle huffed and stomped away, and her little white puff of a dog scurried behind. He laughed and sank his hands into a large root-ball and gave it a yank. "Well, my dear Cheryl. I do believe my work here is done."

He laughed as he watched Gayle's Olympic walking pace flee from view.

Vincent's wheelbarrow overflowed with a multitude of perennials. He pushed it toward the bed of his truck and thrust its contents onto a tarp that lay inside. He returned the wheelbarrow to its proper place and climbed into the truck to head to Janice's. After the heavy rains, replanting would be easy. As he neared Lilac Lane, he noticed Madison strolling across the lawn adjacent to the York Harbor Inn. Her hands were in her jeans pockets and she was looking toward the water. Vincent tapped the brakes with indecision, then took a sharp right into the parking lot of the inn so he could turn around and grab a spot he'd seen along the road.

The sun shined in his eyes, and he squinted to find Madison. He followed the path leading toward the beach and found her seated on a bench. Vincent cleared his throat as he approached. "Hello, Madison." She jerked her head in his direction, and she appeared stunned at his intrusion. "I saw you walking when I drove by. I hope you won't mind if I join you."

Madison scooched over toward the edge of the bench and tapped on the open space next to her. "I don't mind. Have a seat," she said, but her demeanor and her tone of voice didn't seem welcoming.

They sat for a minute or two staring out at the water as a sailboat drifted by. "I can only imagine what might have gone through your head after seeing me this morning in your mom's kitchen." He leaned forward and rested his elbows on his knees, and rubbed his palms together. "You need to understand that I respect your mother, and you, Madison. I would never do anything to jeopardize your mother's reputation."

Madison shook her head and chuckled. "I don't think you need to worry about that. My mother's reputation was jeopardized the moment my father took his own life."

Vincent felt like he'd been sucker punched, and he couldn't understand how what Madison's father had done had anything to do with her mother's reputation. "Please excuse me, but I'm in the dark here. I'm not sure what you're saying."

"What I'm saying is that my mother and I had to hide our faces in shame back then. You would think she'd put the rope around his neck herself."

"I'm sure that wasn't the case. Your mother…"

"Respectfully, Vincent, you don't know the first thing about what my mother would or wouldn't do. Oh, you might think you know her, but I can assure you, you don't."

"And I'll submit, respectfully, that I may know your mother better than you think I do."

Madison raised her eyebrows and rolled her eyes. "Really? You say that after one night with her. And might I add, it's your reputation I'd be most worried about."

"Meaning?"

"I hate to state the obvious, but you're a married man. Or have you forgotten that?" She turned her head away and crossed her arms.

"I understand, but all is not as it may appear." He shifted in his seat, and he could feel the damp bench through his pants, and it reminded him of his wet clothes the night before. "I'd like to explain."

Madison rolled her tongue into the inside of her cheek and refused to look in his direction, but she didn't object, so he continued. "First, my wife passed away about three years ago."

Madison swung her head, and her eyes widened.

"Second, I did not sleep with your mother. I simply stayed the night, on the couch, because it seemed the right thing to do with the storm and my broken-down truck."

Madison bit her lip. "I'm sorry to hear about your wife." She sat up and faced him. "And I'm sorry I jumped to conclusions, but you were wearing my dad's robe and…"

"I understand." He placed his hand on Madison's shoulder. "You don't need to say another word."

Madison sighed. "But I do. I have no right to interfere in what you and my mother do together. I've been away for so long, and being back here makes everything fresh, as if time stood still. I'm right back to nine years ago when my dad…" She cleared her throat. "So, seeing you in my dad's robe just seemed—you know—wrong."

Vincent noticed Madison's lower lip quiver. "I lost my wife to cancer, and that was bad enough, but I can't imagine what you and your mom have gone through." A tear trickled down her cheek. "I'm so sorry you've been dealt this hand," he said and wiped the tear away with his thumb. To his surprise, she leaned over and rested her head on his shoulder, and they sat there in silence, watching the sailboat glide out of view.

"What do you say I give you a lift home?" Vincent said.

Madison sat up and nodded. They rose together, and he wrapped his arm around her shoulders as they walked in tandem to the truck. The silence stayed, but quiet wasn't awkward. It was as if their two hearts beat in understanding of one another, and the rhythm of their hearts spoke for them.

Sorrow is painful, but in time, their hearts will mend.

forty-eight

Vincent pulled into her driveway, and Madison climbed out of the truck and Vincent went straight away lugging the plants out of the back end. She thought of her mom, sitting in the house alone, and felt bad for the way she'd left earlier. But leaving was her go-to remedy.

Yep, she thought. *I lash out and leave.*

Nathan always called it her MO. Thinking back now, she wondered if she'd learned that behavior from her dad. She had to face her mother and carry with her a large dose of humble pie.

She opened the front door, but her mom wasn't sitting in her chair, nor was she in the kitchen or her bedroom. The bathroom door was open as well and worry settled in. *Where is she?* Just as her concern grew, she spotted her mother outside. She stood facing the leaning barn.

Madison stepped outside the back door and trekked the distance to stand at her mother's side.

Janice was stoic as she stared at the barn. She didn't look in Madison's direction and said, "I hate that barn."

Madison took her mother by the hand and stayed quiet.

"It brought you a lot of happiness, though. I'm sorry I had to sell your horse. I know how much she meant to you." Her mother gave her hand a squeeze. "I didn't do it to hurt you."

"I know." Madison understood that now, but as a kid, it just seemed spiteful. "You did your best."

"I tried to tear it down, you know," she said as her steely gaze glared at the dilapidated remnants of the barn. "The night I got hurt. I wanted that painful reminder to go away. I couldn't bear looking at it for one more second."

"So, you weren't trying to hurt yourself?"

Her mother spun her head in her direction, and her eyes grew big and round as saucers. "Oh, heaven's no, Madison. That was an accident. I wasn't thinking, is all. I was in a state of—I don't know—hysteria? When the beam came down, I was in shock. I'd never considered the repercussions."

A quiet release escaped Madison's soul. "I hate it, too, Mom." Her mother's eyes penetrated her own. "What do you say we make it go away?"

"I'd like that. I'd like that very much."

"I'll talk to Vincent about it."

Madison took her mother by the arm, and they walked back toward the house, just as Vincent took the corner. He smiled from ear to ear and set the wheelbarrow down. "Well, would you look at that? Is there a special occasion I've missed?"

Madison grinned in his direction. "You've heard of a barn raising, but have you ever heard of a barn falling?"

Vincent's sideways smile and glimmering eyes spoke volumes. "Seems to me my next project is to tear down a barn."

"*Our* next project," her mother corrected.

"Well, ladies, I guess we've got to get ourselves a plan to tear that sucker down."

forty-nine

Madison left her mom and Vincent to visit with one another while she went to her appointment in Portsmouth. Before long, she was walking out of the bank with a spring to her step. Because of her income, job stability, and good credit, she felt confident she'd be able to take over the note on the house, so the deed and the mortgage could transfer into her own name. This was the cleanest and best way to handle the situation. The question that remained, however, was if her mother would agree to her proposition.

Madison still faced the obstacle of her and Nathan's relationship, not to mention his father's overzealous need to want to help with the overall financial situation. Nathan wasn't ready to give up on them, and Mr. Hawking offered to give her a private loan for the mortgage, so she wouldn't have to go down the road of bank financing. He said it would be a sound investment, but she half wondered if it was because he didn't want to see her out of his son's life completely. The financial ties would certainly link them together, just as her school loan had, and she wanted no part of that again. She needed to do this on her own. In the meantime, she'd continue to make the payments on the house and hope her mother and the bank would let her purchase it.

Madison took in the sunshine. She agreed to meet with Franky for an early dinner, but her incessant phone interruptions, which she ignored while she was with the loan officer, piqued her attention. She fumbled around the inside of her satchel and removed her phone. It surprised her to see the calls were from her mother and not Franky. She would have bet Franky was calling to cancel. Madison's concern grew. Her mother rarely called her. Come to think of it, she'd only been called a handful of times since she'd arrived back home. Madison checked for messages. There weren't any. She attempted to call back, but the cell service was spotty, and her call didn't go through.

Madison glanced at the time. She could still make it home to see what the issue was before meeting up with Franky, so she hoofed it to the car and headed back. All along, she wondered what the urgency was. She shook her head and chuckled. *She probably needs milk.* As she turned down Lilac Lane, she pictured the street as hers, but she had put little thought as to how she and her mother would share the space. She imagined nothing would change in that regard. She certainly wouldn't take over the mortgage and kick her mother out. On the contrary, she was helping her mother keep the family home. The fact that she'd be the owner of record was irrelevant.

An unfamiliar car with a Massachusetts license plate sat in the driveway. She pulled up next to it and peeked into the passenger window. Nothing in it gave away who the driver might be, so she gathered her belongings and hurried to the house. As she opened the door, she gasped. Nathan was sitting on the couch with his hands clenched together, looking as if he were a child who had just been disciplined. His wide eyes caught her attention before she turned her attention to her mom. Her mother wouldn't look at her. Madison thought that if her mother clenched her jaw any tighter, she might break her teeth, so she turned back to Nathan, whose pleading eyes stared back.

"What's going on?" Neither one of them responded. "Nathan? Why are you here?"

Nathan lowered his head and sighed. "I came to give you my support."

Madison's mind flooded with possibilities: support for tearing down the barn, finances, fixing up the house? But the tone of the room said something altogether different. "Has something happened to Lily or Journey?" Panic rose and she could feel her throat tighten. "Are they…"

Nathan stood and came to her side. "They're doing just fine."

"Then what is it?" she asked. Her mother still averted her eyes. "Mom, what's going on?"

Janice came to a stand and glared in her direction. "I understand you are here to buy my home out from under me." Her biting words stung as she lashed out. "I should have known you weren't here for me." She pounded her cane on the floor as she came to meet Madison eye to eye. "You sure had me fooled, Madison. But I see now how like your father you really are. You take and take, just like he did."

"Mom. I don't know what Nathan has said to you, but I assure you, I am not taking your home away from you."

"So, you're not getting a loan to buy my house?"

"Yes. I mean, no. I…"

"You've said all I need to hear." With that, she turned away and walked out of the room.

Madison stood there in shock until fury found its way in. "What have you done?"

Nathan stood there with his mouth open. The problem was, Madison wasn't sure who she was angrier with, herself for not telling her mother sooner or Nathan for butting in.

fifty

The tide was in and the sun lay low on the horizon when Janice stepped out of the house to get some air. Her anger boiled over, and she didn't want to completely lose her temper in front of Madison and her boyfriend, Nathan.

Her eyes surveyed the York River. A lobster boat chugged along the route to Off the Boat Lobsters on the Sewall's Bridge dock. How many times had she visited the quaint family-owned business to purchase fresh lobsters and steamers? The girls were quite young the first time she'd taken them to see the live lobsters being sold out of a cooler and cooked on site under a pop-up tent. The site had grown into a picturesque open-air storefront, and was now well known as a photographer's dream and a lobster lover's delight.

Janice's thoughts trailed back to the only home she'd ever lived in. And even though she'd suffered at the memory of what Charlie had done there, it was still her home.

Her parents were gentle of spirit, hard-working, and generous with their time. They'd cultivated long-lasting friendships and served the York Harbor community in a multitude of ways. She was proud of the family she'd come from as well as the family she'd created. But when Charlie's behavior changed, and after his death, she thought her husband's actions had tarnished the family name. Maybe she didn't deserve the house since she'd brought disgrace to it. Her chest grew heavy as did the knot in the pit of her stomach. Her parents would be humiliated to know what had become of their beautiful home.

Janice pressed both hands on the cane and bowed her head. Her face drained from the realization that she was losing her home, either to the bank or to her daughter. The home's loss would be inevitable because Madison surely wouldn't want to continue making payments on a house she didn't own. She just wished her daughter had talked to her about it. Janice swallowed the lump in her throat. At least if Madison owned the house, it would stay in the family.

As Janice lifted her head and fixed her eyes on the sunset, horizontal lines of pink, orange, blue, and purple burst into a tapestry of overwhelming colors, so brilliant it took her breath away. *Is it a sign?* Maybe. But if Madison were to buy the house, where would she and Madison live? Nathan was here so Madison would surely go back to Ohio with him. But, if that were so, why would Madison bother to buy the house? Or did Nathan plan on moving in with her here? Would that leave her out in the cold? Her questions were piling up, and her angst was building.

Janice strolled back toward the house. Another lobster boat moved through the water. There was a peace about it, and if only for a moment, the vision calmed her heart.

She hadn't had a lobster in ages, and the thought of dipping fresh lobster and steamers into melted butter, corn on the cob, and red potatoes caused her stomach to growl. Her thoughts shifted to Vincent. He'd treated her to a lovely dinner, and maybe she should return the favor. A warmth flowed through her at the possibility.

As she approached the house, she couldn't bring herself to go back in just yet, so she took a seat on a weathered Adirondack chair that overlooked the river. The rest would do her leg some good, anyway. The house stood in the distance and if a house could have feelings, it appeared sad. The grounds, she had to admit, were in much better shape since Vincent had dedicated so much of his time on them. Playing in the gardens had brought her joy in the past, and she hoped that if she somehow still managed to own the house, by the time her leg was fully healed, she and Vincent could work on them together. In the meantime, she'd enjoy the improvements as they came, for however long that was.

What would become of her house? It screamed for attention, and as she thought more of inviting Vincent to dinner, the vast differences between their two homes hit her. Vincent's house was magazine ready and full of light. She pictured herself on his seaside deck, sitting on the sea-foam-colored cushioned chairs around the table, and taking in the vast Atlantic view. She imagined a sunset, like today, with soft music playing in the background, and a glass of wine in her hand, as Vincent placed the lobster feast on the table. Her mind swirled as the entire image played before her. He'd pick up her hand and bring it to his mouth, kissing it softly while he gazed into her eyes, as if she were royalty. She'd giggle and bat her eyelashes, then after dinner, he'd scoop her up and lay her across his bed.

Janice's daydream broke with the sound of a slamming door. Familiar shouts from Madison escaped from inside the house, through the bedroom window, and reached Janice's ears. She shook her head, feeling grateful she wasn't on the receiving end of Madison's wrath for once. Their roles had reversed. This must have been how Madison felt at hearing her parents fighting. Even though Janice wasn't the intended target, in their argument, the angst she felt made her feel as if she was indeed part of their problem. If nothing else, Janice could have been the catalyst for their explosive spat, and she wasn't sure if she should stay where she was, walk away, or try to intervene. Before she could decide, the front door burst open and Nathan barreled out. His face was red, his jaw firm, and his fisted hands were held tightly to his side. He paced in circles and kicked at loose stones, and Janice didn't dare to move.

Madison flung open the door, stormed across the porch, and stomped down the steps to meet him. "So, just like that, you're leaving?"

Nathan turned on a dime. "I'm still here, aren't I?"

Madison jammed her pointer finger into his chest. "We need to talk this out."

"Do we? Seems to me you've said all you needed to say when you slammed the door in my face."

"You're the one that came here with demands!"

Nathan pressed his palms to his forehead, then released them with flair. "I came here to help you see reason."

"No, that's not true, and you know it." She clenched and unclenched her hands, as if attempting to prevent her temper from rising further. "You came here expecting me to drop everything I'm trying to do here, Nathan. You came here to convince me to go back with you."

He took a step back and glared in her direction. "Oh, I see how it is. You can drop everything to come here, to take care of a woman you despise, and haven't spoken to in years, but you can't drop everything to come home to be with me in a place where you belong?"

Janice caught her breath. His words stung. *She despises me?* Janice froze in her seat. The last thing she wanted at this point was to be seen, or be a witness to such an intimate argument. She pressed her palms to her ears, but the pull to listen was too great, so she leaned in.

Her past replayed before her eyes, and Janice's stomach grew queasy. As the movie reel turned, all she could envision were she and Charlie. She cupped her ears with her hands, and slumped with worry for Nathan and her daughter.

Madison's eyes were wild with anger. "Where I belong? You say that as if I'm a possession of yours. Well, I have news for you. I'm not someone you can dictate your demands to." She threw her arms up in the air, waving them madly. "The thing is, I was home for you. Every day I'd wait for you, in hopes you'd see me, hear me." She crossed her arms and tapped her foot. "But you didn't, and you haven't in a long time. Most of the time, you made me feel invisible." She stuffed her hands in her pockets and stared at the ground.

Nathan's face softened. "I saw you. I did."

"Did you? Did you really?"

"You're the one that's been distant, not me. I've asked you to marry me—more than once, I might add, but each time you've rejected me. So, what do you expect from me?"

Madison sat back on her heels, and she tilted her face upward toward his. "I don't know." Her voice was raspy and low. "Honestly, I don't know."

Nathan stepped closer to Madison and tucked her hair behind her ear. "Yes, you do, Madison. You know exactly what you want, and I'll have to accept that, but you need to know that I've loved you from the start. I've wanted you as my wife and to raise a family with you, but you don't want a husband, or a family." He placed his hands on her shoulders and gave them a squeeze. "You'd rather be alone with your grief, and your anger, because you can't believe it's possible to trust anyone, or love anyone without fear of getting hurt in return. Can't you see that you'd rather push people away, to punish yourself, for the things that are out of your control?"

"You don't understand what's it like to lose someone the way I did, so how can you possibly expect me to put my trust in anyone, even if it's you? I've tried to get past it. I really have, and since I've been here, I discovered that it's better for me to live my life by myself, on my own terms." Madison sighed and rested her head on his chest. "Please understand, Nathan. It's what I need to do." He stroked the length of her back, and they became a silhouette. He leaned down and kissed the top of her head, then he slowly pulled away, leaving her to stand alone.

The rental car drove away and Madison collapsed onto the ground and sobbed. Janice wanted to go to her daughter and comfort her, but she doubted Madison would find her presence comforting. Furthermore, Janice wasn't quite sure what she'd say or do, even if Madison was to allow her. It would be a lose-lose situation to try.

Madison slowly climbed the stairs and retreated into the house. Janice shivered. The evening turned cold, and a chill coursed through her as she sat in the chair. She hadn't anticipated being out this long, so she gathered her cane and hoisted herself up from the low-lying seat, and breathed in the cool air. The stars sprinkled across the night sky, and the moon cast its light across the water, causing the lapping waves to shimmer. And even though her heart broke for her daughter, it also broke to know how much Madison hated her. That was her own doing. If she'd only told Madison the truth from the beginning, maybe their relationship would have turned out differently. She cursed Charlie for driving a stake through their hearts. She'd allowed him to win. Even in his death, he continued to win Madison's favor.

The walk across the lawn gave her pause. She wouldn't bring up the house situation with Madison just yet. Nor would she ask about Nathan. Janice thought it best to give them both some space. She'd try to fill her mind with positive thoughts, like spending time with Vincent, even if she were only to watch him tear the blasted barn down.

She took another look at the water. Was Vincent doing the same?

fifty-one

The water lapped the rocks below Vincent's home, but the rhythmic roll didn't calm his unease. Vincent could sense the tension between Janice and Madison in their every action and breath. He was smart enough to know that it wasn't his place to intervene, and yet, he was stupid enough to try anyway.

He leaned his head back in his favorite chair and stared at the starlit sky. Was Cheryl watching over him? Just in case she was, he raised his crystal glass of Pappy Van Winkle toward the heavens. "Well, my dear, you encouraged this mess I'm in. What say you?"

He was just about to take a sip when a rustling sound reached him, and Gayle peered at him from the side yard. He pretended he hadn't seen her.

"Hi, Vinny. Sorry, I couldn't make out what you said."

Vincent sank into the chair, and instead of taking a sip, he poured the entire shot across his lips and swirled the rich, smooth bourbon around in his mouth, savoring it for a moment before swallowing. He closed his eyes and warmth spread through his chest, easing its way down to his stomach. Now, he'd find the will to talk to his neighbor.

"Hello, Gayle. What brings you out?" he asked just as the reason ran across the deck and barked at his heels.

"Sissy, down!" Gayle traipsed across the decking and grabbed the feisty little dog, who yapped incessantly. "No barks." The barking continued. "Sissy, Mommy said no barks." Still, she barked. Gayle glanced down, apologetically. "I'll just put her in the house, and I'll be right back."

Before Vincent could object, she dashed away, yelling a request from her yard. "Vinny, could you pour one of those for me, too?"

He wanted to scream, *no, I don't want to*, for the universe to hear, but he abstained, and set his glass down, only to pick it up again. He'd need another shot to deal with the likes of Gayle Hines.

"Sure thing," he mumbled under his breath. "I'll get you one, but it won't be Pappy. I'm not wasting my good stuff on you." He glanced up at the sky. *I know I shouldn't think this way, my dear, but sometimes, I just can't help myself.*

In a nanosecond she was back. As Vincent prepared her drink, Gayle dragged her fingers through her flowing blond hair and cocked her head back as if she were posing for the latest magazine cover of the rich and famous. Most men would find her attractive, but in an artificial way. Vincent didn't much care for anything remotely artificial. Beauty, in his mind, was simply as nature intended. It wasn't put on, colored over, or pretend. He preferred the grace of aging, a genuine smile. Someone who had a spirit of wonder and was delighted by the simple things in life. He enjoyed seeing a woman's eye light up at seeing a rose bloom, and when she took the time to allow a piece of chocolate to melt in her mouth so she could savor its full flavor. He enjoyed seeing messy hair in the morning and fuzzy slippers. He relished seeing a woman in a pair of rolled up jeans, a loose-fitting sweatshirt with the sleeves pushed up, and wearing a gardening hat and gloves.

He thought of Janice in her simple classic dress, and he smiled. Janice had worn a touch of makeup, but it brought out her natural beauty. It didn't mask the beauty she already had. Even now, he could see her cheeks blush when he'd complimented her.

"Vinny?" Vincent snapped back to reality, and Gayle was giving him an incredulous look. "Have you heard a word I was saying?"

"Forgive me, Gayle. I've got a lot on my mind, which is why I was out here having a drink." He gestured for her to take a seat. "You were saying?"

"You poor dear." She pursed her lips and shook her head, then swished the amber liquid in her glass and took a sip. "I was saying," she said as she rested her hand on his thigh. "Since it's that time of year when all my friends arrive for the summer, I thought I'd throw a soirée to get the season off on the right foot."

Her season-kickoff soirée, boasting the cultural elite, was an annual event. He had to admit that she sure knew how to throw a party, but he hadn't attended one since Cheryl had passed. He'd only attended at Cheryl's insistence, as she wanted to be a good neighbor. Now, he had no desire to do so. All he cared about was being as far away from it as possible. "And when might this soirée be?"

"I'm still mulling it over, but I must insist that you'll be my date for the evening. I'd hate to think of you all alone over here, now that—well—now that Cheryl's gone."

He held back a laugh. She acted as if this was something new. Gayle, at the time, had milked Cheryl's passing for all it was worth, and his attempts at asking her to leave him alone went unheard. He'd been relieved when she'd found someone else to cling onto, and he'd enjoyed her distance immensely. "I was under the impression you were seeing someone."

"Oh, Sebastian?" She waved him off as if it was the most preposterous thing he could have said. "He's moved to Paris, and I had absolutely no desire to go with him. He insisted, but I simply had to turn him down." She downed the rest of her bourbon and thrust her empty glass in his direction. "Another?" she giggled.

Vincent doubted every word she'd said. He thought it more likely that Sebastian moved across the ocean to get away from her. In fact, he considered the probability of his moving to Paris at all was quite possibly a ruse. He rose from his chair.

"That's a shame," he said as he dropped an ice cube into Gayle's empty glass. "I thought he'd swept you off your feet." He poured the bourbon into her glass. "I've always heard Paris was beautiful this time of year."

Vincent placed the glass into Gayle's hand and stood at the railing of his deck. The sea was black with only the reflection of the stars, moon, and the shine of Nubble's light. No ship could be seen, and he couldn't delineate the sea from the sky. He exhaled and took a sip, wishing it was Janice who was about to stand at his side. Janice made him feel like a human being and not a possession.

Gayle leaned on her hip against the banister to face him. She rolled her fingertip along the rim of her glass. In the dim light, her sultry gaze searched his eyes, and he winced. He backed away just enough to give distance, but not enough to insult. She touched her neckline and her touch trailed down her chest at the crest of her cleavage and lingered there.

"I've thought about you a lot over the past few days, Vinny." Her seductive voice sent an icy shiver up his spine. He needed her to leave, and now.

"Thanks for sharing a nightcap with me, Gayle, but it's time I call it a night." He downed the rest of his drink and set it on the railing. "Perhaps you should—go."

She gave an incredulous gasp and firmly placed her empty glass next to his.

"I suppose so." She glared before forcing a smile. "This is good, as I must attend to Sissy. She's probably going out of her mind without me."

The still night broke with a gust of wind, and Gayle pushed her hair out of her face and gathered it to one side of her shoulder and held it there. She sauntered off the deck, accentuating her swinging hips, then turned back in his direction.

"Toodles," she said, with a flip of her wrist, then marched back into her yard.

Her door slapped shut, and he gave a deep sigh of relief. "Toodles."

He chuckled as he strolled into the house. When he walked through the open space, the wine glasses in the glass-front cabinet caught his attention. He instantly thought of Janice and wondered if she'd be up to going out for breakfast in the morning.

Or better yet, he thought, he made a hell of a good omelet.
Yes, it would be best to invite her here. She'd prefer that.

fifty-two

The phone rang, and Madison waited for Franky to pick up. After what she'd done last night, she wouldn't blame Franky if she chose not to answer.

"Well, it's about time I heard from you," Franky said. "What happened to you last night? You had me worried sick. I called a bazillion times, and it kept going straight to voicemail."

"I'm so sorry I stood you up for dinner. I had every intention of being there, but Nathan showed up. On my mom's doorstep. And I lost all sense of—well, everything. Sorry to say, our dinner date hadn't entered my head until this morning. On top of that, I lost track of my phone, and when I found it, it was dead."

"There is such a thing as a landline, you know."

"You expect me to remember your number?"

"Okay, smarty-pants," Madison retorted. "Without looking, what's my number?"

There was a long hesitation. "Fine. You win. You're forgiven. Is he still there?"

"No. We had a fight. And don't you dare say it. I can feel that your eyes are rolling from here."

"I wasn't rolling my eyes. If you must know, I opened my mouth to say something and then I snapped it shut, because my mother taught me that if I didn't have anything nice to say, to not say anything at all."

"And you chose now to listen to your mother and bite your tongue? Honesty, it's as if I don't know who you are anymore, Franky."

Franky laughed, then paused. "So, what happened?"

Madison flopped onto her bed and rested her head on a stack of pillows. "He said he was here to support me, which was a bald-faced lie, because what he did was drop a bomb on my poor mom…"

"Don't say another word. I need to let this sink in."

Franky waited about ten seconds, and Madison couldn't stand the silence. "Okay, enough of your attempt at drama."

"Just a sec. I need to let that sink in."

Madison was exasperated and getting more irritated by the moment. "Go ahead—humor me. What's sinking in?"

"*You* just referred to your mother as *your poor mom.*"

"For Pete's sake, Franky, would you please let me at least get to the crux of my story?"

"But it's so much fun annoying you. But sure, go ahead. Spill it."

Madison flipped over onto her stomach and bent her knees. With her feet in the air, she crossed her ankles and collected her thoughts. "Nathan showed up unannounced and told my mother that I was trying to buy her house. I mean, I haven't even broached the subject with her yet! As you can imagine, my mom was furious, and I can't blame her because she took that as my trying to buy it out from under her." Madison rolled onto her back and punched the mattress with the side of her fist. "But I think his actual goal was to sabotage my plan, so I'd have to go home with him. Can you believe it?"

"That is pretty remarkable."

"I know. Right?"

"What are you going to do?"

"First, I need to talk with my mom to clear everything up, but I was hoping to do that after I knew it would work. The last thing I wanted was to get her hopes up or piss her off unnecessarily. As for Nathan…if I had any doubts before, he's now confirmed my decision. I need to move on with my life, away from him. I can see that now."

"I'm so sorry, my friend."

Madison sat up and walked toward the window. The morning sun reflected off the water, and boats bobbed with the tide. "I hadn't realized how much I've missed being here until I came back, and the sad thing is, I think all I'll want from Ohio are my horses."

Her mind shifted to the barn in her mother's backyard, where her original horse was once housed, and her throat thickened. *Maybe someday I could bring the horses here.* She shook off the thought as impossible. Nathan's family paid for the horses and built the barn. It wasn't her place to ask for them, it wouldn't be right.

A knock sounded on her bedroom door, and it caused her to jump. "Thanks for listening, but I have to go. Someone's at my door." She wondered if it was her mom, or Nathan coming back to try again.

"Sure thing. Call me later," she said, then disconnected.

A soft knock landed on the other side of the door this time. She knew that sound; it was her mom. She set her phone on her nightstand and opened the door. Her mom's green eyes stared back at her. They didn't appear angry, but sad. "I'm sorry,

Mom. I never intended for you to hear about my wanting to buy the house from anyone other than me."

She stepped aside and welcomed her mom into the room, and pulled out the vanity chair for her mom to take a seat.

"So, it's true?" Her mom sat. "You're trying to take my house from me?"

"I didn't want to say anything until I knew, at least on my end, that what I was going to propose to you would work." Madison sat on the edge of her bed and faced her mom.

"Go on."

"What I'm proposing is for you to deed the house over to me, but I need to hear back from the bank first, to assure I'm able to get a loan. That's why I didn't say anything to you yet."

"So, you figured I'd just sign away the family home after you've rejected it for the past eight years?"

"I can see how you might come to that conclusion." She chewed on her lip before continuing. "The way I see it is that I'd be saving the family home. If I stop making the payments for you, the bank would take it, I don't want to keep making mortgage payments on a house I don't own. And as much as this home means to you and me, I don't want that to happen. This house has been in our family for generations, and I always assumed it would remain in the family for generations to come. My assumption was wrong."

"I see, but here's the rub. You've made it very clear that you detest me..."

"I was young, and—" Madison started.

Her mother put up her hand to stop her. "My point is, what is to happen to me? Where am I supposed to live?"

Madison jumped up from the side of the bed and scrambled to her mother's side. She crouched on the floor next to her mother and rested her hands on her good thigh. "I would *never* make you leave your home. It's the only place you've ever lived! I mean, sure, we'd have to make some adjustments, but we are both grown women. I'm confident we'll make it work."

Her mother nodded, and Madison could tell she was fighting back tears and sighed a couple of times, as if to pull herself together.

"What about your sister?" Janice asked. "How would she feel about this?"

"We've emailed. She told me she's a lifer and intends to serve until she is no longer able to, or reaches retirement. Her life is not here and she was actually relieved to know the house would stay in the family."

"She said all that?" Now the tears rolled down her mom's cheeks. "I miss her, Madison, just as I've missed you. She never calls or emails me. I know I pushed the two of you away, and I've had to live with that all these years. Honestly, Madison, I can't help but feel like I'm never going to see her again."

"I don't know about that, Mom," she said as she wiped her mother's tears away. "I miss her, too."

Madison got up and pulled a tissue out of the box on her nightstand, then grabbed an additional one for herself.

Janice blew her nose. "I'm sorry I was such an awful mother. I was only trying to—"

"Maybe we shouldn't go down that road today."

Madison stuffed her damp tissue into her pocket to avert her mother's pleading eyes. Her mom was bursting at the seams to explain the past, but Madison wasn't up for it. Not today. "I think one heavy topic a day is enough, don't you?"

Her mother's red nose scrunched up, and a grin grew. "I suppose you're right about that, and I'm thinking you're also right about the house. It makes sense for you to take the reins on this. So long as you give me your word that you won't kick me out."

"I would never kick you out of your own home. I'm trying to prevent that—remember?"

"You say that now, but…"

"But nothing." Madison gave her mother a stern nod. "We'll make this work," she said, as if to convince herself as much as convincing her mom. *Oh Lord, help me make this work.* "Is Vincent coming over today to start on the barn?"

"Not today. He's lining up some help first," she said, glancing down at her watch. "Maybe tomorrow, though." Her mother's face lit up. "Vincent asked me to his house for a late breakfast." Her cheeks blushed. "But the physical therapist is coming here this morning, so I had to decline his invitation."

"She's coming here? How come?"

"She wants to see my environment and make sure I'll be alright on my own. Apparently, if all goes well, I'll lose the cane." Her mother smiled ear to ear, and Madison couldn't help but share in her hopeful enthusiasm.

"Will that mean you'll get to drive again?"

"Yep," she said, but her excited expression changed and her countenance fell, and she fidgeted with the hem of her pullover.

"I should think you'd be happy to have your car back."

"The thing is—I haven't driven since I hit Vincent in the parking lot."

Madison was at a loss and couldn't imagine why that would be an issue. "And that's a problem, *because?*" Now it was her mom's turn to avoid eye contact. "Talk to me."

"You haven't seen how I was before you got here." She cleared her throat and came to a stand, leaving the cane behind as she approached the window. "I suppose you could say I was more of a recluse." She ran her fingers along the edge of the window frame. "Going out was difficult at best—it got me so anxious that I'd have panic attacks."

Madison tried to envision her mother in such a state. She'd always been confident and steady. In fact, she was a social butterfly, which was something Madison admired about her mom. "Are you afraid you'll have another panic attack, and cause another accident?"

Her mom's shoulders sagged, and her head hung low. "Because if that's what you're afraid of, you need to know what I see." Madison stepped next to her mom's side. "What I see is a strong woman that's been through hell and back, and survived." Her mom nodded and reached for her hand, then gave it a squeeze. "Now, let's say you show this therapist what you're made of?"

fifty-three

Nearly two months had passed since Janice sat behind the wheel of her car, and the feel of the steering wheel seemed foreign in her hands as she tentatively pulled out of the driveway. Madison had suggested she pick a place to go that would make her happy for her first trip out. They'd agreed grocery shopping wasn't it and shared a good laugh over it. So, her first outing would be a visit to Vincent. She made a mental note to thank Vincent again for having the damage on her car repaired.

Janice chose to meander along some side streets, off Lilac Lane, to better take in the views of the water. The detours were short, but they brought back memories, and those memories flooded in with the tide.

As she drove along Organug Road, she smiled. She and Charlie had taken the girls sled riding on a steep slope at the York Golf and Tennis Club. Janice could almost see Hannah sitting between Madison's protective legs as Charlie took a running start, then shoved them over the crest of the hillside. Their screams of joy permeated her thoughts. They did have good times together. She had to remember that. And yet, her lasting impression was always seeing Charlie in the barn. She'd prayed for the image to leave her, but it remained. Having Madison around brought memories of Charlie to the forefront because the two of them had done so much together. However, she was grateful to have Madison home at last.

Janice took the turn leading to the harbor beach and noticed a parking spot straight ahead that gave her the full view of the entire harbor. She pulled in, put the car in park, and fixed her gaze on the beach. The recent storms washed a multitude of rocks onto the shore, adding to the already plentiful stones. Janice didn't dare get out to try to navigate over them, so she sat and watched the waves break and roll ashore, only to recede and start all over again. The mesmerizing waters, with its beauty and dangers, stirred an overwhelming sense of awe. She couldn't help but think life was like the ocean. One minute she was coasting along and rolling with the tide, and the next, an undertow had taken hold of her, leaving her exhausted, fearful, and fighting to stay afloat to survive.

Then, when she lost all hope, she was saved.

Vincent rescued her from more than the accident in the barn. She had to believe that divine intervention played a role. Maybe, as Vincent said, Cheryl *had* spoken to him from beyond and guided his path, but to what end? *And, why me?* Janice felt as insignificant as a tiny crab in a tide pool. There was no denying she wanted more in her and Vincent's relationship, but did he? Or, was he just helping a friend in need? These concerns kept her sitting in the car and not making headway toward his home.

She thought about the day they'd gone to Short Sands and shared a piece of fudge from Whispering Sands Gifts. That was the first time she'd even so much as thought about another man. There was something so special about the way he'd cared for her. A gentleman in the truest sense of the word. As much as Charlie had loved her, so much of their lives revolved around his needs, without a care for hers. Vincent, on the other hand, was good to the bone, and it bubbled out through every pore of his flesh. He showed compassion and generosity with his words and deeds, and he wore the humble badge graciously.

Janice turned the key and triple checked before backing out of the parking space. What had she done to deserve having Vincent in her life? Maybe she was just someone to look after, so he wouldn't feel so alone? Or maybe there was a little something more. At least she hoped there was.

The closer she got to Vincent's, the calmer she felt, which was rather shocking. Janice would normally crawl out of her skin with anxiety about now, especially because he didn't know she was on her way. She wanted to surprise him with the picnic lunch she'd prepared because she had to turn down his breakfast invitation. Janice had made chicken salad with walnuts, grapes, onion, celery, and craisins for their sandwiches. She just hoped he wasn't allergic to nuts. She included some chips, a bottle of wine, some slices of cheddar cheese, apple wedges, and a good-sized piece of fudge Madison had picked up, to split between them.

This, she realized, was also the first time she'd prepared a meal for anyone other than Charlie. Back then, it had become a chore. Now, she was giddy with the task, and the knowledge that the sentimental piece of fudge wouldn't be lost on Vincent.

Janice rolled her windows down as she drove along Long Sands. The temperature was perfect, and she could envision her and Vincent sitting comfortably on his seaside deck. She pictured the sound of the surf, the gentle breeze sweeping across her face. She could hear their wine glasses clink together as they toasted their friendship. He'd gaze into her eyes, and her heart would melt. Yes, this was going to be a beautiful day.

Nubble Road's twists and turns led her straight to his door. She pulled into the driveway and adjusted the rearview mirror so she could see her reflection. Madison was right; she did look healthier. Her face no longer appeared gaunt. Her color was back, and she'd put on some weight. After feeling satisfied, she slid out of her seat and adjusted the lavender sundress she'd purchased at Daisy Jane's.

Janice opened the passenger door to remove her picnic basket full of goodies and grabbed her shawl. She breathed in the salty air and slowly let it out, releasing the tension in her neck and shoulders. Butterflies fluttered in her belly as she knocked on the door; she thought ringing the doorbell seemed too impersonal. After a moment or two, she tried again, and her impatience grew, as did her nerves. Janice considered all the times Vincent had entered her home without so much as knocking, so she tried the door. It was unlocked, so she stepped inside. As soon as she heard Vincent's voice, her anxiety vanished, only to be replaced with a sense of comfort, as if he were her safe harbor.

Janice could see his profile as he stood on the deck, and her knees grew weak. She figured he was on the phone and didn't want to disturb him, so she quietly set the basket of goodies next to a vase of fresh-cut peonies on the entry table and waited until he finished his call.

Her breath hitched when a woman's voice floated through the opened door leading to the deck. She couldn't make out what she was saying, but her body language appeared seductive. The woman held a near empty glass of wine in her hand, and now, what Janice initially thought was a cell phone in Vincent's hand was a wine glass as well. The same glasses she and Vincent used when they'd had dinner together.

Janice froze, and all sense of internal balance and ease she'd felt earlier flipped on a dime. The familiar knot in her gut intensified. Her insides jittered, and her hands shook as she watched the woman flirtatiously press her hand on Vincent's chest, then dragged her finger toward his navel.

The front door couldn't open fast enough, and she couldn't walk fast enough, nor turn the key quick enough to escape from Vincent and his seductress. Tears rolled down her cheeks, and the road blurred before her. If she could just get to the Nubble Lighthouse, she'd be able to pull herself together. *How could I have been so stupid to believe he'd be interested in me?* She wiped her face, but no sooner did she finish, more tears would fall. *I'm a fool.*

The car came to an abrupt halt, and she shoved the car into park. Her grip on the steering wheel met with the same intensity as her pounding heart in her chest. *I'm nothing but a charity case for him.* She rested her forehead on the wheel and sobbed. When her eyes drained of her last tear, she removed herself from the car and stepped toward the bench that sat on the knoll facing the lighthouse. Janice plunked down and stared out at the sea. Waves crashed against the rocks with immense intensity, casting spray into the air, and her skin tingled with its touch as she breathed.

She'd had such hope for today. Even Madison had cheered her on as she left the house. What was she to do? She couldn't go back home, not yet anyway. Madison would know by her red nose and puffy eyes that it didn't go well. Even if she hadn't been crying like a fool, how would she explain her quick return? She couldn't, so she sat alone wishing for someone she couldn't have, while she watched the surf break until she grew too chilly to stay.

fifty-four

Vincent eased away from Gayle, who, by then, had become quite intoxicated. He thought he'd be polite and have one glass with her, but Gayle continued to pour. He'd nursed his Merlot and made the excuse of needing to get some work done for a project, but that meant nothing to her, and she produced another bottle from her tote.

The warmth of her breath puffed against his face, but he could no longer escape her advances without being rude and pushing her away. She greedily ran her tongue along her upper lip and her eyes narrowed as she backed him against the railing. Vincent braced for impact. Her mouth found his, and the feel of her lips was sloppy wet. He could no longer be polite as his mind reeled. *I don't want this. You are not Cheryl, and you're not Janice.*

Vincent grasped her shoulders and put her at arm's length, then took her chin in his hand. "I think that's quite enough, Gayle, and I think we should call it a day."

"You can't be serious, Vinny." She stepped closer. "Seems to me we deserve a little afternoon delight once in a while, wouldn't you agree?" Her words slurred, and she sloshed some wine out of her glass, which caused her to giggle. "Oops."

Vincent recalled all the times Cheryl teased him about their neighbor. "She has the hots for you, my dear. She's like a tigress on the hunt for some fresh meat," she'd say, then she'd hold her hand up, as if they were claws, and she'd growl. He'd always pushed her remarks away as lunacy, but now he could see she was right after all. "Let's get you home, Gayle."

"I thought you'd never ask." Vincent dismissed the comment and placed one of her arms around his neck and grabbed on to that hand while he wrapped his arm around her waist and held her up as they walked side by side through the yard and onto her back deck. He leaned her against the exterior of the house and reached for the door handle. He was relieved to see her door wasn't locked and pushed it open. He reached for her and she fell into his arms.

"Home again, home again, jiggety jig," she said.

"Yes, you are home, safe and sound." He set her down on her sofa. She tried her best to pull him down with her, but Vincent steadied his feet and held firm. "Goodbye, Gayle."

As soon as he stepped outside, he wiped his mouth with the back of his hand to rid himself of the feel and taste of her mouth, and he quivered with the thought of her lips on his.

Vincent reflected on how this day had turned out. He'd hoped to have breakfast with Janice, but that wasn't meant to be. Instead, he'd put his time into plans of removing the Gables' barn. He'd researched the equipment needed for such a project and consulted a friend. All was going well until he stepped onto his back deck to stretch his legs. Gayle had just come back from walking her dog, and before he knew it, she was bounding across his deck with a small tote bag over her shoulder. He'd soon found out the tote's purpose was for carrying wine, and Vincent hadn't seen the harm in sharing a glass with a neighbor. He could see now, that had been a huge mistake to crack that door open. For the most part, he had managed to avoid her little pop-over visits, but recently, there'd been an uptick in the frequency.

Gayle's soirée was coming up, and he'd intended to avoid going at all costs, but it occurred to him that the best way to deter her advances might be to let her know he had eyes for someone else. Yes, he thought, he'd invite Janice to go with him. Satisfied with his decision, he picked up the two long-stem glasses off the deck table, went inside, and shut the door behind him.

The fading sun slipped behind the clouds, and he'd grown cool as the house's warmth dissipated. Vincent shivered and turned toward the kitchen when his eyes caught the sight of a basket on his entry table. He set the glasses on the counter and glanced around the room to see if anyone was there, then hollered out, "Hello?"

Vincent approached the basket and peered inside to see a plethora of food. *What on earth?* He opened the front door, hoping he might spy who had come into his home and left it there, but there wasn't anyone in sight. *It couldn't have been Gayle.* As he fished through the basket in search of a note, he noticed a shawl on the floor, and he recognized it at once.

Janice.

His mind reeled as to why she'd left it there and fled. There were clearly two sandwiches, so he presumed she'd planned on them enjoying this picnic together. He turned and faced the other direction, with his back to the front door. Vincent gasped when he saw what Janice's view would have been had she arrived while Gayle was visiting. His heart sank. He only hoped that Janice had come over when he'd taken Gayle home. Perhaps she hadn't seen them together, and maybe Janice guessed he was away. In his heart, he knew that wouldn't be the case. She would know he'd never leave the house unlocked and the back door open, if he hadn't been home.

The clock above the mantle proved it was too late to salvage a date with Janice. In fact, he doubted she'd want anything to do with him if she'd seen what had occurred on the deck. As he thought of the effort she'd made to prepare such a feast, he was even more shattered to think he'd hurt her. He lifted the picnic basket and carried it to the kitchen and unloaded the contents into the refrigerator. When he saw the little white bag of fudge, it just about did him in.

fifty-five

A storm was coming. Madison could feel it in her bones before she even looked outside to confirm. Dark clouds were rolling in and caused the river to appear black. For a moment, she thought of her mother driving home in a downpour, but considered she'd probably remain at Vincent's for most of the day.

Madison marveled at the change in her mother. She didn't seem as angry as she was all those years ago, or even since visiting her mother in the hospital. Something had changed. Madison had assumed she'd been one of the reasons that caused her mother to be so angry. Now, she recognized her father was quite likely the culprit.

Madison thought of her own relationship with Nathan. She remembered the turmoil they went through when Nathan could no longer work as a firefighter. He'd fallen into a depression of sorts, which caused him to either withdraw from everyone or go to the other extreme. Nathan would drink and become the life of the party. This teeter-totter ride was hard to come to terms with. He loved her, but he'd often-times taken out his frustration on her. He'd snap at her, shut down, and be so caught up in his own thoughts that he sel-dom acted like she existed. Nathan had become a man on his own island. Not until he began working in the family business did he seem to find some semblance of balance—that, and the arrival of Lily.

She recalled her father's behavior. Madison recognized he had shared some of the same traits Nathan displayed. Not that she considered the similarities to the extent of her father's, at least she hoped Nathan would never resort to such an extreme, but she could certainly see why her mother may have tired of the mood swings. And she had two kids to tend to. One of which rebelled at every turn. Still, what possessed her dad to take his own life? She'd always blamed her mother, but now she recognized that her mother was an unlikely reason. Her father was too proud and strong to take his own life because he'd had arguments with his wife—there had to be something more.

A thunderclap shook the old house's windows, and Madison jumped. Once she calmed herself, her thoughts turned to the condition of the house. Why had her mom let the house go downhill the way she had? And why on earth had she placed a mortgage on it in the first place? Her father had a great job with a pension, and Madison presumed her parents were financially stable. Plus, with her mother's inheritance, her mom should have been able to handle whatever the house needed. These questions remained, as her mother's headlights headed up the driveway.

Janice no sooner entered the house when the downpour began.

"I didn't expect you home so soon. Were you trying to beat the rain?" Her mom shivered in the entry as she set her purse on the side table. She wasn't smiling—she seemed indifferent, considering she'd just come from Vincent's. "Did you have a good time?"

Janice pursed her lips and swiveled her head, as if she found it hard to know where to direct her eyes. She stiffened her back and nodded. "It was fine."

There wasn't a chance in hell that her visit with Vincent was fine. Franky always said Madison was as easy to read as a book, but her mother was no different. "Well, at least you made it home before the rain, so that's good."

"I suppose," she said, as she jutted her chin up and walked toward the kitchen. What had happened between the two of them?

"I bet he liked your new dress. You look terrific in it… It's such a flattering fit for you."

Janice pulled open a cupboard and took down a box of shredded wheat. The box was new, and she attempted to open the plastic bag inside. Her frustration grew with each tug, so much so that when it finally did open, the bag had ripped down the middle and popped out of the box. Cereal went everywhere. At that point, her mother lost all composure and threw the now empty bag on the table and stormed out of the room. Madison didn't know whether to pursue her or give her some space, then thought if her mother wanted to talk, she would have, so she chose the latter.

Madison removed a hair tie from her wrist and pulled her hair back to keep it from getting in her face, then retrieved the broom and dustpan from the hall closet, and went about cleaning up the mess. All the while, keeping watch to see if her mom would return. About twenty minutes went by, and she hadn't come out of her room. Madison guessed her mom was hungry, so she took the leftover chop suey out of the refrigerator and made her mom a plate to bring to her room.

She carried a tray of chop suey, a slice of bread and butter, and a glass of milk, then softly knocked on the door. No response. Madison gently pushed the door open. Her mom was sitting at the vanity blankly staring at the mirror. At that moment, Madison saw a wounded woman who was hurting, and Madison felt sorrow for her mom.

"I thought you might be getting hungry." Her mother didn't move an inch. Madison strolled over to the small table in front of the window and pulled out one of the two chairs. "I'll just set it over here, for when you're ready."

"Am I that unlovable?"

Madison pressed her palm to her chest, as if it would suppress the sorrow she was feeling for her mom. She lifted the other chair and carried it over to where her mom sat and joined her.

"What would make you ask such a question?" she said, as she looked in the mirror to see her mom's reflection.

"I should have known better. I guess I'm just someone to be pitied."

Madison raked her fingers through her mom's hair—something she remembered her mom doing for her. "What did Vincent possibly say to you that would have you feeling this way?"

"He didn't *say* anything."

"Nothing?"

"Vincent didn't even know I was there."

Madison knew that feeling. She'd felt invisible many times while with Nathan. "He must have at least enjoyed the wonderful lunch you made for him."

If Vincent was anything, he was appreciative.

Her shoulders sagged, and she buried her face in her hands. "I wouldn't know," she said, shaking her head. "When I left, I forgot the basket."

The defeated woman that sat before her was too much. Madison never thought she'd think this, but she preferred her strong and somewhat abrasive mother. She didn't know how to handle the teary-eyed, needy mom she now had. "You know what, Mom? I think you should show him what kind of woman you are made of, and if he can't see you for who you are, then he isn't worth another minute of your time."

It pained Madison to say it; she liked Vincent.

"Maybe that's precisely the problem, Madison. He does see me for who I am, and who I am isn't what he wants."

Madison shook her head, trying to make sense of it. "Okay, help me to understand. You went to Vincent's house to bring him a lovely lunch. He ignored you, and you left?"

"Not exactly."

"Mother," she growled, "what happened? Just spit it out." Madison could hear her mom using the same expression on her more times than she could remember. *It's official. I've turned into my mother.*

"It's too humiliating to share with my own daughter."

An instant panic shot through her. "What did he do? If he did anything to—"

"It's nothing like that." Janice stood up from the stool and wrung her hands together. "When I got there, I saw him with another woman—an attractive woman." She turned away and looked at the rain pouring down the window panes. "I don't know what I was thinking. You wouldn't know it because he seems so down to earth, but he's a man of means. You should see his ocean-side home. It's absolutely stunning." She exhaled. "Vincent is a single man of wealth, and I'm sure he has a count-less number of women of his ilk seeking his attention."

"Maybe he does, but I can't imagine him liking someone like that. Are you sure you saw what you saw?"

"I may be many things, Madison, but I'm not blind." Jan-ice's face turned stern—an expression Madison was used to seeing. "I've had enough of this conversation, so go find some-thing to do, like measure the curtains." She waved her away.

"Fine," Madison said, but refused to let her mother push her buttons. She gave her mom a teasing grin. "And maybe when I'm done with measuring for curtains, I'll go draw up some plans to update the kitchen."

"You do that. Now, leave so I can eat my cold chop suey."

"I can heat it…"

"Shoo," she said, with a brush of her hand. "Out you go."

Madison left the room and couldn't resist yelling another tease. "I'm thinking of knocking the kitchen wall down!"

Now she hoped she hadn't gone too far.

"Do whatever you want, smarty-pants. Just don't let it hit you on the way down!"

Her mother's laughter followed her down the hall.

She smiled. *Not too far.*

fifty-six

The night was free of stars, and the moon hid. No shadows cast about the hedgerow, and the surrounding homes appeared to be asleep. Sleep eluded Vincent, and only the sound of the sea joined him. The melodic crescendo of waves on the rocks would normally help subdue him into slumber, but not tonight. He sipped his bourbon and thought of Janice. He should have gone to her, but he hadn't, and he tried to wrap his head around why. He could have at least acknowledged receiving the picnic basket.

Vincent had never been unfaithful. He'd never had a hint of infidelity in his marriage, no burning need to "spice things up," or desire to look at another woman. He already had the best, and until now, he hadn't dreamed of anyone else becoming a part of his life. He couldn't put his finger on why he was so drawn to Janice. She didn't resemble Cheryl, and their personalities were quite different. Perhaps their inner strength to endure hardship was what he admired. He had to admit Janice had a tendency to lash out when provoked, but she also had a vulnerability he found endearing. All the same, he hadn't been looking for anyone in the romantic sense. Yet here she was, taking up space in his mind and in his heart.

He zipped up his sweater, and his thoughts turned to how he and Cheryl had met. Vincent wasn't looking for anyone then either. At that time, his Boston-based architectural firm was preparing for a merger, and he was giving a lecture on how to incorporate modern design in historical settings. Cheryl had been sitting in the back row and she counter punched many of his points with astute clarity. Before long, she'd made her way toward the front row, and the next thing he knew, they were sharing an éclair from Mike's Pastries on the North End. They'd talked about things that made their hearts sing. Cheryl's passion was interior design, and his was landscaping, and the desire to be a bestselling author. She'd become his muse, and his writing took off.

The bourbon was long gone by the time Vincent went inside to settle in for the night. There really was no comparing Cheryl and Janice. They were unique in their own right. He loved being helpful and needed, and he liked how Janice showed her vulnerabilities. She was real, unlike other women he'd met who only cared about their looks, money, and stature. Janice was in his life for a reason. Was his meeting Cheryl at a lecture hall purely serendipitous, or the fender bender with Janice in the parking lot totally random? He doubted it, and he simply couldn't ignore that fact.

He washed out his cocktail glass and the two wine glasses from earlier in the day and placed them on a drying rack. His eyes caught a glimpse of the wicker basket, and he came up with a plan. Finally, he grew weary enough to call it a night and prayed his sleep would be restful.

As he drifted off, a vision of Cheryl clutching Janice's scarf floated through his mind. She'd placed the scarf into his hand, then lifted his hand to his heart. She held it there and gave him a nod and a smile. Slumber came.

Vincent woke, and his first thought was of Janice. He hoped she'd be excited today was the day they'd start removing the items from the barn, so the teardown could begin. The dilapidated barn was an eyesore. He wondered why Janice and Madison preferred removing it versus having it repaired. The barn still had some good bones left in her. But if tearing it down was what they wanted, then tearing it down was what he would give them.

In the kitchen, coffee cup warm in his hands, Vincent's mind went back to the time he'd overheard one of Janice and Madison's arguments. He'd never come out and asked Janice what led to her driving into the barn's post. He didn't think it was his business to ask. But since they'd grown closer, he wished he knew the circumstances. Vincent also recalled an insinuation by Madison, suggesting Janice's accident wasn't an accident at all, but an intentional act.

Vincent removed the picnic basket's contents from the refrigerator and placed the items back in. The significance of the barn must hold more meaning than Janice's accident or of Madison's horse. His thoughts shifted to the time Janice forced him to leave her property. *I was looking at the barn that day.* Yes. That must be where he her husband killed himself. Everything made sense.

A set of note cards lay in Vincent's writing desk drawer. He pulled the bundle of floral-and-bird-printed blank cards out and fished through them until he found the one he was looking for—a seagull perched on a pier post. He took to his pen and scribbled down what came to mind. After being satisfied with what he'd written, he tucked the note card in the small envelope and placed it in the picnic basket, then headed outside with his floral snips. A collection of peonies, hydrangeas, zinnias, and daisies formed a delightful bouquet. Vincent tied a piece of twine around the stems and nestled the bouquet in the basket and set it in his truck before making sure he had the tools he'd need for the day.

Blue skies and a few fluffy white clouds overhead made for a perfect day to spend outside. He glanced at the time on his dashboard and hoped he and Janice had time to share a private lunch before the hired help arrived. He needed to set things right with Janice. He only hoped he wasn't too late.

fifty-seven

Janice checked the time and paced back and forth between the living room at the front of the house to the kitchen's back door. Each time, she peered out the windows awaiting Vincent's truck. Time wouldn't go by quick enough to tame her anxiety. Madison, on the other hand, was already in the barn, dragging out tools, old furniture, and various other items into the yard. She'd been sorting them into groups to keep, to donate, and to throw away.

As the minutes ticked by, Janice could no longer attempt to set her mind at ease. She riffled through the cabinets in search of chocolate. Certainly, she thought, there must be a piece somewhere. Her thumb brushed along the lid of a serving dish in the back of the cabinet, but the dish was too far to reach. She pulled out a step stool and carefully balanced on the top step while clinging to the cabinet's lower shelf for stability. This wasn't wise, but chocolate soothed her nerves. At least she convinced herself it did. A sweet tooth was better than smoking.

Success!

A wadded-up bag of dark chocolate chips lay inside the serving dish. She'd once hidden them from Charlie because he always scoffed up the chips before she had a chance to bake. Janice didn't even care that the chocolate chips were years old.

The door burst open. "Good Lord, woman! What are you doing up there? Are you trying to kill yourself?" Vincent's booming voice caught her off guard, and she lost her grip, causing her to sway. He jumped and grabbed hold of her just in time. "Are you out of your mind?"

His eyes were wide as he held her in his arms.

"If you must know, I was getting some chocolate," she said breathlessly. "And I would have been perfectly fine if you hadn't burst in here like a wild beast."

"You scared me half to death, Janice. If you'd fallen…"

"But I didn't. Or at least I wouldn't have." He still clung to her. "Would you like to put me down now?"

"Actually, no. I would not." He tossed her over his shoulder.

"What—what are you! Where are you taking me?" She pounded on his back with her fists and kicked as best she could as his arms held her legs against his chest. "Put me down!"

"I will soon enough."

Janice could no longer contain her fury. "I don't know who you think you are that you can manhandle me like this? Maybe you can get away with this with your other lady friend, but I assure you, you cannot with me."

"I don't know," he said as he traipsed through the yard carrying her like she weighed nothing. "Seems to me I'm doing just that."

Janice gave up the fight, just as he opened his truck's door and plucked the picnic basket from the front seat. He carried her and the basket to an old wooden bench tucked under a tree. That vantage point offered a view of the river, the side of the house, and the barn, which was precisely why she'd chosen that spot for the bench. Vincent dipped his knees and placed the basket on the middle of the bench, then pulled

Janice back into his embrace and gently set her next to it. Her anger now diminished. "You found my basket."

"How could I have missed it?"

Janice's face flush with embarrassment. She attempted to sweep her messy hair out of her face when Vincent reached over and did it for her. "I wasn't sure you'd show up today."

Her previous concerns about him blew in the wind, tangling up her thoughts.

Vincent's hazel eyes gazed into hers with such calm and care that she couldn't look away. "Why wouldn't I?"

Janice sucked in a breath and exhaled. She didn't want to say it, but her feelings for him outweighed her anxiety to not. "I saw you yesterday—with that other woman—and I figured you might be too tired today, or maybe you might have made other plans."

He cupped her cheeks. "I said I'd be here, and there is no place I'd rather be."

"But…"

"But nothing." He nodded and softly kissed her between her eyes, and held his lips there. The warmth of his mouth eased away her fears as he pulled away. A smile grew, and he removed an envelope from the basket and handed it to her.

Janice's hands trembled as she opened the pale blue envelope. A sketch of a seagull donned the front flap. She carefully flipped it open.

Dearest Janice,

Ocean tides roll in and out and never repeat the same wave. Ever since their existence, they've moved and flowed, creating different paths, breaking new ground, and changing course, leaving all that they've touched changed.

I picked this card because I am moved by the image of the seagull as it watches over the water, as if it's waiting for the seas to be just right. Its knowing wisdom, in a symbolic sense, moves to where the best resources thrive. We, as a people, often deny ourselves the ability to thrive because we remain in our comfort zones—where we feel safe—but not a seagull. They fly out of their comfort zone and take risks to find freedom and safe harbor in the storms and tides that turn. They master the winds and soar above the fray. I believe this is what we must do, Janice. The seas are right, and we must set aside our fears and stop clinging to pasts we cannot change.

I'm fond of you, Janice, and I dare to weather the storms with you. You, like the sea, have touched me and allowed me to change. And as with the seagull, please allow me to be your safe harbor.

With an infinity to hope,
Vincent

Tears flowed down Janice's cheeks, and she couldn't catch her breath. She stared at the dilapidated barn in the distance, and fear burned in her heart. *He is too good for me. I don't deserve this beautiful man. He's better off without me.*

All she could think to do was shake her head *no* as she slid the note back into the envelope. She wanted to love him more than anything else in the world, but all she would do is bring him pain, and he deserved more than she could give. She closed her eyes and the words, "*I can't,*" slipped past her lips.

Janice clutched the card to her breast, and she left him to sit on the bench alone. As she turned the corner to enter the house, Vincent sat with his elbows on his knees, his hands covering his face, and his shoulders sagging. She'd hurt him, but he was better off this way. Someone out there was better deserving of his love than she was. She turned toward the door and went inside, then headed to her bed and grieved for a love she wasn't brave enough to grab hold of.

fifty-eight

adison rolled an old tire into the yard and wiped the sweat off her brow with her arm. Her shirt was covered in grime and even with her hair in a ponytail, hair clung to her neck. She glanced up to see Vincent laying a bouquet of flowers on the back steps, then walking toward her. He carried a basket, and as he grew near, he waved it in the air. She brushed off her hands and walked to meet his elongated stride.

"Whatcha got there?" she asked, then noticed his puffy eyes and red nose.

"Lunch. I'm not feeling very hungry and thought it shouldn't go to waste."

"You don't look well. Are you alright?"

He rubbed his eyes. "Must be allergies or something."

Madison thought of how her mother looked when she'd come home from Vincent's the night before, and he appeared as though he'd been put through the ringer. No doubt, her mom's doing, but she didn't dare broach the subject, especially knowing he chose to tell her his bout of tears were because of allergies. She believed it was *something* else. "Do you still feel up to working?"

He nodded and stomped toward the barn just as a pickup truck with two men inside climbed out.

"Perfect timing," Vincent said, as he shook their hands,

then introduced them to Madison. They went straight to work, securing the barn's frame so it wouldn't collapse any further before emptying the rest of the contents.

The day's cleanout continued by hauling items to the dump. Things too nice to throw away were placed in Vincent's pickup. He planned to drop them off at Savers or Goodwill before heading home. Janice checked in from time to time to see the progress and to confirm that everything they were getting rid of was acceptable. She offered refreshments but each time, they kindly refused them, except for Madison.

Madison stood in Lily's old stall. Remnants of hay lingered in the corners, and the feed trough still hung on the wall. She ran her hand over the roughhewn barn boards. Oh, how she missed spending her days there. She breathed in the memories. She and her dad hammered every nail to create the stall. Madison rubbed her thumb nail. She smiled recalling how many times she'd bashed her thumb with the hammer.

She wandered toward the back of the barn and found an old fish stringer and net hanging on a peg. On one of the shelves sat her small tackle box. She brushed off the dust and opened it up to reveal the booklet of flies she'd purchased and tied by hand. Madison pulled one of the flies out, recalling when she'd sat on the picnic table near the back of the house wrapping the feathers and hook with fine thread and wire. Her dad marveled at her skill. Her father no sooner said *attagirl* when her mother called for them to come in for dinner.

Madison placed the holder back into the tackle box and tucked it under her arm. *This is a keeper.*

The day drew to a close, as did her last vision of the barn as it stood. They'd emptied all that was left inside, leaving only the skeletal remains of the structure. Tomorrow the barn would be no more.

She stood back and stared at the looming frame, casting shadows. She felt numb from exhaustion, or maybe the empty barn and all it represented caused her body to feel indifferent. She sat down on the dewy ground and wrapped her arms around her bent knees. The barn creaked and groaned with each gust of wind.

Madison focused her eyes on a particular beam and post and became transfixed by the way they lay at an unnatural angle. The same beam her father used to end his life, and the one that almost took her mother's. How many times had her dad contemplated killing himself there? Did he methodically plan it or was it on impulse? A knot formed in her stomach as she thought of all the times she'd innocently looped Lily's harness on the iron stake her father had pounded into the post that supported the beam. Little did she know at the time the immense pain that beam and stake would bring.

She rested her chin on her knees. *Why here, Dad? The one place that brought me so much peace?* Madison blinked back her tears. *Were you looking for peace, too?*

Madison picked at the blades of grass by her feet. The need to understand weaved its way through her thoughts. Oh, how she loved that barn and her dad. She wondered if the barn somehow symbolized his love for her? Or worse, did he choose the location because the barn was the only thing that stood in the way of the two of them spending time together? Was he punishing her? Her breathing was shallow. Her throat tightened.

Madison closed her eyes, hoping that he'd speak to her and give her some answers. He loved her; she knew that. He wouldn't have done it to punish her, but as irrational as the thought was, she couldn't shake it away. There was nothing rational about suicide. She'd read about depression and how those that suffer from it only think about escaping. Madison wasn't even sure her father had suffered from depression or that it had caused him to take his life. Did he kill himself out of fear? Her eyes popped open. What could he have feared? She'd always thought of him as strong. But she was a kid then, and she guessed all dads seem fearless to their children. Her dad had never served in the military, or had a traumatic experience like Nathan had, so she hadn't considered PTSD, and yet, other factors could have come into play to cause it.

Madison pounded the ground and came to a stand. *What's done is done, and I will never know.* There was no one to blame but her father. He did what he did, for whatever reason, and she needed to accept it and move on. She was tired of having his suicide define her, and she refused to let the way her father died be her legacy.

A sound of footsteps came up behind her and stopped at her side. Her mom's arm wrapped around her. They stood silently for a few moments, then her mother turned them toward the house. Without a word, they headed to the back door.

Madison broke the quiet. "How have you lived with that barn all these years?"

"I haven't lived since then—until now," she said, as she rested her head on Madison's shoulder.

Madison embraced her mom. She could smell the familiar scent of lavender in her mother's hair. She could feel the warmth of her mother's touch and her heart beating in time with her own. Her heart grew heavy. "I've missed you, Mom."

"I've missed you, too, my girl."

They broke their embrace and entered the house. The aroma of fresh thyme, tarragon, and rosemary in the kitchen brought her back to her childhood. "Smells amazing."

A roasted chicken sat on the counter, waiting to be carved. Whipped potatoes warmed in a pot and roasted carrots covered in tin foil sat atop the stove. But the aroma of baked apples in the oven nearly brought her to tears. "What on earth prompted you to do all this?"

"It's the only thing I could think of to do to say thank you."

Madison took her mother by the hands and searched her mother's eyes. "It's wonderful, Mom. This has always been and will always be my favorite meal. You doing this means so much to me. Thank you."

"You're welcome." Janice beamed. "Now, go wash up and try not to dawdle. It's getting cold."

Madison skidded off to the bathroom and jumped into the shower. The warm water washed away the filth, but it also seemed to wash away something more—an internal ache she'd carried around since her father's death. The running water gave her a sense of renewal and freedom from whatever guilt she'd borne. Maybe her dad did answer her while she sat on the lawn. She could fully breathe again.

Remembering her mother's need for her to not dawdle, Madison wrapped up in her towel and ran to her room to dress. By the time she made it to the kitchen, the table was set, Vincent's bouquet adorned the center, and her mom sat waiting. Madison's first thought was she'd be reprimanded. "Sorry I took too long."

"It's okay. I sprung dinner on you, so I expected it would take you some time. I wasn't sure what you'd want to drink."

Madison poured herself a glass of water and sat down. Then they heaped their plates and settled in to eat.

"I saw you talking with Vincent today, but I'm guessing it didn't go too well." She popped a carrot into her mouth while her mom pulled apart a biscuit and slathered on butter.

"I'm not sure how it went, to be honest." She laid the butter knife across her plate and took a bite of her biscuit.

Madison tried to read her, but her mom's face remained focused on eating. "It looked like you were reading something. Is there anything you'd like to share?" She, too, grabbed her butter knife as she waited for a response.

"He gave me a card with a handwritten note. He's a writer, you know."

"Is that so?" As much as she wanted to learn more about his writing, she didn't dare ask. Her focus was to try to help her mom open up and not derail her. "Am I to guess it was a Dear Jane letter?"

Her mother sighed and looked at the ceiling. "Not exactly," she said, then scooped up a spoonful of potatoes.

"Oh?" Madison took a drink, and her mom moved potatoes around on her plate.

"It was—well, I suppose—it was more of a love letter of sorts."

Madison about spit out her water and swallowed hard. "Mother!"

Janice brushed Madison's enthusiasm aside. "Like I said, the card was a kind of love letter, but not in the traditional sense."

"That makes sense. Nothing about him seems traditional to me. Or maybe that's exactly the kind of man he is…traditional?" She jabbed another carrot. "Think about it. He's been wooing you by helping you. Don't you see? Some men show

how much they care about someone through their works. A handwritten letter is definitely traditional."

"I see what you're saying, but what you don't understand is the way he wrote it."

"Good grief, Mom. I would give anything to receive a handwritten note from someone who cared for me. Why does it matter how he wrote it?"

"He wrote about seagulls, the ocean, of moving past our fears, timing, and being together. That kind of stuff."

"And?" Madison asked, then noticed her mother's chin quiver.

"But how can I let him take a chance on me? Don't you see? He's too good for me, and I'm not about to let him destroy his happiness and his way of life for me."

Madison noted her mother's determined eyes and stiff upper lip.

"He deserves better than a woman who couldn't keep a man happy enough to not kill himself." Janice grabbed her cloth napkin and wiped her mouth, slid back her chair, stood up, then threw the napkin on the seat. "I've gone and lost my appetite."

Madison jumped up from her chair. "Oh, no you don't. You sit your butt back down."

The startled look on her mother's face nearly stopped her in her tracks, but she wasn't about to let her mother win this battle. "I think I've seen enough of you sulking about and tak-ing all the blame for what Dad did. And I'm sorry for the heartless things I've said to you in that regard, but I was an idiot. *You* cannot own it anymore. *I* cannot own it anymore. So, I suggest you find your appetite and share this wonderful dinner you've worked all day preparing because I have no intentions of eating it by myself."

To Madison's surprise, her mother picked up her discarded napkin and sat back down.

"Did anyone ever tell you that you're a lot like your mother?" Janice asked.

"More times than I care to mention." Madison laughed, and she raised her glass. "To two stubborn women who are trying their best to make a better life for themselves."

Her mother raised her glass. "Here, here."

They clinked, and she smiled.

"So, are you going to write back?" Madison asked.

"Don't push it, young lady."

fifty-nine

Vincent picked up Janice's shawl, grateful he'd forgotten to take it out of his truck when he'd gone to Janice's that afternoon. The fabric felt silky to his touch, and the pattern, with its different shades of purple, soothed him. The colors reminded him of one of his flower beds. He ran the shawl through his fingers as he reflected on her reading his note. He wasn't heartbroken about her reaction. In fact, he half expected her response. Still, he'd hoped for something more. Her rejection hurt. Vincent thought they had gotten to a point where she was ready to move their relationship forward, but he now realized his instincts were off. Or, perhaps he'd chosen the wrong place. He also never actually addressed the situation regarding his neighbor, Gayle.

He slid open the atrium glass door to his deck and drank in the full moon. The moon's reflection over the water caused him to feel small and insignificant. And when the Nubble's beam cast out its light to meet the stars, he thought of the note he'd written. Who was he to say he could be Janice's safe harbor, when he barely had enough light in him to shine? Who was he kidding?

Vincent rested his forearms on the railing and shook his head. *How am I going to get through tomorrow?* It tore him up when Janice avoided eye contact all day. Her rejection compelled him to plead with her to *see* him—to trust him—but he didn't want to make matters worse. So, he focused on the task at hand. Vincent accomplished his goal of completing the work of emptying the barn, but with every action, Janice invaded his thoughts. Now, he hoped tomorrow wouldn't be a repeat of today.

The wind caught the shawl, and it seemed to spring to life in his hands. Had Janice not rushed away the day she'd delivered the basket, he imagined they'd have had a delightful afternoon of laughter and thoughtful conversation. They might have chatted about what the future could hold if they were *together*, in the romantic sense. *Romantic sense?* Vincent grinned at the idea of him and Janice as a couple. Until a few months ago, he'd never dreamed of inviting the thought of any relationship. But here he was, with his brain preoccupied by a complex woman that turned his world upside down.

He folded the shawl as best he could, while fighting with the wind, and retreated to the living room when an idea for a book crossed his mind. Vincent stopped in his tracks to cement the idea firmly in his brain. He glanced at the time, and the wind flew from his sails. It was too late to write, if he had any hope of arriving on time for the barn's teardown in the morning. The book would have to wait. Instead, he pulled out one of his leather-bound notebooks and jotted down a few ideas, so he wouldn't forget.

Janice

Lost in the sea of despair until happiness found me.

Finding home.

When beauty is more than skin deep.

When lonely hearts are no more.

The last line he scribbled—*when lonely hearts are no more*—slipped into his innermost being and found comfort there, he realized he no longer wanted to be alone. He had friends and a handful of ladies that sought his attention. But the loneliness that caused his once vibrant life to turn into a dismal gray wouldn't disappear with frivolous, superficial relationships. He wanted—needed—someone in his life that sparked a flame and nourished the depth of his humanity.

He relished the time he shared with Janice. Even when she acted cantankerous, she stirred something within him. He didn't like predictability and stagnation. Vincent enjoyed adding a sparkle to Janice's eyes with the simplest of actions. He wanted to learn what made her tick, what set her off, what caused her to feel frightened and anxious, safe, and loved. Had he fallen in love with Janice? The revelation didn't frighten him. The declaration inspired him with renewed and unfettered determination to seek Janice's affection and write once again.

Vincent no longer cared about the late hour. Even if he stayed up through the night, he'd be at Janice's on time with energy to spare. He sat down at his desk, flipped open his laptop, and wrote with exuberance as words flew across the pages. Vincent found his muse in Janice, and even though Janice wasn't on board just yet, he had hope for a future with her.

• • •

Morning broke, and stunning rays of color poured across the sea and sky. He forced himself to stop writing his novel—an uplifting book of love unlike anything else he'd ever written.

Vincent, still wearing the same clothes as the day before, stretched his arms overhead, and linked his fingers together, then rolled his head back. The cracking of his neck relieved his tension and stiffness from sitting so long. He widened his arms and gave one more stretch before jumping up to refill his coffee mug.

A quiet knock on the deck's glass door startled him. His tension came back at the sight of Gayle. Her hands cupped around her eyes as she pressed her face into the glass. Vincent shrugged with a sigh and sluffed to the door. "Good morning, Gayle."

"Good morning, Vinny," she sang, then entered the room with a flourish. "I hoped I'd catch you before you headed out for the day," Gayle said with a teasing smirk. "Seems there wasn't any need to rush from the looks of you."

Vincent glanced down at himself and ran his fingers across his scruffy chin. "I was up all night writing," He gestured toward his desk. But his need to explain himself irritated him more than her presence. "What brings you over on this fine morning?"

"Well, as you know, my soirée is this weekend." She glided across the floor and came within a few steps of Vincent. He shifted his coffee mug to create a barrier between them. "I was thinking," she said as her index finger poked him in the chest. "You should be my date. Wouldn't that be nice?"

Vincent couldn't find the words as she stared at him with an expectant smile. She winked. He backed around the counter to bide him some time to think and create some additional distance. "I'm flattered. I really am, but I already asked someone else to come with me to your party."

"How disappointing." Gayle stuck out her lower lip in an exaggerated pout. "I'm sure your *friend* could reconsider your invitation."

This, he thought, was the exact reason Janice attracted him more. He stuffed his hands in his pockets and stepped toward Gayle. "Sorry, but I believe she's already bought a dress for the occasion. I'm sure you must understand what a disappointment that would be for her. Wouldn't you agree?"

The incredulous look on Gayle's face made the fact that he just lied bearable. Lying was a vice that he detested, and yet, here he was doing just that. He hadn't planned to go to her soirée in the first place, but it occurred to him that if she saw him with Janice, Gayle might finally get the picture and leave him alone, then find some other man to cling on to. Plus, Janice could see for herself that he and Gayle weren't involved. All he had to do was persuade Janice to go with him, which, as things stood right now, seemed highly unlikely. But he had a few more days to get back into her good graces.

Gayle strolled across the room and stopped when she came to his desk. She paused, resting her hand near his notes, then spun to face him. "I suppose you're right. Besides, it'll be nice to meet your new friend." Gayle tapped her index finger on his notepad. She smiled, then waved goodbye before heading out the door.

"Toodles," he said under his breath and shook his head before heading to the bathroom to take a shower.

The foamy shaving cream fell off his razor with each pass under the water faucet. He thought of Janice and her anxiety. *What have I done?* There was no way she'd go to a party. Getting her to go for a ride with him to the beach was hard enough. *But she did drive all the way here—by herself—so there's hope.*

The refreshing shower awakened him with renewed energy, and he was chomping at the bit to see Janice. He just hoped she wanted to see him.

sixty

*J*anice prepared a couple of fried eggs and avocado toast sandwiches for her and Madison as she waited for Vincent and the others to arrive. She no sooner sat down at the kitchen table than Vincent's truck pulled up. Her insides churned in anticipation at seeing him, but the taste of anxiety took hold. Would he be happy to see her, or did her response to his lovely note yesterday put a cloud over his otherwise cheerful disposition? She set down her uneaten sandwich and hollered to Madison. "Your egg sandwich is on the table."

Janice stepped outside to greet Vincent. She shaded her eyes from the morning sun and shakily gripped the step's handrail as she descended the stairs. Janice's heart skipped a beat at his jovial smile, and her nervousness dissipated with each step he took in her direction. At last, he stood by her side.

"Good morning," she said.

"And so it is," Vincent said, as he glanced at their surroundings. "Good morning."

"If you haven't eaten, I made an extra egg sandwich. It's in the kitchen, if you'd like it."

Vincent rubbed his stomach. "Come to think of it, I didn't take the time to eat. I'd like to take you up on that."

"Terrific. I'll go get it for you. Be right back."

Janice backed away with a spring to her step. Madison

stood in the kitchen, eating her sandwich while she poured her coffee. Janice breathed a sigh of relief at seeing her own sandwich resting on her abandoned plate. She scooped it up. "It's for Vincent," she said, then grabbed a napkin. Madison looked on with a sideways grin, and Janice could feel her cheeks warm.

"You go, Mom."

"Stop that. It's the least I can do. He has a big day ahead of him, and he said he hasn't eaten breakfast."

"And now, neither have you." Madison chomped a big bite off hers and mumbled with a full mouth. "Too bad you didn't make one for yourself." Madison smirked, and Janice headed out the door.

Vincent was already at the barn. He wore a pair of brown Carhartt pants, a sage green T-shirt, and the same work boots he'd worn since he'd stepped foot on her porch to fix the floorboards. He's a complex man, she thought. One minute he's fashionably dressed in an Oxford shirt with the sleeves rolled up, Chinos, and boat shoes, and the next, he's a down-to-earth working man.

Janice admired both looks. He was sexy no matter what he wore. A flutter formed in her stomach as she envisioned him in nothing but a towel, but she came to her senses, pulled herself together, and hurried to bring him his now cold egg sandwich.

A pickup truck towing a large tractor pulled into the yard. Vincent took a huge bite and finished off his sandwich, wiped his mouth with the back of his hand, then jogged to meet the driver. Janice recognized him as one of the men from yesterday. Vincent helped him unload the equipment, and before long, they went to work, carefully yanking off the tin roof with crowbars. With each section of the barn getting dismantled before Janice's eyes, Charlie's death lessened its hold on her. Soon she'd no longer have the physical reminder of one of the worst days of her life looming over her. Janice's chest wouldn't grow tight each time she stepped in the barn's shadow. She felt lighter—freer.

Madison was sitting on the bench, watching each board getting ripped from the barn's frame. Janice strolled over to Madison and joined her. "I thought you might be in on all the action," she said, then caught a glimpse of a tear-stained cheek. "Oh, honey. This must be hard for you to see?" Janice's previous relief at seeing the barn disappear was eclipsed by the heartache her daughter must be feeling with the barn's demise.

"Yep." Madison rolled her lips into her mouth and looked to the sky.

Janice took Madison's hand. "That barn brought you a massive number of wonderful memories. I hope you'll be able to focus on those."

"I wish—I—I wish the memory I had in there with Lily was all I could think about, but all I can see is Dad."

"I see him, too, and that's why the barn had to go. We don't need that memory every time we look at it." She gave Madison's hand a squeeze. "I'm hoping in time, the memory of his death will ease."

Madison pulled her hand away and tugged at her shirt's hem. "It's been nine years, and the pain is still so new."

"Maybe that's because you've been away, and seeing the barn again made it all come rushing back so it seems fresh."

Madison nodded, then her gaze drifted away to something unknown. Perhaps her mind was visiting the scene of that horrible day.

"I told myself I didn't need to know why he killed himself, but I do, Mom." She exhaled and her shoulders sank. "I've blamed you all these years, but looking back, I know there had to have been more to it than that."

Janice's heart pounded as if it were ready to fall out of her chest. *She still blames me, and that's okay. She needs to know the truth.*

Janice blew out a breath and shifted to face Madison. "I've always tried to protect you from the truth, because I know how much you adored your father, and believe it or not, I loved him, too." She stared Madison in the eyes. "But I see that was a mistake."

Madison's lip quivered. "Did he do it because of me?"

Janice felt as though the world had swallowed her up and spit her back out. "My goodness. No! He was your biggest fan, and he loved you so much."

"Then why?" she pleaded and tightly hugged herself, as if she were protecting herself from being ripped and torn apart as well.

"Well, you obviously know I have money troubles, right?" Madison nodded. "That's because your dad had a terrible gambling addiction. I tried my best to hold everything together for a long time. He'd promised to get help and stop, but each time I helped him out, he'd float right back into it. I know how hard not having money was on you girls. There were so many fun things we wanted to do with you, but no sooner would I save the money for a vacation or buy you new clothes, that the money would disappear. So, I made excuses."

"That's why you sold Lily."

"Yes." Her shoulders sagged. "You have to know I tried everything I could to not have to sell Lily, but she cost too much to feed, and with the vet bills, I couldn't keep up. The house had to take priority. I hated to sell her. I really did."

"I'm sorry, Mom."

The words *I'm sorry* coming from her firstborn eased the welled-up self-loathing she'd carried with her. "It's okay. I understand. You were a kid, and you didn't need to know all that stuff."

"I was a teenager, which was probably worse because I treated you so horribly."

"I'll give you that, but you also worshiped your father. And, truth be told, I recognize I treated you horribly, too. I'd become bitter and angry. I took my bitterness out on everyone I loved, including your father. And because of that, I lost you, Hannah, and even my friends. My counselor once told me I have a tendency to act passive aggressively."

"You don't say?" Madison threw her a big grin and nudged her shoulder.

"Who knew?" Janice said with a chuckle.

"Thank you for sharing all that with me, Mom, but it doesn't explain why he killed himself."

"I don't think we'll ever fully know the truth, but I think once he convinced me to take a loan out on the house, then gambled all that money away as well, he must have thought there was no way out."

"What about your inheritance?"

"Your dad didn't have access to that, and once I realized he'd used the loan money from the house, I vowed I'd never enable him again. I refused to give him my inheritance." A knot grew in her stomach. The guilt in saying those words aloud caused her to tremble. Janice could no longer catch her breath.

"Mom? What's going on?"

"It's my anxiety." She sucked in some air and slowly blew it out. "Just give me a minute." She held up a finger, then slowly breathed again. Once she composed herself and breathed regularly, Janice didn't see condemnation in Madison's eyes—she only saw compassion.

"You have blamed yourself for all these years, haven't you?" Madison asked.

Janice nodded. "Your dad told me he owed some bad people a lot of money. He begged me for the inheritance, and I refused to give it to him. I loved him. I wanted to help, but I couldn't have my father's hard-earned money get gambled away. That money was all we had left to our name, Madison." Janice couldn't hold back her tears. "He'd even lost his job because he stole from the company to feed his gambling addiction. I'd thought of taking a job, but I was afraid if I left the house, he'd find something of value, and sell it to get more money to gamble away. Maybe that was extreme thinking, but it scared me to leave the house." Janice's body trembled again. "And all that didn't matter after all because I ended up having to sell your sweet horse, just to get by." She trembled more. "If I'd only agreed to—"

Madison wrapped her arms around her, held her tight, and whispered. "It wasn't your fault. You must believe that, Mom. It wasn't your fault."

They held each other and cried.

sixty-one

The last barn board of the day dropped to the ground with a resounding thud. Every muscle in Vincent's body ached, but he imagined his aches and pains didn't compare to the anguish he witnessed earlier in the day between Janice and Madison. He wished he could magically make things better for them, but he was no magician. Vincent had hoped the barn's teardown would be a good thing. It was what they wanted, but their emotions appeared to say otherwise.

He waved goodbye to the help. As they drove away, he removed his work gloves, then threw them on the front seat of his truck. He pulled out his one-gallon jug of water and took a few big gulps before heading to the house to see how Janice was holding up.

Daylight faded into a purple sky by the time he knocked on the back door. Janice greeted him with a smile. He smiled in return.

"Come on in," she said. Considering the day she seemed to have, her pleasant demeanor surprised him. Vincent stepped in to see two place settings on the table. "I'm hoping you might join me."

"Nothing would please me more." *There is hope.* Vincent opened his hands, palm side up. "I should wash up first. I'm a filthy mess."

He pointed toward the hall and she responded with another smile. Her happiness took his breath away.

The shroud of sadness that they'd worn for far too long seemed to lift, and light broke through an otherwise dim future, attempting to reveal something beautiful in its place. He practically skipped down the hall to clean up. *Yes*, he thought, *there is hope right here on Lilac Lane.*

The mouth-watering aroma of fresh-cut tomatoes and basil filled his senses when he arrived back in the kitchen. Janice placed an ample-sized Caprese salad and avocado slices, with grilled asparagus and chicken in the middle of the table. "That looks refreshing."

"Oh good. I ran to the farmer's market they have at the York Chamber of Commerce earlier. I'd forgotten all about those until Madison mentioned it." She brushed her hair behind her ear. "I hope it's enough for you after working so hard today."

"It's perfect," he said, knowing anything Janice put in front of him would be perfect, so long as she sat at his side. "And look at you going to a local farmer's market."

"Kind of silly, but I confess, I'm proud of myself." Her cheeks blushed. "Go ahead." She slid her chair closer to the table. "Dig in."

He picked up his fork, perplexed by her change in demeanor since his last attempt at wooing her. She might wish to pretend the note he'd given to her didn't exist, but her reaction to his written words ate at him. Vincent wanted to address the note, but more importantly, he needed to talk about what Janice may have interpreted when she saw Gayle at his home, because he feared if he didn't, they'd have no chance at a romance.

Vincent watched Janice eat her salad. She didn't appear self-conscious, as he often noticed with other women. Janice seemed relaxed, and he thought that was a good sign. As much as he didn't wish to spoil their time together, he thought there was no time like the present to broach the subject.

"Janice." She raised her gaze from her plate to meet his eyes. "You know I like you, right?"

Janice's eyes grew wide. She gulped and nodded.

"And there isn't anyone else I'm interested in." She gave him a sideways glance. *She doesn't believe me.* "I think you may have seen me and my neighbor, Gayle, the evening you delivered your thoughtful basket to my house. And I imagine you may have assumed we were—we…"

"Lovers?" she said nonchalantly.

Vincent choked on his own spit, and his eyes watered while he tried to control a cough and gain some composure. "Yes. I mean no. What I mean to say is…"

"You're not?"

"We are not." Vincent took a drink of water, and Janice's eyes narrowed. "Most definitely not."

Janice turned away and poked at her salad. "So, you commonly have ladies over for drinks, and I shouldn't read anything into that?" She glanced up with her full fork in her hand. "Or maybe having women stroking your ego is just common practice in your neck of the woods."

Here's the curt untrusting Janice I know. "I can see why you wouldn't trust what I'm saying, but I can assure you, I am a trustworthy man. In fact, there is nothing more I value than being a man of integrity."

"I'm sorry, but I will not be made a fool of again. I've trusted in a man too many times, especially when the obvious stares me in the face, and you see where that's gotten me."

Vincent teetered on the verge of anger and compassion, and he wasn't sure which side of the seesaw he'd land on. He caught her gaze, but she diverted it away. Janice had shared little about her late husband, but he knew enough to gather his death shattered her in more ways than he could ever imagine.

He rested his fork on the table and reached for her hand. She didn't pull away. "I'd hoped I'd earned your trust, but I can see you need some convincing." He leaned in. "My neighbor, Gayle, the same woman you saw at my house, is having a party, and I'd like you to be my date."

Janice jerked her hand away, and fear washed over her face.

"Absolutely not," she said, as she fumbled with her napkin.

"I'd be right there with you, and I promise I won't leave your side."

"But I—I… You've seen what I'm like around a lot of people. I hit you with my car!" Janice slid her chair back and paced the floor. The napkin spun around in her hands like a fidget toy.

Vincent got up from his chair and took a few steps toward her. As she turned in her pacing stride, she came face-to-face with Vincent, and nearly body slammed him. He stumbled back and fell into the arms of Madison, who'd stepped into the kitchen.

"Whoa there," Madison said as she thrust him forward. She jutted her smiling face from one to the other. "Am I interrupting something?"

Janice threw her arms up. "I give up. Now I'll just get tag-teamed." She slumped over to the table and took a seat.

Madison's twisted grin gave Vincent all the encouragement

he needed. "My neighbor is throwing a party, and I've asked your mother to be my date."

"Mom." Madison thrust her hands to her hips. "That's fantastic! You should go. Ooh, and it will give us a reason to go shopping again." She rubbed her hands together greedily.

"I'm not going to any party. And you already forced me once to go shopping with you, and I'm not about to do it again."

"But we had fun. Didn't we?"

"You might have, but I crawled out of my skin until I got back to the car."

"And you got a beautiful new dress to show for it."

Vincent watched their exchange and became more amused by the moment. Seeing them getting along was refreshing. "Maybe you could wear that new dress to the party." He stepped closer to Janice. "That way, you won't have to go shopping again."

"A sundress is hardly the type of dress I would wear to a party—at Gayle's."

"Gayle?" Madison asked. "Do I know this Gayle? Is she one of your lady friends you used to meet, for your luncheons?"

"Certainly not!"

Madison shrugged. "I'm just asking."

"Well, it's a stupid question."

"Seriously?" Madison tutted.

Vincent had whiplash from their back and forth. "Gayle is my neighbor, and she throws a soirée every year to celebrate all her seasonal friends who arrive back in town."

Janice's mouth flew open. "A soirée?" Her eyes grew wide. "Like a fancy evening party?"

Vincent wasn't sure how to respond. He needed to de-escalate Janice's panic, but words escaped him.

"That's even better," Madison interjected. "Don't you see? It's easier to blend in at night, and it's much easier to sneak out if you get too overwhelmed."

"That's right. If you get overwhelmed"—he placed his hand on hers—"and I'm sure you won't. But if you do, we'll go over to my place and take a breather."

"I think you'd have a much better time if I didn't go." Vincent saw Janice grimace. "What I mean to say is…"

"I know what you meant, and I can assure you I wouldn't have a better time without you." He gave Janice a wink. "In fact, if you don't go with me, I won't go at all."

"Mom, go. Really. You used to love going to parties, and it'll be good for you."

"Fine. I'll go," she snapped. "But you better give me your word that you won't leave my side—ever. And if I start to…"

"I promise." He crossed his chest with his finger. Janice rolled her eyes. "I'll even pinky swear that you'll be stuck with me the whole night. And when you want to leave, we'll leave."

Janice smiled. In that moment, Vincent couldn't be more proud. And yet he hoped his urging her to go wouldn't be a huge mistake and set her progress back.

"This is getting weird," Madison teased. "I'll just—head outside, and leave you two googly-eyed lovebirds to yourselves." She couldn't resist giving her mother a wink before she headed out the door.

sixty-two

All that remained was the empty spot in the yard where the barn once stood. Madison reached down and grasped a handful of dirt and sifted it through her fingers. The damp soil was cool to her touch, and she thought of her father buried under the earth in the cemetery. The last time Madison stood at his grave was the day soil fell through her fingertips on top of his casket. She still hadn't seen his headstone, and she questioned if she ever would.

All the reminders of her father were long gone. The scent of his aftershave, the smell of whiskey on his breath, and her memory could no longer hear his voice or laughter. His fishing boat and truck no longer sat in the yard. And now the barn that once brought her so much joy had vanished. She thought she'd find peace with its removal, but the pain of her father's death lingered. She fought back tears.

Madison glanced at the house. Her bedroom window curtains blew in the breeze, and she recalled all the times she'd peered out to see her horse trotting around in the corral.

She missed her horses. They'd provided comfort when she wept with grief, and was in need of companionship, when the ache of feeling alone was too great to bear. She didn't have to justify or make excuses for her tears with them. They didn't judge or try to fix her or her situation. Now, as she stood in the yard of her family home, there was nothing but an empty space on the land and in her heart. The weight of regret lay upon her shoulders. *Maybe someday I can build a new barn and bring Lily and Journey here.* She chewed on her lip and shook her head. *Who am I kidding?* In a matter of days, her childhood home would become hers, along with the mortgage and the cost of upkeep.

Have I made a mistake?

The house seemed larger, and overwhelming as it loomed before her, but there was no turning back now. She was staying, and that was that.

The image of Nathan, as she told him goodbye, tugged at her conscience. She'd known him for nearly nine years, and that had to stand for something. Madison did love him, but over time, she felt more alone with him than without. Even so, she refused to accept their time together was a waste. She'd grown to believe everything happened for a reason, and now, more than ever, she needed to hang on to that truth.

She scooped another handful of earth, and a glimmer caught her attention. She knelt and a silver chain peeked out of the soil. She gently pulled, and the pendant she'd lost dangled within her grasp. Tears of joy poured down her cheeks as she thought of Hannah.

The day she'd given Hannah the matching necklace seared into her memory. Leaving her behind to run off to Ohio was one of the hardest things she'd ever done, and now she felt a piece of Hannah was with her once again.

Madison clutched the necklace to her heart as she thought of saying goodbye to her father at his grave, to her sister, Franky, and her mother. *So many goodbyes.* And now, Nathan. She sighed wishing she'd said goodbye to Nathan differently.

Madison pulled her phone out of her pocket and Nathan picked up after the second ring.

"Hi."

"Hi," she said. Her nerves flipped and twirled inside out.

"I'm sorry," they said in unison. Madison couldn't believe her ears. "What do you have to be sorry about? I'm the one that left you."

"You were right to leave when you did," Nathan said. "And you are right to stay. I shouldn't have pressured you."

Madison quietly cried at his admission. "Thank you for that. Really. But I was cruel in how I handled you coming here. You'd come all this way, just to have me turn you around to go back."

"I should have called you first. That's on me."

She wiped her cheeks. "Please know I will always love you, Nathan."

"You better," he said with a half-hearted laugh. "I love you, too."

"I never pictured us ending up like this."

"Me either, but I thought about what you said the entire way home, and you are right. We've drifted apart, and I'm sorry for my part in that. I guess I blinded myself to the obvious. I think we both went through the motions of what we thought we should do, but that wasn't enough for either of us."

"Yep." She gulped back the lump in her throat. "You must understand how much you and your family mean to me. I'm beyond grateful for the life I've had in Ohio. Goodness, we've pretty much grown up together, and we've shared remarkable moments that I will cherish for the rest of my life."

"We sure have." Nathan paused. "You know you will always be welcome here, and sooner rather than later because I need more drawer space. I don't look as good as you in your jeans, so you'll have to get 'em outta here."

Madison laughed.

"Your Stetson hat and boots though," he said, and gave a light whistle. "I'd look pretty sexy in those."

"You stay away from my cowboy hat."

"Only if you promise to come back…for a visit. You have to see how Journey's grown, and Lily misses you. She told me so this morning when I fed her a bunch of carrots."

"Thank you. I hoped you'd say that." Relief shattered the weight she'd worn for far too long. "And when I visit, I promise I'll make my world-famous apple crisp for you."

The line grew quiet, and Madison was at a loss for words. "Thanks again, Nathan. I couldn't imagine my life without you in it. You mean too much to me. Love you."

"Me too, you."

Tears fell again. "I've got to run, but feel free to call anytime."

"Will do."

The line went dead, and Madison felt relieved, knowing they would remain friends, and that relationship certainly made her job with Hawking Equipment more comfortable as well. She had to tell Franky.

Madison snuck in the front door and ran up the stairs to grab her handbag. Laughter filled the house, and the sound stopped her in her tracks. She hadn't realized how much she missed hearing her mother's laughter until now. She made a mental note to email Hannah and tell her about the recent goings on, then she got in her car and called Franky.

"Hey, Mads, what's up?"

"I'm craving an ice cream cone. Care to join me?"

"Sure. Let's take a walk to the Village Scoop. I swear my mother's purposely trying to fatten me up with all her home-made cooking. Honestly, I feel like I'm in college again, and I've put on my freshmen fifteen."

Madison laughed. "Don't be ridiculous. You look perfectly healthy and beautiful, as always."

"Oh, my. Why are you so—complementary? What's happened?"

"I'll tell you all about it. I just pulled in. See you in a sec."

Madison slid out of the car in a hurry and came face-to-face with Franky's brother, Ryan, standing there holding a tool bag. His tall, lean, muscular physique came as a surprise, and she had a hard time keeping her mouth from gaping open.

"Well, if it isn't long-lost Madison Gable."

She eyed him up and down. "You've, ah, changed."

"Crazy, right? I don't know how it happened." He looked down at his ripped torso. "One day I woke up and…"

Madison rolled her eyes. "Always the comic. It's good to see you haven't completely changed since our days in high school." She couldn't get over seeing him. No more braces, pimply face, and lanky arms. He carried himself with confidence and ease. "It's great to see you."

"You, too. Hey, how's your mom doing?"

"Oh, my gosh, I'm so sorry. Thank you for taking care of her. She's doing great."

"I'm glad to hear it."

"Honestly. If you and the rest of the team hadn't helped my mom get to the hospital the way you did, I doubt she'd be with us." Madison shifted her stance. "I'm confused, though. I could swear Franky told me you're a veterinarian."

"I am, but I volunteer as an EMT when I can, which is rare. When the call came in that day, I happened to be here."

Franky bounded down the stairs. "Ryan, Dad's getting impatient. Says he needs the socket wrenches pronto."

Ryan glanced at Madison. "Another thing that hasn't changed." He laughed and swung his arm around her and gave her a sideways squeeze. "Great to see you, Madison. And please give my best to your mom."

"Will do."

"So, what's up, my friend? Is it about you and Nate, or your mom and Vincent? No, wait, it's you and your mom. I want all the details."

Madison laughed. "How much caffeine have you had?"

Franky's eyes popped. "Enough."

"Come on." Madison pulled her by the arm. "You need to walk some of that off."

Franky jogged a couple of steps to catch up. "I'm still waiting?"

"I called Nathan."

"Ooh. Do tell."

The brisk walk to The Village Scoop gave plenty of time to fill Franky in on all the details of the day. By the time they held Death by Chocolate ice cream cones in their hands, Madison sat back on the bench, devouring the cone, and felt satisfied at the direction her life was taking her.

"So. You and Ryan seemed to hit it off." She gave Madison a side-eye and popped the last of her cone into her mouth.

Madison spun in her seat. "Absolutely not, so don't you even think of going there." She took her last bite of cone, then tossed her napkin in the trash as Ryan's insanely gorgeous pecs linger in her mind.

sixty-three

*J*anice glanced at the time. She pressed her hand to her stomach and focused on the watermark at the base of her bedroom window. *Focus.* She pushed air out of her mouth, then slowly breathed in through her nose and repeated the exercise. All the while, wishing today was tomorrow, so the party would be a distant memory instead of overwhelming her with anxiety. *I can do this. It's just a party.*

Madison was correct. She'd attended tons of parties when Charlie was alive, and for the most part, she'd enjoyed them. Of course, that was before he got fired from his job. Once that happened, the rumor mill followed. She'd heard hushed conversations that ended when she'd approached, but she caught snippets. *I hear he got thrown out the front door. They should have arrested him.* But after his death, going to parties was out of the question because the gossip became intolerable. The thought of facing the same judgmental faces she'd seen at his funeral was more than she could bear. So, she'd stayed home. To her relief, it didn't take long before the invites came to a stop. Now, here she was, waiting to be picked up for an oceanfront soirée, of all things.

Her jitters didn't relent as she stood in front of the full-length mirror. She checked and rechecked every inch of her magenta-colored jumpsuit. Madison told her the sleeveless split neck flattered her breasts, and the flowy, pleated front with a tie belt accentuated her slim waistline. Janice was pleased the jumpsuit had pockets, so she could hide her trembling hands. She tucked a loose strand of hair back in place.

Janice smiled in the mirror to confirm she didn't have lipstick on her teeth, when Madison's reflection appeared behind her.

"You look absolutely beautiful." Madison leaned over her shoulder. There she was, staring at herself and Madison side by side. Janice couldn't help but think Madison was a younger version of herself. She smiled.

"Connie did a fabulous job with your hair." Madison stepped back to examine her hair more closely. "Aren't you glad I talked you into getting it professionally done?"

Janice had to admit the decision was a good choice. Even though she'd fought, tooth and nail, insisting she'd managed to cut and style her hair on her own for many years, and how there was no need to pay someone else to do it. But Madison harshly reminded her, in no uncertain terms, that she would not be going to a soirée with her hair shoved into a hair tie. "I'm happy you twisted my arm, but don't think for one minute that you can continue to boss me around."

"I'll do what I want." She grinned, then her eyes shot open. "Oh, my goodness. I almost forgot. Be right back." Madison darted out the door and ran down the hall.

Janice slipped on her nude-colored sandals as Madison entered.

"I thought I lost this, but I found it in the dirt where the barn was." Madison draped her necklace around Janice's neck and latched the clip. "I gave Hannah a matching one the day I left for Ohio. The necklace has our birthstones on it."

Janice touched the pendant that sat at the hollow of her throat. She gasped. *Madison's and Hannah's birthstones. My daughters' birthstones.* "I don't know what to say?"

"I thought, if you wore it tonight, maybe you'd find comfort knowing we were both there with you."

Janice trembled and couldn't hold back her tears. "Thank you."

"Don't go messing up your makeup." Madison ran her thumb over her cheek.

"You're bossing me around again," she said as tears of joy continued to flow. Janice didn't care if the rest of the night was an utter failure. Because this moment, right now, was more than she could have ever dreamed of. She wasn't alone any longer. Janice had her girls with her, and even though the sentiment was figurative, it didn't matter. The meaning was real.

"I'm getting you a tissue so you can clean up, and I'll entertain Vincent until you're ready."

Janice wiped her cheeks. "He's here?"

"I just saw him step out of his car, and he's as handsome as you are beautiful. Which is saying a lot."

Janice gave Madison a quick hug and watched her leave the room. *She's back. She's really back.*

The necklace around her neck brought her a confidence that had eluded her for far too long. She pulled the pendant to her lips and gave it a kiss. Janice's heart beat calmly in her chest. "I can do this."

Vincent stood with his neck craned to get a closer look at a photo hanging on the living room wall. He and Madison hadn't noticed she'd entered the room, so she took the moment to take him in. Vincent looked distinguished in his lightweight gray suit jacket and white dress shirt with the top two buttons left undone. His neatly trimmed salt-and-pepper goatee and hair that shone by the glow of the lamp complemented his look. She wanted nothing more in that moment than to run her fingers through his silky locks. Janice had heard the expression *he took my breath away*. She finally understood.

Janice approached and noted the image he'd fixed his gaze on. A formal family portrait taken during happier times. "I don't think I was much older than Madison is now when that was taken."

Vincent gazed in her direction. "And you look just as stunning now as you did then."

Janice's chest swelled at the compliment. "Thank you. And you look quite dashing yourself, Mr. Vincent."

"Alrighty then," Madison said. "I'm just going to go back to my room and finish some work I have to get done. You two have a great time." Madison pointed her finger at Janice. "And I better not see you until the wee hours of the morning."

The warm evening and light breeze brushed across her shoulders as they walked to the car. He opened the door for her and she slid inside. Her previous calm nerves made themselves known, and she took a deep breath while Vincent walked around the car to join her.

Vincent's cologne and the car's leather interior gave off a rich, yet subtle, combination of sophistication she found intoxicating. Here she was, going to an oceanfront soirée to join society again. Never in her wildest imagination did she see herself in this position with this beautiful man at her side.

"Are you ready?" he asked.

"I think so." She couldn't believe those words crossed her lips, but Vincent had the ability to set her mind at ease. She'd soon stand on a deck surrounded by the scent of rosehip and peonies in the air, while watching the sun set over the water. She imagined a glass of champagne in her hand, music playing, and laughter. But her mind spun out of control after they drove by the home of one of her former friends.

Barb could be there. They'd met at the Union Bluff for drinks or luncheons over the years. The Bluff was only a stone's throw to Vincent's. *Who else could be at the party?* Janice attempted to slow her breathing. *Jacky. What if Jacky's there, too?* Her hands grew clammy. *They're gossips.* She rubbed her thighs with shaking hands. *They'll tell everybody about Charlie. They'll stare.* Her chest tightened. *I can't do this.*

Janice pressed back into the seat and gripped the car door handle to brace herself as panic rose.

"Turn around." She gasped for air. "I need to go home."

Vincent pulled in to the first parking space he came to along Long Sands Beach, and slammed the car into park. Within a flash, he'd flung open her door and came to her eye level. "Talk to me, honey. What's going on?"

His kind eyes begged for understanding.

"What if there's people at the party that I know?" she asked.

Vincent took her hands. "That's in the past, sweetheart. That part of your life is over. It's time for you to live again." Vincent didn't let go. He didn't break eye contact. "I've got you." He leaned in and embraced her with such care, as if she were a small bird within his grasp. His tenderness and empathy, without the ability to truly understand, overwhelmed her. He stood up and pulled her to him.

"Come with me." Vincent walked to the edge of the sea wall, facing the vastness of the ocean. The bright orange-and-yellow sky over the horizon lay out before them. He took a step behind Janice and wrapped his arms around her waist, and rested his chin atop her crown.

"Isn't that view awe inspiring, Janice?" His calming, low tone reverberated through her body. She nodded. "Take in the vastness, the multitude of color, its scent. Breathe in."

She breathed.

"The sea is many things. The water can be calm on the surface, but underneath can breed turmoil. And sometimes the surface isn't calm at all. The waves can crush walls of stone, turn over ships, and take lives. I think sometimes that's what life is like."

"The world we live in can be scary, but it can also be as beautiful as that sunset. Isn't that what makes life interesting?"

She relaxed her shoulders.

"Without fear, there can be no strength. Without worry, there can be no hope, nor would there be joy without tasting sorrow." Vincent turned her to face him. "And without hate, we wouldn't recognize love when it stares us in the face," he whispered.

Tears rolled down her cheeks.

"Don't you see? It really doesn't matter what the people at that party think of you, or me either, for that matter. They don't know you like I do. If they judge you, then they aren't worthy enough to see your pain, because what I see in you is more beautiful than any sunset."

Janice's heart leaped out of her chest. "You can't mean that? I can be so miserable—needy."

"I most certainly do. Even when you're a cranky pants." He smiled and lifted her chin to face him.

She desperately wanted to believe him. With everything in her, she wanted to believe. She'd never known anyone as kind as the man that stood before her. "I don't deserve you."

"That's where you're wrong."

Vincent pulled her hands to his lips, and his warm lips caressed her skin. They tingled under his touch as he tenderly kissed each hand. "I'm just as broken as you are. Everyone is at some point in their lives. Let them think what they want, Janice. You don't need to defend yourself, and you certainly don't need to defend what your husband did. *He* killed himself. Don't let him kill you, too. You're strong. A survivor. And I'm going to stay right by your side. Like I promised."

Janice melted into his arms, as jagged cries escaped her limp body until she felt release. A peace washed over her, as he kissed the top of her head.

"What do you say we get back in that car because I want to dance with you under the stars and tell the world how much you mean to me?"

Janice couldn't speak. She had no words to express how she was feeling. How do you tell someone thank you for taking a lonely broken heart and piecing it back together with grace and wisdom? How does one reveal the magnitude that this moment has meant? She had no words. She could only show him with a kiss. A kiss unlike any she'd given before. A kiss filled with passion, gratitude, and love. A kiss Vincent reciprocated with an intensity that nearly brought her to her knees, then she stepped away and walked back to the car.

Without so much as a word, Vincent opened the door and helped her inside, then slid in beside her and started the engine. As if God ordained the moment, Don McLean's

"Starry, Starry Night," played on the radio. As the words rolled across McLean's tongue, his melancholy lyrics clung to her with new meaning. She would not succumb to despair. No matter the cost, she would live to see beauty in sunsets, in the eyes of her daughters, and in a caressing touch. She'd enjoy the feel of sand between her toes, the scent of lilacs in the spring.

She was given a second chance, and she needn't worry about what the others thought of her any longer. They were not of her concern. She'd make the most of this life, and she'd enjoy sharing her life with the man who sat beside her, for as long as he was willing—her Vincent.

The party was alive with chatter and clinking glasses. Vincent took Janice's arm in his as they descended the stairs to Gayle's deck. He stopped before they turned the corner and he peered into her fiery green eyes. "Have I told you how stunning you look tonight?"

Janice rested her head on his shoulders and gave his hand a squeeze. "Thank you."

"I'm proud to have you at my side, Janice." They turned the corner, and Janice's grip intensified. "You've got this, my dear." She nodded.

Gayle grabbed two glasses of champagne and headed their way. "I'm so happy you could make it, Vinny." She eyed Janice and gave a forced smile. "And you must be Vinny's special friend, Jenny."

"Janice, her name is Janice, and yes, she is pretty special to me."

Gayle winced, and handed over the two champagne flutes. "Welcome to my humble abode," she said, then directed her attention to Vincent. "Please indulge yourselves to *anything* you might wish." She gave him a quick wink, then glanced toward Janice. "You too, dear," she said before flitting off to mingle with her adoring click.

"And now you've met Gayle." He chuckled. "She's more bark than bite."

"I hope you've had your rabies shots," Janice said and grinned.

They moved toward the buffet. "Do you see anyone you know?" Janice scanned the decks, then her gaze stuck on one woman.

"That woman over there." She nodded in the woman's direction. "She's Claire, but I don't see her husband." She wrenched her neck to look for him. "Oh." Janice sighed. "Barb's here, too."

Claire and Barb. He tried to recall ever meeting them, but neither of them rang a bell. Vincent patted Janice's hand. The women glanced in their direction. "What do you say we rip off the Band-Aid?"

Janice's eyes popped open. "You can't mean what I think you mean."

"Indeed, I do. Once you introduce me to your 'friends' then we can be free to enjoy ourselves. Let them see the Janice I see. Besides, I've heard I'm a pretty good catch, so you've got that going for you, too."

Janice gave him a teasing slap on his shoulder. "That's one of the things I love about you. You're humble."

"I'm happy to hear there's things you love about me. Please, tell me more."

Janice bit her lip, a nervous tic he'd noticed Madison do a thousand times. "I like—love—your confidence, and can-do attitude."

"And?" He didn't ask to boost his ego. He simply wanted to know how she felt about him. It relieved him to know he hadn't been missing the cues of their attraction toward one another. He'd grown to adore the woman at his side.

"And, I love how you make me feel when I'm with you."

He tipped her gaze toward his. "And I love how I feel when I'm with you, Ms. Gable."

Her eyes sparkled. "I hope that's really you talking and not the champagne."

"Oh, it's definitely me. One hundred percent me. Let's do this thing." She nodded and he escorted her toward the two gawking women.

Janice put her chin up and strutted over, initiating hugs. "My goodness. It's so wonderful to see you. It's been way too long." The ladies appeared gobsmacked at first, but then complimented her outfit and hair. "Barb, Claire, this is Vincent Clark." Janice wrapped her arms around his bicep and gave it a squeeze. "He's my *very special* friend and date this evening," she said, to which they fell over their tongues. Janice gave him a wink. "Well, what do you say we leave these lovely ladies and partake in all the scrumptious appetizers."

As he and Janice walked away, he heard the women's whispers. "I can't get over the change in her. She looks fantastic."

"They were talking about me, weren't they?" she asked as they neared the buffet.

"Yep."

"I told you. They are some of the worst gossips I know. Honestly, I don't know why I was ever friends with them in the first place."

"I don't know. I think some gossip is just fine."

Janice turned on her heels. "How can you say that?"

Vincent leaned in and gave her a kiss on the cheek. "There's always room for gossip when good things are being said. They think you look fantastic."

"No way! You heard them say that?" She beamed from ear to ear.

"Oh, and they said they think your boyfriend is a great catch."

"They didn't." She gave him a side-eye.

"No, but you have to admit, I am."

Janice inched up and pecked him on the cheek. "Indeed, you are."

Vincent could no longer hold back the tension that built inside of him. He needed release. He nestled her in his arms, and as her eyes followed his gaze, he leaned in and tenderly kissed her lips. The taste of sweet champagne mixed with the scent of her lavender hair, and he savored every moment as she returned his passion. He thought he'd died and gone to heaven.

He was still basking in the glow of the kiss when Gayle sauntered over toward them.

"Well, you two seem to be enjoying yourselves."

Vincent didn't miss the glowering shot she gave Janice. "We are. Thank you, Gayle. You've really outdone yourself."

"Yes, Gayle. Your place is stunning, and I admire all the effort it must have taken for you to pull off such a wonderful event."

Vincent looked from Janice to Gayle and back again. He couldn't get over the woman before him. She'd blossomed before his eyes, and she bloomed with confidence. She trampled on the weeds of fear and worry. Vincent couldn't be prouder.

Gayle lit up with the compliment. "Planning this soirée has been laborious, to say the least, but knowing everyone is enjoying themselves makes my effort worth every sleepless night I had to make it happen." She rested her hand on Janice's. "We simply must get together sometime, you and me. You should definitely join me for one of my yoga classes?"

Gayle whipped her head to see a new guest arrive. "Oh, the senator's arrived." She dashed off in his direction.

"You sure know how to get on Gayle's good side," Vincent said.

"Flattery will tamp down ill-harbored resentment every time."

Vincent and Janice finally filled their plates, and before long, they danced the night away under the starry moonlit sky. He would never grow old from hearing Janice's laughter, tasting her lips, or the feel of her body within his arms.

sixty-five

Morning broke as Vincent sat in the Adirondack chair on his deck. He held his usual morning coffee in his hand as he gazed at the Atlantic. The briny scent and the cool mist of the sea clung to his arms and face. He unrolled his sleeves from the dress shirt he'd worn the night before and sipped his brew. Had last night been a dream? Vincent replayed the evening.

As Vincent reminisced, he noticed Gayle walking Sissy on the beach. He waved and Gayle gave an enthusiastic wave back. His coffee was now empty. He stood and leaned against the railing as Gayle and her dog jogged in his direction.

"Mind if I join you?" she shouted into a gust of wind.

Vincent gestured for her to come up.

Gayle labored to catch her breath. "Wow, that was a tough walk on the way back. Especially since I'm still recovering from last night." She picked Sissy up and pulled a treat from her windbreaker's pocket. "I'm happy you and your friend enjoyed yourselves."

"Indeed, we did." He smiled recalling how much. He tipped his empty coffee cup. "Can I get you a coffee?"

"I'm good. Thanks. Maybe a glass of water?"

"One water coming up," he said. She followed him into the house. "Is tap, okay?"

Gayle pulled out a bar stool and rested Sissy on her lap. "After a walk like that, I'd drink out of your garden hose." She laughed. "I heard through the grapevine that your friend—Janice, is it?" He nodded. "Anyhoo, I hear she's a widow, in the most tragic way imaginable. Honestly, if that happened to me, I don't think I'd ever be able to show my face in society again. Poor dear."

Vincent bit his tongue as water filled Gayle's glass. "Janice has been through a lot, but haven't we all?"

"Well, sure, but we lost our spouses because of illness, not…"

"Every loss of a loved one, no matter how the loss was made, is great." He slid her glass across the bar. "It's the grace, fortitude, and perseverance in how we handle that loss I find compelling. Wouldn't you agree?"

Gayle's gaze drifted to Sissy, and she stroked her back. "I suppose you're right. Your special friend was rather brave to attend. I like her."

Images of Janice flashed through his mind, from the first time he'd laid eyes on her, in the supermarket parking lot, to the stunning woman that stood before him last night. "Janice most certainly is."

"Well, then. It seems as if we both got what we were looking for. Haven't we?"

"Oh?"

"You have your new—Janice, who seems to have inspired you to write again. I've seen your light on, like I used to when Cheryl was alive. And I have a new travel…companion. Me and the senator are planning a rendezvous."

"It appears we have."

Gayle hopped off the stool. "I must run. I have some

shopping to do. Toodles." With that, she was off, like the gust of wind that brought her in.

Vincent carried his coffee back to the deck. He thought about what Gayle had said. *I got what I was looking for.* The funny thing is, he didn't know he was looking for anything. Maybe he'd looked for a muse, so his passion to write would return? No. What he'd really been seeking, without realizing it, was to feel needed.

Two seagulls soared by in tandem. Perhaps he needed to fill the void of loneliness. There is a time and place to be alone, he thought, to meditate, consider, to think, but those times are purposeful. Loneliness, however unintended, can wreak havoc on the soul.

Vincent's eyes drifted to the sky. "Thank you, my dear Cheryl, for opening my eyes to not withering away like a flower without water. Thank you for encouraging me to love again," he whispered to the breeze.

His gold wedding band caught the sun. Vincent slipped the ring from his finger and turned it to read the inscription. *Till death do us part – VC & CC.* He set the ring in the palm of his hand and gave the symbol of love a kiss before closing his fingers around it, then put the ring into his pocket. "Thank you for loving me enough to let me go."

Three weeks had passed since Madison's mother's debut back into society. Since then, she and her mom closed on the house. And today was the first celebration she'd host as a homeowner. The closing was uneventful, but the peace she felt afterward, at saving the family home, nearly moved her to tears.

Vincent and Franky, along with Franky's mother, buzzed around the kitchen, helping to prepare dinner before Janice got home from Gayle's yoga class. Madison, however, busied herself decorating the dining room with purple streamers and table linens. She set a fresh bouquet at the center of the table, then ran back to the kitchen to watch Mrs. Murphy frost the cake.

Madison scooped a teaspoon of the frosting out of the bowl and stuck it into her mouth.

"You know, Madison, you are not too old for me to smack your hand like I did when you and Franky were kids."

"Sorry, but you make the best frosting ever." Madison stuck out her tongue. "Is my tongue purple?"

"Yes, and it serves you right."

Madison watched the clock. She bounced her leg and tapped the table as the ticking of the clock captured her attention.

A car pulled up, and Franky jumped up and ran to the window. "Your mom's here!"

Vincent slipped out of the house and met Janice at her car. He carried her yoga mat and stepped toward the front door.

"Your mom looks confused," Franky said.

"She's used to coming through the kitchen door. But I thought it would be better to have her come through the front."

Franky scurried to the table just as Vincent opened the door. When Janice stepped inside, they yelled, "Surprise!"

Janice gasped and brought her hands to her mouth. Her eyes, like saucers, took in the room.

"Happy Birthday, Mom!" Madison's stomach did flip-flops. Her mother's reaction was what she'd hoped for.

"You did all this for me?" she said, as she gave out hugs. "The table is so pretty!" She ran her fingers over the lilac-colored napkins, then notice the bouquet. She looked at Vincent. "Are these from your yard?"

"Nope," he said with a broad smile.

"They couldn't be from mine. Could they?"

Vincent rocked on his feet and shook his head. The smile remained.

"Look at the card, Mom," Madison said, then motioned for everyone to have a seat at the table.

Janice sat down and tugged the small card from the flowers. She pulled the envelope open and slid the tiny card out. Her lower lip quivered and tears welled up in her eyes as she read the contents, then Janice brought it to her chest. She smiled through her tears.

"Well, what does it say?" Madison asked.

Janice's jagged breath hitched. "It says, *Happy Birthday. I'm sorry I couldn't be there to wish you a happy birthday in person, but I'll be seeing you soon! Love, Hannah.*"

Janice wiped her joyful tears, and Madison blew her mother a kiss from across the table.

Laughter filled the room as they dug into fresh lobsters and steamers from Off the Boat Lobsters with sweet corn on the cob, red potatoes, and clam chowder. Then Madison and Franky cleared the table while Janice, Franky's mom, and Vincent drank their coffee.

Franky turned off the lights, and Madison carried the cake with lit candles into the room. A robust round of "Happy Birthday to You" rang out.

"Make a wish, Mom."

Janice glanced toward Madison's and Vincent's expectant eyes. "I don't need to. My wishes have already come true."

The room fell quiet.

"Blow out the candle already," Franky said. "I want that cake!"

sixty-seven

Happy Birthday to me.

Janice tugged on a streamer and it floated to the table. The guests were long gone, and Madison lay sleeping in her room. She glanced over at Vincent on the couch. He appeared to be dreaming a glorious dream, as a smile rested on his face. She picked up the note from Hannah and reread the message. "I'll see you soon." She savored each word and their meaning. Soon she'd be laying eyes on Hannah. She'd get to touch her cheek and hear her voice, from just a breath away.

Only in her wildest dreams did she envision the life she now had, compared to the one she left the day she attempted to erase the past. The empty space in the yard still held what Charlie did in her heart, but her heart now beat with fulfilment and joy for a wonderful future. Her sorrow would always be a piece of her, but as Vincent once said, she could never truly experience joy without tasting sorrow.

Janice plucked a flower from the vase. She rolled the flower between her fingers, taking in the scent. The sweet perfume filled her senses. *I am alive. I am loved. I am free.*

THANK YOU FOR READING

Lonely Hearts on Lilac Lane

To learn more about Karen's books, insights,
upcoming events, blog, and more:
www.KarenCoultersAuthor.com

Join her Newsletter @
www.KarenCoultersAuthor.com/newsletter

Follow her @
www.facebook.com/Karencoultersauthor

www.instagram.com/Kcoulters

Email her @
KarenCoultersAuthor@gmail.com

Invite Karen to your Book Club @
www.KarenCoultersAuthor.com/book-clubs

Your review of *Lonely Hearts on Lilac Lane* and Karen's other works would be greatly appreciated, as they provide readers with valued information. Your review will also aid in Karen's novels reaching a greater audience. Reviews can be accepted anywhere books are sold, as well as social media.

www.KarenCoultersAuthor.com/books

www.ingramcontent.com/pod-product-compliance
Lightning Source LLC
Chambersburg PA
CBHW021241190726
48289CB00005B/1423